THE CHOIR

THE
CHOIR

JOANNA TROLLOPE

RANDOM HOUSE

NEW YORK

All rights reserved under International and Pan-American Copyright
Conventions. Published in the United States by Random House, Inc.

Originally published in the United Kingdom by Century Hutchinson Ltd.
in 1988.

Library of Congress Cataloging-in-Publication Data

Trollope, Joanna.
The choir / Joanna Trollope.
p. cm.
ISBN 0-679-44454-8
1. Choirs (Music)—England—Fiction.   2. Cathedrals—England—
Fiction.   3. Clergy—England—Fiction.   I. Title.
PR6070.R57C46   1995
823.914—dc20   95-11612

Manufactured in the United States of America on acid-free paper
2   4   6   8   9   7   5   3
First U.S. Edition

For Ian

Full lasting is the song, though he,
The singer, passes: lasting too,
For souls not lent in usury
The rapture of the forward view.
—George Meredith

Acknowledgements

Needless to say, all the characters in this novel are entirely fictitious, but there are several real people to whom I owe a great debt of gratitude for their time and experience, and for the chances they gave me to learn at first hand about life in a cathedral choir. I should like to thank most warmly the Reverend Alan Charters, headmaster of the King's School, Gloucester; Mr. John Sanders, organist and director of music at Gloucester Cathedral; Mr. Harry Mudd, managing director of the Abbey Recording Company; Mr. Andrew Shenton, organist and director of music at St. Matthew's Church, Northampton, who allowed me to sit in on the recording session of Daniel Ludford-Thomas, B.E.T. Choirboy of the Year.

Joanna Trollope
Gloucestershire

THE CHOIR

1

NICHOLAS ELLIOTT, WHO HAD HAD MANY REVERSES IN HIS YOUNG life, pushed open the inner door of the cathedral porch, and heard the singing. It was early, not much after eight in the morning, and outside the cathedral there had been no sound but the wind and a few gulls looping, crying round the tower. Now, with the felt-padded door softly shut behind him, he could hear nothing at all but the singing, far off but very clear. They were singing Palestrina's "Tu es Petrus."

He began to walk rapidly, on tiptoe, across the back of the nave towards the north transept. In the corner of the transept was a door he had opened every morning for four years, which gave on to a flight of stone steps that led up to the practice room. That room was where they were singing now, twenty-four choristers among the music stands and the dust, with the miniature cricket stumps on the disordered mantelpiece, the stacks of psalters on the scuffed benches and chairs, the engravings of past organists askew on the walls. When Nicholas had been head chorister, he had stood and sung beneath William Goode, vastly fat and hugely benign, who had played the Aldminster organ from 1782 until 1801.

The door at the foot of the staircase was open. The singing had stopped.

"And what," said the voice of the organist clearly from twenty feet above Nicholas, "is that sharp doing there, may I ask?"

Memory filled Nicholas's mouth with the taste of stale Weetabix imperfectly brushed from his teeth in the early-morning panic. He could hear his mother, as they dashed erratically along the city's ring road, shrieking that she would never have countenanced his being a chorister if only she had *known*—

"If it's three-two, Wooldridge," said the organist, "what is it? Come on, come on—"

"Three minims, sir?"

"Now find that anthem. The Batten one. It's the one you will sing in procession. Listen to this note. Now, a nice round O—"

Probably, in fact certainly, he was playing the same old Steinway up there, with its keyboard facing the huge diamond-paned window blurry with dust and its top heaped with sheet music in sliding piles.

"Look," the organist said, "the altos have got the tune. Haven't they?"

Nicholas could smell the smell up there, dust and paper and boy. He was sick with envy. Under his hands he could feel his old copy of Byrd's "Magnificat" in its thin stiff red covers, with the cathedral crest stamped on the title page and NOT TO BE TAKEN AWAY underneath in purple ink.

"Now," said the organist, "we haven't much time left. Tallis. 'If Ye Love Me.' Right up to 'commandments' in one breath and you've got to do a bit of counting. All right? All right, Hooper? First time round that's only two beats—"

Five minutes later, when the organist came down the steps to the transept, in a skirmishing crowd of boys amiably bashing at each other with carrier bags and fiddle cases, he found a perfectly strange young man on a bench by the wall, gripped by a paroxysm of weeping.

"I gave him to Sandra," Leo Beckford said to the headmaster of the King's School at break.

"Who did you give to Sandra?"

"The chap I found in the cathedral this morning. He said he was a chorister here once, head chorister in 1976. I've looked him up, and he was. I was awfully moved by him. It seems to me that he was seeking sanctuary, somehow. Are you listening?"

"Sorry," Alexander Troy said, "not really."

"I know he isn't your responsibility really, but as an old boy—"

The headmaster twitched his gown more securely on to his impressive shoulders.

"Tell Sandra. She's so competent. I expect she'll feed him."

"I *have*. She did. She sent him into breakfast and he was overjoyed that it was still bacon and tinned tomatoes on Wednesdays. Are you all right?"

"No," Alexander said, "I am not but I can't talk about it just now, not even to you. Sorry."

When he had plunged out of the common room, Leo knew that his own protective colouring had, as usual, gone with him. Leo disliked the common room; he had no place there, not being on the staff, and he only came in to find the headmaster or to do battle, to explain, as temperately as he could, to one master after another, why choir practice must take precedence over football practice and cricket practice and rowing practice and athletic practice. He began to move towards the door and somebody said, "Beckford," and he unwisely said, "Yes," and the athletics coach (who taught woodwork in winter) said, "About Wooldridge, Beckford—"

"Not today."

"But—"

"We sing Monteverdi's 'Stabat Mater' in evensong. It has three treble parts. Wooldridge is the second-best treble we have. He can jump about any time."

"I hope you know," the athletics coach said, losing his temper in an instant, "that you musicians are a total irrelevance in the modern world."

Leo looked at him.

"Is that so," he said, and left the room.

In the corridor, Sandra Miles, the headmaster's secretary, was pinning notices on to the Gothic bulletin boards that had hung there since the building went up in 1850. She was small and pretty, with prim little shirt collars turned down over the neat necks of her jerseys and a bell of disciplined pale hair.

"I spoke to the HM," Leo said, "but he doesn't seem to be taking much in this morning."

Sandra looked at once soberly discreet and self-important.

"I don't think this morning is the morning to trouble Mr. Troy."

Leo grinned at her.

"Don't you call him Alexander?"

Sandra blushed rose pink. Beneath her Marks and Spencer jersey, her heart sometimes called him darling, and after two glasses of Liebfraumilch, lover.

"Ho-ho," said Leo, and then, in order not to tip the teasing into taunting, said, "What have you done with our refugee?"

"I've given him to Mr. Farrell to help mark out the running tracks. He seems awfully pathetic. He hasn't anywhere to go."

A bell rang and immediately the hubbub of a resumed morning began to swell around them.

"Mr. Godwin remembers him," Sandra said confidentially, having put the unused thumbtacks into a neat square in a corner of the board. "He never used to see his father, and his mother was terribly neurotic and used to turn up on parents' evenings and make scenes and cry all over everyone. And then he went to find his father in America and he had married again and had got a new family and they wouldn't take him in. Then he got a place at Oxford—Mr. Godwin says he can't think how except on the strength of his voice—and they threw him out after a year for failing some exam or other. And now he can't get a job. He told me he doesn't know what he wants to do. Pathetic, really."

"I suppose I could give him a bed for a bit," Leo said uncertainly, thinking of the deep litter in which he lived and which he never noticed unless it was to be subjected to outside scrutiny.

"Oh, don't bother, Mr. Beckford—"

"Leo."

"Leo—it's all right. I've seen matron and she's putting him in the sick bay for a night or two, because that's almost empty, what with this being the summer term. He can do odd jobs for now, and one more for meals won't break the bank. The Cottrell twins don't eat anything as it is. Mr. Farrell said to remind you that he needs Wooldridge for the hurdles this afternoon."

"Mr. Farrell," said Leo, "can boil his head, and I have virtually told him as much. Sandra—"

"Yes?"

"Sandra. Is Mr. Troy all right?"

She looked at him with her clear blue glance and there was real sadness in it.

"No," she said, "I don't think he is. But we must none of us interfere," and then she went quickly and lightly away from him down the red and ochre tiles of the corridor and left him, disconsolate, by the notice boards.

The door between Sandra's own neat office and the headmaster's study was open, and she could see a corner of his disordered desk and the vase of flowers she put there faithfully every Monday. This week it was three very pink peonies—from her mother's garden—and he had already knocked them over twice, once soaking the pile of *Choir Schools Reviews* waiting to be sent out to the parents of the choristers. He was on the telephone. Sandra heard him say, "No, there is no clue. She simply went. I hoped she was staying with you."

He was talking to his brother-in-law. The "she" was Mrs. Troy, Felicity. Sandra closed the communicating door and went back to her typewriter. Sandra's mother had said that Felicity Troy was a person of real quality, and Sandra's mother was right. She had a most distinguished face, an elusive and remarkable mind that could, and did, produce excellent poetry, and an air of eternal youth. Sandra had seen her walking dreamily across the turf of the cathedral close early one summer morning in her usual swirling skirts and shawls, with her feet bare and her hair loose, and even though Sandra knew she was forty-seven, she had looked unaffected and dignified and imperishably young. The boys loved her. She had gone like this before, of course, when troubled or stifled—Sandra had gingerly tried to use the word "mystic" in describing her—but never so suddenly or silently. Once she had gone to a friend's cottage in Shropshire, and another time to stay in a remote and tiny convent in Suffolk. Sandra thought that when the headmaster looked as if he could bear a remark upon the subject, she would remind him comfortingly of this. In the meantime she would get on with his letters, beginning with the one to the lady producer at Granada

Television who wished to come down to Aldminster for a series she was making on elitism in education.

Nicholas Elliott, hammering in two white-painted posts to mark the end of the hundred-metres track, was accosted by a broad and affable Labrador.

"I hope you don't mind dogs," the dean of Aldminster said.

Hugh Cavendish had been dean of the cathedral when Nicholas was head chorister. He was much the same—upright, grey-haired, well-groomed, with the air of a country squire about him. Boys who went to the deanery in Nicholas's day reported a pair of guns in his study—Purdeys—and rod clips in summer on the roof of his car and the fairly regular arrival of a delivery van from Berry Brothers and Rudd of St. James's.

"Down, sir," said the dean.

The Labrador flopped immediately into the pose of a Landseer lion. The dean turned a smile of enormous charm upon Nicholas.

"I believe you are Nicholas Elliott."

Nicholas's face was illumined.

"Do you remember, sir—"

"No. To be truthful, I don't. But I have just met Mr. Beckford in the close and he told me about you. I am glad that it was your instinct to return to Aldminster."

"There seemed nowhere else—"

The dean allowed a tiny respectful pause to follow this admission, and then he said, "And I expect you have spoken to Mr. Troy."

Nicholas looked awkward.

"There seems to be some sort of problem this morning."

"I don't suppose any day in any school passes without one. Come and see me. You remember where the deanery is?"

"Certainly, sir."

"Come and have a cup of tea with Mrs. Cavendish and me."

"Thank you."

"Heel!" the dean said to the Labrador.

"He's terribly well trained, sir."

"He is—when my children refrain from undermining him."

A memory of last night's row filled the dean's mouth with sourness. Cosmo—removed from the King's School for disruptiveness and now whipping up anarchy in Aldminster's best comprehensive—Cosmo had come into the deanery drawing room, prodded the Labrador arbitrarily out of a profound slumber, and begun to haul him towards the door. The dean said sharply, "Where are you taking that dog?"

"To watch *Picnic at Hanging Rock* with me. He's read the book, you see, and now he'd like to see the film—"

Mrs. Cavendish shot out a hand and gripped her husband's arm. "Huffo—"

The door shut loudly behind the boy and dog.

"I cannot *bear* this whimsical humanizing of animals," the dean had said furiously. "It demeans both the human and the animal."

"He only does it to provoke you, Huffo—"

"Don't call me Huffo."

"And you *are* provoked."

"Yes," the dean said, "I am," and then he had gone up to the little attic room, which the children had painted black, where they kept their television and the squalor of their wayward culture, and he had had a full-volume shouting match with Cosmo. Cosmo had won by putting on a tape of UB40 tremendously loud and then lying peacefully down on a bean bag and smiling up at the ceiling. On his way down to the drawing room, the dean had sat down on the staircase and had a moment of black despair, so filled with self-disgust that he could not even, for the moment, pray. The Labrador had waited in good-mannered sympathy two steps below.

He held his hand out now to Nicholas Elliott.

"About four. After evensong. We shall look forward to seeing you."

He would not, he resolved, walking away across the playing fields towards the green dome of the close, whose gentle summit the cathedral rode like a great ship, think about Cosmo. He would think instead about the organ, that great tour de force of restoration that was nearing completion, which would give Aldminster the distinction of possessing about the only double-case seventeenth-century organ to survive in its bold and original glory. He had adored those three years. Day after day he had gone exultantly into the cathedral while the Victorian overpainting of the pipes and pipe-shades and cornices came away to reveal the vigorous colours of the Restoration, tassels and flowers and birds, oak trees and roses, a girl holding an apple, King David playing exuberantly upon the harp. He had made it his business to understand the infinite ingenuity necessary to insert a modern organ into an ancient case, and was very happy to have the organ builders instruct him in the use of different metals for different pipes, and extol to him the wonderful advantages of an electromechanical organ. With them he rejoiced over the unique size of the Pedal Open stop—"Eighteen twenty-one," he said in awe to his wife, who was trying to telephone the window cleaner—and the soundness of the original choir case and exclaimed over the unsympathetic hands that had perpetually rebuilt the instrument for two centuries. It had made a bond between him and Leo Beckford that ordinary intercourse would hardly have achieved between men so unlike.

He paused at the edge of the close and looked up. There it was on its green summit, incomparably moving and majestic. He would never tire of it, never feel any labour too great for its preservation and restoration. No dean of Aldminster had ever known more about this cathedral than Hugh Cavendish or cherished its fabric with such zeal. He walked slowly down its great length, and then down the gradual slope of the close beyond to the dignified eighteenth-century ashlar face of the deanery.

His wife was on the telephone six feet inside the front door. He hated the instrument's being in the hall—so uncivilized.

"Must fly, my dear," Bridget Cavendish was saying. "It's the day for the fish man. Fish Monday, community shop Tuesday, Evergreen Club Wednesday, never a dull moment . . ."

At three o'clock, Alexander Troy took some of the younger boys for ancient history. That way, he got to know each boy in the school. A lot of them, he thought, looked extremely tired, almost strained, which was wrong for nine-year-olds on a summer afternoon who had only played cricket since lunch. They were doing the Peloponnesian Wars. Nobody was concentrating well. After a while, Alexander gave up and read them an extract from Mary Renault's *The Last of the Wine*, and three out of seventeen went gently to sleep on their desks. When the bell rang he had an impulse to say, "Sorry I'm not much fun today," but there was no need; they had a childish acceptance of authority, good or bad, and would not think to judge him.

Sandra met him in the corridor outside.

"Mrs. Troy rang."

"What, now? Is she on the telephone now?"

"No. She wouldn't let me fetch you. She said to tell you she was very well but that she must be alone for a while."

"Sandra. Sandra, why didn't you *fetch* me?"

"Mrs. Troy said not to."

"Haven't you the wit to see when it is right to disobey?"

Sandra opened her mouth to say that Mrs. Troy would only have hung up if she had left the telephone to fetch the headmaster, but shut it again. He looked so utterly wretched.

"Was that all she said?"

"Only that she probably wouldn't stay in London."

"Where is she in London?"

Sandra said falteringly, "She didn't say."

"And you didn't ask?"

"No."

Sandra said timidly, "Remember when she went to Suffolk—and then when she went to the cottage at Picklescott. And when she saw Daniel off to America and stayed in London then—"

Alexander was abruptly smitten by the unwanted, unbidden reflection that neither his wife nor his only child seemed to want to stay permanently near him. He said with an effort, "Mr. Beckford says we have a homeless old boy in our midst. I'd better see him. Do me good to see another victim of the arbitrariness of life."

"He's gone to tea with the dean, Headmaster. I saw him going across the close a few minutes ago."

"I thought he was *our* piece of news."

"I expect the dean has only borrowed him."

Alexander looked down at her gratefully.

"Fetch a bemused old clergyman a cup of tea, there's a good girl. What a prop and stay you are."

"And who," said Mrs. Monk, who ran the kitchen, looking at Sandra's illuminated face a minute later, " 'as been giving our Miss Miles red roses, then?"

The dean opened the door of the deanery to Nicholas. Inside, in the stone-floored hall lit by a marvellous Venetian window on the graceful staircase, the Labrador waited, and a tall man in a purple cassock.

"In your day," Hugh Cavendish said to Nicholas, "Bishop Henry was here. Now it is Bishop Robert. Bishop, this is Nicholas Elliott, who was our head chorister ten years ago."

"I am glad you have come back," the bishop said.

Nicholas said, "Yes," and felt feeble.

"I was in Calcutta ten years ago, while you were singing here."

Nicholas nodded.

"What has brought you back?"

"Well—I—I ran out of money and I couldn't think where else—"

"We are going to give him tea," the dean said encouragingly.

"Ah."

Robert Young moved forward and took Nicholas's hand.

"Come and see me. You remember where the palace is."

"You are all being so kind."

"It is what we are here for."

Nicholas said suddenly, "I wish I hadn't needed to come, you know, I wish I could have managed—"

"When you have about three weeks to spare," Bishop Robert said, "I will tell you a few things I can't manage. Not managing is part of the human condition. And now I must return to the palace my poor wife can hardly manage."

When the door had closed behind him, the dean said, "We give him a chauffeur-gardener and he will hardly use him. We put two cleaning women into the palace and they have been sent to work at the council offices, which of course they are thrilled about because they get forty pence an hour more, and Janet Young does it all herself. If the palace garden wasn't visible in part from the close, I don't suppose he would use Cropper at all. And as for the House of Lords . . . Now, come in and have tea. We eat it in the kitchen."

The kitchen table bore the kind of tea Nicholas knew about only from old-fashioned stories set in prep schools. He wasn't sure he had actually ever seen a plate of bread and butter before. Mrs. Cavendish, who was large and handsome and wore a print frock and pearls, was very gracious with him and told him that she had spent her girlhood in the bishop's palace in Wells, just in case he mistook her for other than a member of the church's aristocracy.

"Dog collars all my life, you see." She gave him a roguish glance. "Do you think I might *break out* one day? Have some plum jam. I made it myself. Is that the telephone?"

"It is," the dean said, "and it is bound to be for you."

As she left the kitchen by one door, another opened, and a black-clad boy with rusty spires of black hair slid in. He looked at Nicholas and said, "Hi."

"Hi."

"What," said the dean in a voice of suppressed outrage, "have you done to your hair?"

"Dyed it," Cosmo said. "A packet from Boots. It's Gothic."

"*Gothic.*"

"Black is Gothic. So are these." He lifted his feet and displayed pointed suede boots laced up round silver studs. "I'm a Goth now. See?"

The dean seemed paralysed. Cosmo held out a thin hand smeared darkly with hair dye and smiled at Nicholas.

"I'm Cosmo."

"I'm Nicholas—"

"Go to your room."

"Jesus," Cosmo said, "not *again.*"

Bridget Cavendish came back from the hall saying, "It was Denman College. They want me to lecture on drying flowers again." She saw Cosmo. "How simply disgusting you look."

He looked pleased.

"I know."

"I have told him to go to his room."

"I'm a Goth, Ma."

"Don't shout, Huffo. He can't stay in his room until he is back to normal. Nicholas, you aren't eating. Have some coffee cake. Women's Institute. Frightfully good. Cosmo, go and wash."

Cosmo moved to the sink.

"In the cloakroom."

"I'll take Ganja, then. Come on," he said to the dog. "Wash paws time. I say, *he's* black. He's a Goth too." He turned to Nicholas with a smile as full of charm as his father's. "Father calls him Benedict, after the saint, but I call him Ganja. Don't I, Father?"

When he had gone, Bridget said, "Cosmo is fourteen. I'm afraid his elder brother and sister egg him on a bit. Now, I want to hear all about *you*. Have some more cake?"

When Nicholas left the deanery the sun was slipping down the west face of the cathedral and filling the panes of the great window with copper-coloured glass. He felt extremely full and equally disorientated. Everything was the same: the same interesting buildings formed their picturesque ring round the close; the same green grass flowed smoothly down from the cathedral on all sides, dotted with the same sorts of tourists reading the same old guidebook; and there in the southwest corner was the gap in the buildings where the Lyng began, the ancient highway that ran a steep mile from the cathedral to the estuary, lined with ancient lime trees and new green litter bins. The first of the bins was visible from the close. It said "Please Throw It *HERE*!" on the side. What a surprise and irrelevance it must be, Nicholas thought, to the ghosts of the medieval citizens of Aldminster toiling up the Lyng to their devotions; but then, medieval litter was biodegradable.

He walked across the close to the top of the Lyng and looked down. The estuary gleamed down there beyond the roofs and office blocks and industrial buildings, its sunset-glittering surface pierced with the bony silhouettes of cranes on the docks. He looked at it all critically. The city was pretty ugly really, redeemed only by the hills on which it was built. He never used to think it was ugly, but that was one of the penalties of growing older, that you stopped accepting things and started judging them. That was particularly true of people. That was why he didn't think about his parents much, because the hero father had revealed himself to be callous and dull and the heroine mother to be an hysteric. He scuffed at the grass and noticed that one of the layers in the sole of his trainers was peeling away from the next one. So what. Here he was, twenty-three, penniless, without ambition or qualification, full of Women's Institute coffee cake, and shortly to be walking barefoot. Nowhere to go but up. Or down, where there wasn't even any cake. He was touched by the small glamour of his predicament. He turned away from the Lyng and, adopting the jaunty survivor's air of a modern Huckleberry Finn, began to lope around the edge of the close, back towards the King's School.

"I've given you a poor welcome," Alexander Troy said to him later.

"That's all right, sir."

"A parent has given me a bottle of whisky. I'm going to have some. Will you join me?"

Nicholas said he would love to. They were in the headmaster's sitting room, which Nicholas remembered for its three-piece suite covered in fawn cut moquette and a triangular fifties table whose legs ended in yellow plastic bobbles. Now the room looked like the cover of a Laura Ashley catalogue, a rustic, cluttered realization of the Anglo-Saxon idyll, where long sprigged curtains crumpled on to the polished boards of the floor and every corner contained an object of battered charm. Alexander scooped a cat out of a wicker chair draped in a faded patchwork quilt.

"Sit there. It's more comfortable than it looks. We are so lucky to have this house."

"I remember the guidebook saying it was the best in the close."

"It probably is. The plasterwork on the stairs is perfect. You must come and see—the intertwined initials and emblems of the couple the house was put up for in about 1680. Do you like water in this?"

"Please . . ."

Alexander passed him a tumbler and sat down opposite in a large chair he immediately dwarfed.

"My secretary tells me that you have been rather handed about today like the prize in pass-the-parcel."

"The dean gave me tea. The bishop was there when I arrived."

"A lovely man," Alexander said.

"He didn't seem a bit stuffy."

"Doesn't know the meaning of the word. Did Sandra tell me you were head chorister once?"

"Yes," Nicholas said, and tears pricked his eyelids. "Yes, I was."

"My dear fellow—"

Nicholas said desperately, "Everyone is being so *kind*—"

"Yes. They would be. Very difficult for you, though. Being grateful is exhausting work. Have you kept up your music?"

Nicholas shook his head.

"Don't you miss it?"

"I forgot about it. Then I went into the cathedral and heard them singing some Palestrina this morning and I could remember every note and I missed it so much I nearly fainted." He stopped and then said abruptly, "Sorry."

Alexander looked longingly towards the piano.

"Would you sing a bit for me now? A bit of Bach perhaps? I'd like to play—"

"Do you mind, sir, if I don't. Not right now."

"I was thinking of 'Now Let Thy Gracious Spirit.' "

"I'd have to try it to myself again in the bath first," Nicholas said in a tone of deliberate lightness, observing the headmaster's sudden dejection of face and spirit. "Then I'll have a go. Mr. Beckford said you were very interested in music."

"I read music at Cambridge. Then I went to theological college in Wells and now, after various false starts, here I am, most logically. Mr. Beckford is an outstanding organist and much too modest."

"I wished I was back in the choir, this morning," Nicholas said. "I *wished* it."

"Because it was safe?"

"Because when you do it, your life is quite taken up by it, and other people think you are right to do it, because of the music."

Alexander got up and poured more whisky into both their tumblers.

"It's the professionalism, isn't it? Nobody ever questions that. And of course, sacred music always seems to me such a perfect outlet for boys, platonic, unphysical, unalarming yet richly satisfying because it is something they can do so wonderfully."

Nicholas drooped over his tumbler.

"It's the only thing I've ever been able to do."

Alexander surveyed his own weariness for a moment and decided he had not the energy to take on the intimacy of his guest's misery just now. He said instead, "Would you think I was overdoing it if I told you that I believe the choir to be the soul of the cathedral?"

Nicholas looked awkward and said he didn't know. Alexander got up.

"Don't worry. I'm not about to catechize you and ask you about the relevance of God to today. But you ask the boys what they think about music and the cathedral. And God, for that matter. Ask an outstanding probationer we have, Henry Ashworth, one of the most promising voices I've heard in years coupled with one of the most straightforward personalities."

With his head bowed Nicholas said in a mutter that he supposed people only believed in God because they were afraid not to, but he supposed music must be a help, he wasn't sure, really, but it was sort of comforting, wasn't it . . .

Poor fellow, Alexander thought, looking down on him, poor lost fellow. He put a hand under one of Nicholas's arms.

"Time matron was tucking you up and ticking you off. Have you got something to read?"

Nicholas stared at him in despair.

"I don't read much—"

"Here. Have *Private Eye*."

"I'm sorry," Nicholas said. "I'm sorry—"

"What for?"

"Oh, turning up like this, being so hopeless, refusing to sing, not reading, being so *wet*—"

Alexander put a hand briefly on his shoulder.

"Actually, you're rather a comfort to me. And I'm sure your state is only temporary."

"Thank you, sir. Good night, then, and thanks for the whisky."

When he had gone, Alexander went to the piano and played some of the Bach chorale that had been singing in his head for an hour. Then he got up and found a sheet of paper in the waxed elm desk Felicity had unearthed in a junk shop and restored herself, and on the paper he wrote:

My most dear Felicity,

Three things in life keep me going: God, music and you. Luckily, two of those things do not seem to fail me, but you may imagine that when you withdraw I can only go along but limpingly.

Always and entirely yours,

Alexander

Then he tore the paper into tiny fragments, dropped the pieces into the empty grate, and took a third and unwise glass of whisky to bed with him.

2

"THE ASSAULT COURSE WAS FANTASTIC," HENRY ASHWORTH WAS saying to his mother, "and then we were nearly late for evensong because we lost Hooper and there was only two minutes to get robed up so we just rushed in in our wellies and nobody noticed till afterwards when the dean saw and he said 'WELLIES!' in an outrageous voice so it was worth it."

"Outraged," said Sally Ashworth absently because she was reading a letter. It was from Henry's father in Saudi Arabia, where he was on a two-year contract helping with the technical installation in a new hospital outside Jeddah, and it smacked of untruthfulness, as all Alan's letters now did to Sally.

"So my gown's muddy," Henry said. "Can I have a choc bic?"

Sally pushed the tin across the pine table. There was a lurking boastfulness in Alan's letter. What was it that impelled him to show off his conquests, however indirectly, to the one person he had no business to show them off to?

"I got the top C in the Sanctus today," Henry said, nibbling neat half-moons out of the rim of his biscuit, "bang on. The assault course was really amazing, my legs are nearly dropping off. Will you help me with my English?"

Sally looked up at him with a gaze heavy with what preoccupied her.

"Have you got a headache?"

"Sort of," she said.

He put his biscuit down.

"Shall I play?"

"Yes. Oh, yes. Oh, Henry . . ."

He slid off his chair and padded across the rush matting to the piano.

"Choppers? A prelude?"

"Lovely, anything . . ."

He began to rummage through the music on top of the piano and said hurriedly, with his back turned to her, "I'm going to be a full chorister."

"*Henry!*"

"Next month. It's a special service, me and Chilworth. We get presented to the dean. Better not wear wellies *then*."

She put her hands on her hips and regarded him, beaming.

"Henry."

He ducked his head.

"I am so pleased. You can't think. I knew you would be one day, but not so soon. You've only been a probationer half the time Chilworth has. Did you have to have another test?"

"No, thank goodness. Mr. Beckford just said, 'One test was quite enough, thank you.'" He struck an attitude. "'Ashworth, sing A flat. Ashworth, sing A double flat. Write down this two-part tune, Ashworth, which I shall play only three times. Who, Ashworth, are the major composers of Tudor church music? And, Ashworth, what is *sforzando*—'"

"Mr. Beckford doesn't talk like that."

"He did ask me those things—"

"What happened to my Chopin?"

Henry brandished a thin book of music at her.

"Do you want to know what he said to me today?"

"Yes, actually."

"Well," Henry said, settling himself on the piano stool, "I was chasing Wooldridge in the cloisters and out came Mr. Sims who is only chapter steward but thinks he is more important than the bishop and he said we were hooligans and Mr. Beckford came and said yes we were hooligans which was a pity for a man of *gravitas* like me who was going to be a full chorister. And Mr. Sims said he don't deserve it sir and Mr. Beckford made us say sorry and then he said I've got to be measured for a surplice."

There had been a young man with Mr. Beckford, a young man who had said "You don't know your luck" when he heard about the surplice, but Henry did know his luck. Henry knew about his voice and about music, if only because he saw the contrast in Chilworth, who wanted to play soccer on Saturday afternoon, not rehearse, and who said he might leave the choir anyway, after a year, because he thought the Lenten music was too mournful. He swung round on the piano stool and opened the book of preludes and Sally leaned her elbows on the table and regarded his grey wool back with love and pride.

He played well, a little fast, but that was a sign that he was tired. They both got tired in term time, up for daily rehearsals, in and out of the cathedral all week for extra practices, Saturday afternoons without fail, seven sung services a week, school, homework. At least being so involved with Henry helped to fill the gap Alan left, not so much by his physical absence as by his deliberate separateness from her, his pursuit of his own unhusbandly, unfatherly life. Yet he loved Henry—in a way. Sally had heard the bishop say once, from the cathedral pulpit, that there are so many, many ways of loving. But what were you to do when your way and your partner's way turned out to be so different that neither could see the other even meant love by it? She shoved Alan's letter under the plate that had held Henry's tea-time sandwich and wished fiercely for a husband who would be her *friend*.

Henry stopped playing and turned round, grimacing on a yawn.

"Bath and bed," Sally said.

Henry's eyes strayed with ill-disguised desire towards the television.

"No," Sally said.

"Just *EastEnders*—"

"Particularly not *EastEnders*."

"Please—"

"No."

"I couldn't sleep, it's far too early."

"Bed is for rest as well as sleep."

"Television is *very* restful—"

"Henry . . . ," warningly.

"Do you *know*," he said, suddenly brightening, "that if you stretched your lungs out absolutely flat, they'd cover a tennis court?"

"How revolting."

"I knew you'd say that. Chilworth said his mum'd say how interesting because she refuses to be shocked."

"That must be very disappointing for him."

"She's a teacher," Henry said.

"Oh?"

"She wanted to go on strike with the others at Horsley Comp but Grandpa talked them out of it."

Grandpa! They looked at each other.

"You must tell him," Sally said, "about being a chorister. Go on, Henry, telephone, quick, quick."

Frank Ashworth lived in the top flat of a block built on the site of a Victorian terrace known as Back Street, where he had been born. Front Street had become the main waterfront for the part of the docks whose face it was his aim to lift, and Back Street ran parallel behind it. The entrance to the block was precisely over the patch of yard where Frank's father had grown leeks, huge, woody, prize-winning monsters banked up in the black earth to produce their massive unearthly whiteness. Frank had lived away from the docks for only three years when Alan's mother, seizing upon his rising public profile, had insisted that they move out to Horsley, the up-and-coming Aldminster suburb whose vanishing meadows had once been the grazing grounds for Saxon horses. Frank had hated Horsley. He had disliked its isolation from the city and despised its frail gentility. After three years, Alan's mother had allied herself to a garage owner and been taken away in a Jaguar to a house in Edgbaston, and Frank had returned to the docks.

He started a transport business. It prospered, sturdily but undramatically. It supported Frank and a workforce of fifteen, including drivers, and it paid for Alan to go to Malvern College, where he insisted, incomprehensibly to Frank, that he wished to go. His relationship with Alan was ever precarious, always in danger of drowning in Frank's real sorrow that he seemed unable to pass on the depths of his own beliefs to his son. When Alan grew to be eighteen and used his first vote for the Conservatives, Frank felt real pain, not so much for the political choice but because he knew Alan had not really decided, had not thought properly about it, had just let his thin public school veneer prevail. His mother had given him a gold signet ring for that birthday.

"You'd be a fool to wear that," Frank had said. "You'll be spotted. Not by your voice, but by the fact you haven't any bottom to you."

Alan was slightly afraid of his father. The flat was full of books and Alan wasn't used to books. What his mother called books Malvern College had called magazines, and what they had called books were seldom seen in the house in Edgbaston. But Frank read his books. He read Shakespeare and Marx and James Joyce and Gibbon, and the love that he might have put into family life, had he had any, he put into his city. The city council was at least Labour, and he, a third-generation socialist, was its most forceful and diligent councillor. He battled for parks and trees and pedestrian precincts and street lighting, for schools and the disabled and the elderly, for the use of the whole city by its people. His present scheme was to convert the old inner dock, on Front Street, made redundant by the demands of modern ships for more sophisticated anchorage, into a pleasant waterside place where barges specially equipped for wheelchairs could be moored, and a bandstand erected, not for the trumpet and horn brigade, but for folk groups and jazz quartets. When he had done that—and here, in his musings, he would cross his wide sitting room from its western view of the docks to its steep eastern view up the hill to the cathedral—he would open up the close, that unnatural, unjustifiable sanctuary, to the people of the city to whom it belonged.

Halfway up that hill, in a friendly Georgian terrace that had seen better days, Alan and his wife, Sally, had bought a house. Alan had not wanted to live in the city, he had found a pair of cottages he wanted to convert in a village ten miles outside, but Sally wanted a job and, in any case, had had enough of the country in her girlhood, confined to a small village with her mother. In the end Alan's being abroad so much had decided it, and they had bought the battered house in Blakeney Street. Sally went to work for an antiquarian book dealer who also ran a small wholesale wine business from his basement. A strong mutual respect existed between Frank and his daughter-in-law; he was careful not to step in to supply the lacks caused by Alan's absences, but he could not but be pleased when he was appealed to. He felt that it was at least in part to Sally that he owed the dignity and affection of his relationship with his grandson.

"What'll they pay you for all this honour?" he said to Henry now, over the telephone.

"Sixpence an evensong—"

Frank grunted. After a pause, he said, "That's about sixty pounds over five years. How many hours a week?"

"Seven public services and about eighteen hours' practice. Same as now. Grandpa—"

"Mm?"

"I'll have to have a ruff."

"You'll look a right little ticket, won't you?"

"Mum says are you coming to see us."

"What, now? Is she looking tired?"

"Wiped out," Henry said cheerfully.

"Tell her to go to bed with a stiff Scotch. I'll see her another day."

"She says can she have a word. Half a sec—"

Sally said clearly, "Won't you come and have a Scotch with me, to celebrate?"

"Have you eaten?"

"I sort of picked at Henry's tea—"

"I've got a steak here. Shall I bring that?"

"Yes," she said, suddenly hungry.

"I'll not stay long."

"I'd like to see you . . ."

There was a pause and then Frank said, "Clever little chap," and rang off.

His refrigerator was full of the solid, uncompromising food he had always preferred; it was full because he liked food. He took out the steak, a couple of big tomatoes, a piece of tasty cheddar, and a paper bag of huge open mushrooms, which, though still travesties of proper field mushrooms, were a marked improvement on the anaemic little white buttons that abounded in supermarkets. He found five pound coins as a tip for Henry on this particular day, and carried the whole lot down to the eight-year-old grey Rover that was one of the best-known cars in the city and was regarded indulgently by most traffic wardens.

Sally had laid the table in the big all-purpose ground-floor room in Blakeney Street, and had pinned up her heavy hair rather loosely and changed her pink sweatshirt for a black one. She didn't kiss Frank; they never had. Henry, on the other hand, hopping around in tracksuit pyjamas, put his arms round his grandfather's neck and kissed him with warmth.

"Hold out your hand."

Frank put the pound coins in a ring on Henry's palm.

"Whoopee," Henry said.

From the stove, Sally said, "And thank you, perhaps?"

"Thank you *very* much."

"Where's this voice come from," Frank said, "that's what I'd like to know."

"That's what I like about it," Sally said, unwrapping the steak, "not knowing, just having it."

"Don't you put garlic on that."

"Mr. Godwin stinks of garlic," Henry said, "all the time. We can't breathe in Latin. Will you come to my service?"

"Try and keep me away."

Henry looked awkward. His grandfather did not believe in God. "You won't mind?"

"Mind?"

"Being in the cathedral?"

"Why should I mind? I've often been in it. It's my cathedral. It's a beautiful place."

"Mr. Beckford says it isn't in the first division of English cathedrals, but it jolly well ought to be near the top of the second."

"Bed," Sally said, above the frying.

Henry squirmed on the arm of Frank's chair.

"Shall I play you something?"

"Something quick, you monkey, then bed."

Henry rushed to the piano.

"I'll play you the Gloria, syncopated, then it sounds like Chinese music, listen—"

When he stopped, he shouted, "Ying tong yiddle I po!"

"How old are you?" Frank demanded.

"*Nearly* eleven."

"You're a twit. Anyone ever told you?"

"Only you."

"Henry," Sally said, warningly, "cheek."

Henry stooped and kissed his grandfather.

"Night—"

"Night, old fellow."

"Mum, Mum, night—"

"I'll come and tuck you in. Don't forget your teeth."

The door banged behind him. "Ying-tong-ying-tong-ying-tong," sang Henry on the stairs and then, without a pause, the first line, clear and strong, of the "Magnificat."

"Is he really good?" Frank said.

"I don't know. I'm not musical enough to know. But he has only been a probationer for six months. The whole thing has been so sudden, even realizing he could sing at all—"

She carried two plates of steak across to the table and put them down opposite each other.

"This is a treat. Henry and I eat sausages and eggs mostly. As for a joint—there's no point for two."

There was an airmail letter propped between the salt and pepper mills.

"Any news from Alan?"

"Yes," Sally said. "Read that if you want to."

"I wouldn't do that."

"I probably shouldn't say this to you but I can't help feeling that the arrangement Alan and I have is not what marriage is *for*."

Frank looked at her. She was a good-looking girl and she didn't lack courage. His heart smote him for her but all he said was, "It wouldn't be like you to give up."

She motioned him to sit down and pushed the dish of mushrooms towards him.

"I didn't say anything about giving up. All I said was that I think marriage is not about living as we do, quite separately. Well, not for me, anyway."

Frank took a bite.

"Would you like him to come home?"

There was a pause and then Sally said, "Not particularly."

"Is there something you would like me to do?"

"Thank you," she said, and smiled at him, "thank you, but you can't. I just thought you ought to know my state of mind. That's all. Come on now, what's the gossip from the city?"

When he left Blakeney Street, Frank took the Rover up the Lyng to the close and parked it behind the sixteenth-century almshouses, which now held the county archives in one half and a firm of solicitors in the other. There was no moon, but the sky was light still behind the black bulk of the cathedral. Frank looked at it with affection. He was rather afraid that in old age the idea of a god was going to become more natural to him and that even now, the fact that the cathedral was a spiritual building set it apart, gave it a significance and a stature that it would not have had if it were a castle or a moated manor crowning the close's green dome. But then, that very stature alarmed some of the people of Aldminster; he doubted that more than a few hundred citizens regularly used the cathedral and he felt a huge moral indignation, as well as a great sadness, that they should be daunted by something that had been put up by men like them for men like them.

The close was very quiet. It was much quieter than the Lyng at ten o'clock at night, much quieter than the docks or the newly cobbled precinct where he had fought alongside the junior chamber of commerce to bring in wine bars and eating places, to keep life there, after the shops shut. And here was the close, this great green lung offered up to the heavens high in the heart of the city, empty of people, absolutely empty, no sign of life beyond a few quiet lights shining from windows or from the wrought-iron arches over gateways. Beautiful, yes, in its quirky, unplanned way, harmonious, severe, but dead, *dead*. No drunks, even, nor drug addicts gasping away in furtive corners, as they did in the graveyards of the city's churches at night, propped against tombs, half dead themselves, some of them. Ivies grew in those churchyards, and yew, and both made rank black holes to hide in, but the smooth sweep of the close afforded no shelter; try to hide there and the empty grass would of itself offer you up to whatever was watching you from up there behind the stars. The old hobos would tuck themselves in corners of the buttresses sometimes, but then they, in their wandering free-dom, had nothing to hide, no score to settle by self-destruction. There was one up there now. Frank could see him, a black bundle in the angle made by the south porch against the walls. He'd go up to him in a minute and give him a quid or two and chat a bit. The last one he'd talked to had remarked that though it was a fine cathedral, it couldn't, to his way of thinking, hold a candle to Wells. He had smelled like an old wet dog with rotten teeth.

Frank had been glad to see him. He was glad now to see the glow of another tramp's cigarette and to observe, silhouetted against the dim light of the far end of the close, the black outline of what was undoubtedly the dean taking his dog for a late-night run. Frank shook his head. Nice enough fellow, the dean, but as far removed from the world of ordinary men as if he were not one himself. All that breathed for him was those stones up there, block upon block, while all Frank could see was the hands that had put them there, every one in its place. He turned away and made for the headmaster's house, instinctively drawn, as so many people were, by its particular charm, as well as its quality. Two lights were on, a faint one on the first floor, a stronger one in the two long windows beside the front door. The curtains had not been pulled. Frank could see in quite clearly, could see Alexander Troy in an armchair, with a clipboard and papers on his knee and a bottle of whisky beside him, and through the glass he could hear most strong and distinctive choral music, which Henry would have told him was Benjamin Britten's *War Requiem*. Troy looked extremely solitary, and at first Frank's sympathy was aroused, and then he raised his eyes and looked along the lovely length of the darkened house, unused and empty. "Bloody waste," Frank said to himself. He clenched his fists in his trouser pockets and glared at the unconscious Alexander. "Bloody *waste*."

When Frank had gone, Sally Ashworth cleared up a bit and turned on the television and turned it off again and made a shopping list for the next day and fed the cat and put the sheets in the washing machine, ready to turn on in the morning, and then went upstairs to look at Henry. He lay like everyone's idea of a child asleep, humped in a prawn shape under his duvet with only a crest of hair visible, giving off an aura of being most thoroughly asleep. Beside him, on the floor, lay the grey woollen trail of his school clothes, a comic book about Asterix, and a crumpled photocopy of Masefield's "Cargoes" with "Learn by heart for Tuesday's prep" written across it in Henry's still-babyish hand. Above his bed he had pinned a large photograph of the choir on an outing to Worcester, and had drawn a large red arrow from himself to the white margin, where he had written "Henry Francis Ashworth aged 10." There was also a photograph of his parents, posing self-consciously for him in the front doorway, and dozens of the cat, who was called Mozart and had a distinct sense of humour.

Sally had done the room up during a phase of trying to *throw* herself into interior decor. It didn't last long, because real life reasserted itself and the vast bouquet of dried flowers in a willow basket she had carefully put as a focal point in the hall proved to be directly in Henry's flight path from front door to kitchen, as well as to contain, Mozart insisted, untold menaces within its rustling depths. She had stripped and waxed all the wood in Henry's room, covered the walls with paper striped like mattress ticking, laid rush mats on the floor, bought a bean bag and a cork pinboard and an anglepoise lamp. Three years later, Henry had strewn his pervasive but impersonal masculine detritus across the room, all but obliterating its careful, liberal good looks. Tonight, she noticed that he had clearly been helping the rush mat to unravel, for a long pale snake of it was uncoiling from the central mass and making for the door. The anglepoise was bent, the pinboard was empty except for thumbtacks arranged to say "A Team," and Henry had said a few days before that he would very much like it if his walls could be brown. *Dark brown.*

She bent over him, tucking the duvet closer. His hair needed washing. His hair *always* needed washing.

"Night, night."

He grunted. He seemed suddenly very far away from her, separated not just by sleep but by his talent, by music, this thing she could admire and enjoy but could not share, Henry's own thing. The digital alarm clock by his bed said that it was hardly ten o'clock. On an impulse, Sally went quickly downstairs and picked up the telephone.

"Who?" said Leo Beckford.

"Sally Ashworth. Henry's mother. I'm sorry to ring so late—"

"Is it late?"

He looked about him vaguely as if the time and its consequences would somehow surface helpfully out of the chaos of the room. He had been writing an article on the qualities to be looked for in awarding organ scholarships, and as usual, his mind refused to change gear with ease.

"I just wanted to ask you about Henry—"

"Yes," Leo said.

"Is—is he really good? Or just a bit better than most?"

Henry's voice burst abruptly into Leo's memory, singing the Agnus Dei. Leo's mind cleared.

"I should rather say, Mrs. Ashworth, that his voice was outstanding."

"That good?"

"That good. It will, of course, ripen in the next two years."

He could not recall Henry's mother. He was not conscious of mothers much, beyond their obligations to fetch and carry his choristers and his irritation with them if they failed to make that a priority. Sally Ashworth said, in a voice suddenly full of emotion, "You see, I do so want his life to have a chance of the first rate, and if his voice, even if it's only for his boyhood, is so good, it will help him escape being mediocre, it will lift him, do you see—"

Leo said gently, "Do you think this is the right moment, or the right medium for this sort of conversation?"

There was a pause, and then Sally said humbly, "It was an impulse. To ring you. I was so thrilled to hear that Henry was to be a full chorister, but I felt so far away—"

"You could," Leo said with an effort, "come to a choir practice, if you like."

"I didn't think you were keen on mothers' doing that."

"To be honest, I'm not. But you seem to want to involve yourself in Henry's music, and I am offering you a chance, if you think that is what is best for him."

"You don't—"

"The cathedral choristers are professionals, Mrs. Ashworth."

There was a silence, and then Sally said in a voice of resolute cheerfulness, "Do you know, Mr. Beckford, that I think I am making rather a fool of myself. I am so very pleased to hear your good opinion of Henry, and I am grateful to you for talking to me. Thank you so much. Good night."

She put the telephone down. At the other end, Leo stood and held the humming receiver. What was it she had really wanted, with her funny mixed manner, all at once forlorn and gallant? He put the telephone down. She had aroused in him the same puzzled sympathy as poor Nicholas Elliott, still doing odd jobs about the school, with everyone intermittently and fruitlessly wondering what to do with him next. Leo himself wondered if he ought to take Nicholas in. His gaze strayed over the room, the chairs and tables laden with books and papers, the wastepaper baskets overflowing, cases and bags and boxes lurching where he had left them, and the whole loosely knitted together with a trailing crochet of electrical cables from lamps and heaters and record players. Perhaps Nicholas could sort it out a bit. Leo imagined himself opening the door of the room to Nicholas and saying, "All that can be said for this mess is that it would be worse if I were still married."

And that, at least, was no more than the truth.

3

When the headmaster of Horsley Comprehensive—a man whose unquestionable commitment to education was gradually being soured by the unlovely cocktail of aggression and apathy in the school that he was forced to drink—wrote to the Cavendishes to ask for an interview with them about Cosmo, Bridget said at once that they should deal firmly with him. The dean assumed she referred to Cosmo.

"Certainly not, Huffo. I mean Mr. Miller. Dealt with sensibly, as we do here, Cosmo is very little problem. He must learn to do the same."

The dean bowed his head over his toast and marmalade.

"Cosmo," he said in the measured tones of one hanging on to the last shreds of self-control, "is a nightmare of a problem exacerbated by your idiotic indulgence of him."

Bridget opened her next letter, gave the dean a humouring smile, and said, very kindly, "Nonsense."

When the dean had first met Bridget Mainwaring, she was still living at home. She was not only living in it, but running it, for Bishop Mainwaring was a widower. To step into the palace in his day, even in the early sixties, was to enter the world of Barchester, a Grantlyesque world of gentlemanly assumptions and comforts. The bishop's handsome, capable daughter with her ready laugh and inexhaustible energy had seemed to Hugh Cavendish the mainspring of this civilized, beeswaxed, flower-filled household, a woman who instinctively understood both God and mammon. When he had wooed her and won her—no very arduous task, for she was thirty-two, very eager, yet very exacting as to the breeding and calling of her suitors—he discovered that she thought God was a part of mammon, a kind of high moral gloss available to put upon the good things of this world. He also discovered that she was not teachable, that she lacked not only any kind of self-awareness but, even more dangerously, the smallest atom of humility. Bringing with her a vanload of lovely furniture and rugs and pictures from the palace— "Daddy won't be entertaining on anything like such a scale without me"—she swung into action to make the various houses of Hugh Cavendish's career into the unmistakable dwellings of an aristocratic nineteenth-century clergyman of private means. She ran parishes in the same way, arousing waves of fury and admiration, and filled her nurseries with babies, whom, since they were, as her children, extensions of herself, she could not for the life of her see objectively. Hugh Cavendish ate well, slept and dressed in perfectly laundered linen, trod gleaming floors, and inhaled stephanotis and jasmine and potpourri, and watched the wife of his bosom envelop herself in a hide of complacency so thick that no human weapon had power to penetrate it. He sometimes wondered if she even *saw* Cosmo, quite literally; whether, when her eyes rested upon her youngest son—a triumph, born when she was forty-two—she saw not the reality of his macabre sooty hair and clothes but a fantasy of tweed jacket and corduroys and well-polished brogues. She said now, "I shall go and see Mr. Miller. Don't you bother."

"I should like to see Mr. Miller."

"My dear. You haven't a minute."

"I shall make a minute. I have every sympathy with Mr. Miller."

"Poor dear man. Such a very varied school—"

"I have every sympathy for Mr. Miller over Cosmo."

"Huffo!"

The dean rose.

"It must be a wretched problem indeed to have Cosmo in one's school."

"Huffo—"

"Don't call me Huffo. I shall take Benedict for a run."

Bridget smiled again.

"Don't worry about Mr. Miller. I'll telephone the moment I've opened my letters."

"Please do not. I will telephone when I return from my walk."

He called the dog from the kitchen, collected lead and stick, and left the deanery by the front door. He had not even reached the gate to the close before he heard his wife's voice on the telephone, asking with her unmistakable commanding friendliness, if she might speak at once to the headmaster.

Humankind had failed the dean. He had meant to love his fellow man, had believed not only that he could, but that it would be easy because he wanted to, but he had found, to his dismay, that most of his fellow men simply were not lovable. Their deviousness he might have forgiven, their unscrupulousness and even cruelty—the world was after all a harsh place and drove a man to very basic behaviour merely to survive—but their oafish vulgarity, their unashamed preference for the crude and the shoddy, fell little short of disgusting him. Standing in the cathedral he would picture to himself the original medieval congregation, drawn from its holes and hovels, gazing in rapture and awe at the brilliance and beauty of this holy place; the souls of such people seemed to him very precious. Then he would walk out into the close and be confronted by tourists in trainers, a litter of hamburger boxes, and couples who never entered a church necking on the grass, and he would be filled with rage at their evident intention *not* to strive towards beauty, indeed, their intention to turn their backs upon it.

And if these were not enough for Hugh Cavendish to bear, these bitter disappointments in both his marriage and his mission, what of the added blow of his children? Brought up in a careful atmosphere of worthwhile objects and standards and sounds, well educated, good-looking, every one, and with above-average brains, they had formed themselves instinctively into an aggressive union that seemed bent upon overthrowing the dean's traditional rule. Fergus, the eldest and cleverest, was a loudly proclaimed atheist, the assistant editor of a satirical magazine for which *any* tradition was automatically a target. He lived with a very beautiful actress who was coal black and had two small brown children by a former Indian lover. The next in line, Petra, sculpted vast metal beasts in a warehouse shared by a Welsh painter older than the dean, whose wife broke into the warehouse regularly and wrecked anything of Petra's she had strength and time to destroy. It worried the dean to see how much Petra drank. She drank roughly, like a man, in a man's quantities. Ianthe—the dean had a photograph of Ianthe in his dressing room, taken when she was four, dressed in a smock from Liberty's and laughing at him out of an apple tree—Ianthe had been left five thousand pounds by a godmother, and had invested it, with three friends, in a record company. The company was called Ikon.

"Do you *know* what an ikon is?" the dean had demanded of Ianthe.

"Of course. It's an image. That's the point."

"But it is a *sacred* image!"

Ianthe shrugged.

"Oh, that again," she said.

At least Ianthe had no bizarre lover, if you did not count a frail young man called Adam who followed her about lighting her cigarettes and laughing tremendously at almost anything she said. She was horrible to him, but he still followed her. She was horrible to him because she was in love with Leo Beckford, and Leo made it plain, had always made it plain, that he thought she was a childish pest. She was the only one of the dean's children who worked hard, and she worked slavishly because she meant to make a success of Ikon and prove to Leo that she was really a wonderful modern woman.

And then there was Cosmo. Cosmo who smiled at people and was never put out, and whose whole heart and soul were bent upon overturning whatever seemed ordered or harmonious or constructive. He was the most demonstrative of their children, beloved by every parishioner since babyhood, and seemed to the dean to be not so much his own son but rather a character created by John

Wyndham. Cosmo, the dean felt, was deeply dangerous, and Mr. Miller, battling to hold his craft steady in a hurricane, should be given every help. Indeed, at this moment, whistling Benedict back from his insatiable Labrador's interest in a litter bin, the dean felt his loyalty lay more with Mr. Miller than with either his wife or his son. He would telephone Mr. Miller and see him alone, if necessary without Bridget's knowledge.

He turned for home and his eye swung with relief and joy across the west end of the cathedral. There lay the answer, there lay all that was good and right and beautiful. To that edifice the dean would give all he had to give; there was no doubt now in his mind, after all these years of disillusionment, that that great building was most literally the house of God, the only place where He could possibly live.

Frank Ashworth dressed with particular care to go to the deanery. He did so not out of respect but out of expediency; his friendly old cardigans would not carry as much weight in the dean's study as the subdued suit Sally had helped him buy in the closing-down sale of the old gents' outfitters where, he remembered, his father had bought a black hat for his mother's funeral. Frank was allergic to anything sartorially remarkable and had only been persuaded into the suit because it was in his bulky size and cost only sixty pounds, and because Sally said it was the dullest suit she had ever seen.

When the dean opened his door, wearing a grey cardigan with his dog collar—Frank was not to know it was cashmere—the prospects for the interview seemed to Frank to promise well.

"Mr. Ashworth."

"Good of you to see me, Mr. Cavendish—"

"Not at all, only too pleased. Here, do sit down—"

There was a bowl of roses on the dean's desk, and a welcoming dog on the hearth rug, and a sherry decanter and glasses glittering on a tray in the sunlight.

"Sherry?"

"Not for me, thanks. Doesn't seem to agree with me."

"Gin? Gin and tonic?"

"The tonic," Frank said slowly, "will do me very well."

A cut-glass tumbler was put beside him, heaving with ice and lemon and bubbles.

"Your very good health—"

"I've come with a proposition, Mr. Cavendish."

Hugh looked reflectively at the ceiling.

"I imagined you might have such a purpose in mind."

"The people of this city don't have sufficient use of the close."

Hugh's gaze left the plaster rose on the ceiling and fell swiftly on Frank Ashworth.

"That is their choice, Mr. Ashworth. The close is open to everyone, as is the cathedral. They choose, of their own free will, other parts of the city."

Frank said calmly, "Because they know they are not welcome."

"Not welcome! Absurd."

Frank took an unhurried swallow of his tonic water.

"They feel that the close is not for them. It's too grand. They've nowhere to go in the close that's their own."

"It is all their own," the Dean said with an effort.

"I repeat. They are not made welcome. They feel out of place."

The dean got up and walked to the window. From the hearth rug, sensing an atmosphere, Benedict watched anxiously. The dean came back.

"Perhaps, Mr. Ashworth, we mean different things by welcome. The cathedral is a sacred building in which reverence for God and His worshippers is made manifest by silence and unobtrusive movements. Those who do not profess the Christian faith are most welcome in the cathedral, but on account of the reasons I have just given, they are not welcome to run or shout or play games or loud secular music. The same respectful behaviour—respectful of other humans as much as the Almighty—is somewhat naturally expected in the close, which, owing to its proximity to the cathedral, is not quite like any other public park."

"Quite so."

The dean waited.

"I'm not suggesting the close should become like the Lyng Gardens. I'm only suggesting that it shouldn't frighten people off." The phrase "stuck up" presented itself to Frank, but he was a professional at unemotional argument, so he dismissed it.

"I've a proposal."

"Ah," said the dean.

"The headmaster's house of the King's School is, I believe, the property of the dean and chapter. It's a big house, Mr. Cavendish, some fourteen or fifteen rooms? It is at present occupied only by Mr. and Mrs. Troy, who have no children at home and use perhaps six rooms. I would like to propose to the council that we make the dean and chapter an offer for that house, and turn it into a meeting place for the city, a crèche, a coffee shop, a magazine and newspaper library, even an art gallery for local artists—"

The dean fought down the kind of rising panic induced in him by conversations with his wife.

"This—this seems all most novel. Would—would it be some kind of club?"

"I shouldn't like to see that. I want to see the close made unselective—"

"I must consult others, you know, but I hardly feel very sanguine, Mr. Ashworth. The house is probably the best we have in the close, and the headmaster must be fittingly housed, you know, he has obligations—"

Frank stood up.

"Would you put it to the next chapter meeting?"

"Well, yes—well, I suppose I must since you request it, but really the proposal does not seem to me in the least suitable, or indeed necessary—"

"If you lived in the city proper, you would see that it was necessary."

The dean came to stand close to Frank and peer into his face.

"What about the almshouses? The records could surely be stored elsewhere, and the council already owns half that building—"

"It would be nothing like as suitable. It has no garden. I'm not a man for second bests."

The dean withdrew a pace.

"I assume," he said coldly, "that your proposal is made with open and honourable intention? You are not, are you, threatening any kind of compulsory purchase order? Because I must tell you that our statutes protect us there, the statutes granted by Henry the Eighth—"

Frank moved towards the door. When he reached it, he paused and looked back at the dean.

"I wouldn't threaten, Mr. Cavendish. I wouldn't need to. All I'm doing is suggesting that we might do each other a bit of good."

"A bit of *good*?"

"I would think that house is worth a tidy bit and you are always short of money in the close."

"I think that is no concern of the council, Mr. Ashworth."

Frank shrugged.

"Well," he said with the appearance of unconcern that his opponents on the council had come to dread, "it's only an idea. Give it some thought—but it's only an idea."

When Sandra came into Alexander Troy's study to say that the dean was on the telephone, wanting to discuss a matter of some delicacy, Alexander's reaction was irritated.

"Tell him that I am in a meeting and ask him to make an appointment."

Sandra had an annoying regard for the strict truth.

"But you are not in a meeting. I've said you are free."

"Then I am teaching."

"But you are not!"

He said crossly, "This is an idiotic conversation."

She drooped. There was no point in telling him that he had made it so.

"I'll do what I can—"

"Oh," he said in exasperation, "of course I'll speak to him," seizing the receiver on his desk. "Yes? Yes?"

Sandra went back to her office. Mrs. Troy had now been gone for ten days and there was no word from her beyond a postcard reproduction of a Turner from the Tate Gallery with, on the back, an indecipherable postmark and the words "Don't worry." Alexander was carrying that postcard about like some talisman and she had seen him poring over the postmark endlessly and fruitlessly. Perhaps she must try to regard it as a compliment that his temper was so short with her; he was never irritable with the boys, after all, and he must be allowed to let steam off somehow. But how strange it was, with a strangeness that was very fascinating, to see a clergyman as vulnerable as any other man in such a situation.

"They're real people, you know," Sandra would say to her friends. "Underneath they are. They just can't show it." And then confidentially, "It's really hard on the wives, you know."

Before she came to work at the King's School, Sandra would not have believed that clergy wives behaved like other wives; surely clergy wives had a kind of moral elevation that rendered them immune from resentment, neglect, jealousy, or frustration? Did they not automatically and joyfully share in their husbands' commitment to God and humanity? She had once suggested this diffidently to Felicity Troy in a rare moment of intimacy while mopping up a flooded washing machine together, and Felicity had said, "I think you should look at what you see, not at what you expect to see. Perhaps Victorian evangelizing missionary wives felt like that, but now—"

Sandra had started looking, and it had become compulsive viewing, this quiet observance of marriages round the close. Of all of them, perhaps the bishop and his wife came closest to her early preconception, but then, the Youngs were an essentially private couple, and who could guess what struggles went on in the palace behind those tall windows that Janet Young laboriously polished herself? They were as private as the Cavendishes were public—you only needed half an eye to see how managing Mrs. Cavendish was and how she thought her children so perfect she'd let them roam the streets looking like hippies, while she went off to London once a month, all Jaeger suits and pearls. But then, she had money. It made all the difference. Sandra knew that most of the wives of the diocesan clergy managed on about the same money as she earned as a secretary, and she lived at home and had a boyfriend who had old-fashioned ideas about her not paying for much, so her money wasn't much more serious than pocket money. But clergy wives had to eat and dress and keep warm and bring up a family on that sort of money, and the parishes didn't like it if they pleaded poverty; Sandra knew that at first hand because her mother's parish out at Coombebrook had got very hoity-toity when the vicar had asked for help with logs and coal for the winter. No wonder most of the wives went out to work, and no wonder they then had so little time or energy left for parish work and thus couldn't share in their husbands' lives as once they might have done. Sandra had long conversations with her mother about this, which got them nowhere, really, because her mother was so very old-fashioned in her views.

She was, for instance, very stuffy about Felicity's disappearing acts, as she called them, but Sandra knew better now, herself. She hated to see Alexander caused pain, but she knew that Felicity's life was hard in a way that nobody who didn't know it at first hand could possibly appreciate. If you weren't very careful with each other, God actually could get in the way of a marriage, because it was clearly easier for some men to be more in love with the Church than with a woman. God had His impersonal side. He didn't feel neglected or exploited or have headaches, and making Him the priority, always, had the world's sanction. The world applauded you if you did wonderful parish work and was sorry for you if your wife was neurotic or busy or unsupportive; but what the world on the whole didn't see was that the parish didn't cost you one-hundredth part as much emotionally, however much you cared about it, and therefore to give your time to it instead of to a wife and family was, in essence, an escape.

Alexander came out of his study.

"The dean is coming in at six. Be a dear and fly for a bottle of fino sherry, would you? I've only got an inch of Mr. Cottrell's whisky left and I'm sorry I was cross."

Sandra said impulsively, "You mustn't take Mrs. Troy's going personally, you know. Because it isn't. It's to do with Aldminster and the close and the Church." She blushed tremendously. "I'm sure I'd do the same if I was her."

There was a pause, and then Alexander put a five-pound note down on Sandra's desk.

"Funny you should say that. I often think I shouldn't mind running away for a bit myself if I could. There's the sherry money—sprint, will you, or the shops will shut and I'll have to offer him Nescafé."

"I had a most peculiar visit this morning," Hugh Cavendish said. "Rather caught me on the hop, I'm afraid. Frank Ashworth came and gave me a spiel about the close being unwelcoming to Aldminster citizens, and then said he wanted the council to be able to buy a property here to make some sort of social centre where people could feel at home. He didn't, of course, beat about the bush. He said that this was the house he had his eye on."

"*This* house!"

The dean had recovered himself since the morning.

"Naturally I made it very clear that it does not even begin, as a proposition."

"Is he *serious?*"

"In essence, yes. I don't think Frank Ashworth says anything idly, which is why I must report it to you, and to the next chapter meeting. I think he will pursue the idea and we must be armed. I've already thrown out the idea of the almshouses to him."

Alexander got up and went to lean against the mantelpiece.

"I am absolutely appalled. Why does everything have to be down-graded, why is 'excellence' a dirty word, why are people allowed to behave precisely as they like and are even pandered to and provided with a beautiful setting to defile—"

"I think," the dean said smoothly, "that Frank Ashworth is an old-fashioned socialist and believes in the essential goodness of humankind."

"You don't believe that!"

The dean said nothing.

"Have you come here," Alexander said loudly, "to tell me that you intend to propose the selling of this house to the council at the next chapter meeting?"

"On the contrary. I have come to warn you of what Frank Ashworth has in mind and to discuss with you our tactics when he returns to the fray, which he surely will."

"Is the council behind him?"

"If it isn't now, it soon will be. We must present a united front. The canons won't be a problem, I'm glad to say."

"Is this house covered by the statutes?"

The dean said carefully, "I thought it was, but I fear I was wrong. There *was* a revision of cathedral property under Cromwell, but of course this house is just too young for inclusion in that."

Alexander sat down again.

"It was good of you to come. I am, after all, the headmaster and must live where I am told."

The dean leaned forward and said in a very different and solicitous voice, "My dear fellow, I can't tell you how sorry I am—"

"The pressures build up, you know," Alexander said hurriedly, desperate to prevent his mentioning Felicity's name, "you know how they do—"

"Indeed, indeed—"

"I'll think about this proposal. Perhaps the almshouses really might—"

"If anyone should speak to you, perhaps you would say that the matter is under review by the dean and chapter?"

It dawned upon Alexander that the purpose of the dean's visit had in truth been to condole with him over his vanished wife rather than to consult him over Frank Ashworth's proposition, which, after all, he had no power to affect, one way or the other. He said rather heartily, in an attempt at gratitude, "At least we have the launch of the organ to look forward to."

The sun rose in the dean's countenance.

"That will be a great event. The tickets were completely sold out two weeks ago."

He stood up and put a hand on Alexander's shoulder.

"To tell you the truth, I see no point in selling this house. So rest assured. If the council have money to burn, they can erect some purpose-built leisure centre." He paused. "And I will pray for good news for you."

When he had gone, Alexander poured himself another glass of sherry and then walked the length of the house to the fearsome Victorian larder and put the bottle on an inconveniently high shelf so that he wouldn't be tempted to have any more. Then he went back to his study for the few minutes that remained before the evening prayers he held once a week for the school, which were compulsory for the under-fourteens, voluntary for the seniors, and usually surprisingly well attended. He put this down not so much to godliness as to the boys' instinctive recognition of the particular and mysterious atmosphere of evening worship; you could see by their faces how many of them were moved. If he needed to chastise a boy, an interview after compline was usually successful on both sides.

Felicity often said to him how enormously romantic she found men and boys to be. "Look at them," she would say to him when the school was gathered before them. "They really believe in the possibility of their dreams. They really do." She had sounded so yearning, almost envious. He knew she dreamed dreams and that the only outlet for the near-visionary outbursts of her imagination was these poems, worked over endlessly and painfully. He also knew of her immense womanly practicality, a realism that must sometimes have seemed to her an enemy to her poetic perception. And yet both were rooted in her, made her up, made her the elusive and adorable person she was and also, probably, drove her near to despair, drove her to run away as a physical release from a locked-together combat of mind and spirit. Perhaps—he turned the idea over gingerly in his mind—perhaps it nearly broke her up not to be able to believe consistently in her dreams and visions. He wished she would talk to him about it. He wished she would tell him what, if anything, about their way of life, or indeed *him*, she could not bear. She had always been self-contained, which had given her a graceful dignity that was one of the things that had drawn him to her at the outset, but as she got older, she had dug deeper into herself, and he had to resort to her poems to try to understand and they were often most obscure. She never reproached him; she always smiled and was loving but *lightly* loving, almost absentminded sometimes. It was alarming how much he missed her. Suppose that this time she did not come back, and suppose that the council compulsorily bought this lovely house and he was put into the empty flat at the top of the school's main building, where he would grow to dread the holidays and doubtless take to the bottle?

He straightened himself abruptly. This would not do. He had always announced that next to hysteria, he abhorred self-pity in anyone. He would go upstairs and brush his teeth vigorously before he went down to compline because the boys so delighted in sniffing the air like hounds to detect, gleefully, the faintest breath of alcohol around any member of staff after six o'clock at night. "Glugging gin in cupboards," Leo Beckford had once said, "the minute the clock strikes six. That's what they think we do."

Ianthe Cavendish, down from London for the weekend, made the taxi drop her at the top of the Lyng. That way, she could slip round the close of the deanery via the little sixteenth-century yard on the northern side, where the chapter office was and the cathedral works yard, and where, in a pair of lurching timbered houses, the organist and the assistant organist lived side by side. The assistant organist, Martin Chancellor, had a wife and a baby, and a basket of lobelias and striped pelargoniums hung outside his front door and his knocker was polished and there were three clean empty milk bottles in a special little crate on the step. The curtains were drawn, and no doubt behind them Martin and Cherry Chancellor—who both taught part-time in city schools—were marking books or watching BBC2 with the washing-up done and the baby asleep and breakfast already laid for the morning.

Leo's curtains were not drawn, as Ianthe had known they wouldn't be. In fact, there was only one curtain, as Leo had taken one down once to wrap up a friend's fiddle for a journey to London and the curtain had never come home again. He had a centre light and four lamps and he was sitting at the piano with a score and a pencil, wearing a green T-shirt that said "Warwick University Ski Club" on the back, which was typical of Leo, since he had never been near either Warwick University or a ski slope in his life. The walls of the house rose straight up from the cobbles of Chapter Yard, so Ianthe could lean her elbows on Leo's windowsill and gaze without hindrance. If she tapped on the glass, he'd be unlikely to notice—she had never in her life known anyone who concentrated as Leo did. In her best fantasies she imagined that intensity of concentration focused entirely on her; it would be like being consumed by a wonderful flame. She gazed at him, at his thick, rumpled hair and the knobs on his vertebrae through the T-shirt as he hunched over the keyboard, and his lovely narrow bottom on the piano stool and his really intelligent hands—she could only see the right one properly—moving knowledgeably over the keys. It was a real turn-on, standing watching him secretly like this. She'd think of it when she saw him come in to the cathedral on Saturday for this service to celebrate the restoration of the organ, and he'd be in his surplice and might even have brushed his hair, and only she would know about the private messy lovely Leo underneath.

She banged on the window. He didn't hear, so she banged again, more loudly, and he turned around crossly and came to open the window and said, "Go away, Ianthe, I'm working."

"How did you know it was me?"

"Because it's Friday and I saw your mother today in Sainsbury's."

"Can I come in?"

"No."

"Five minutes?"

"There's this huge concert service tomorrow and a thousand last-minute things—"

"I'll only stay a second, I *promise*. I've got some vodka."

"You drink too much, you and Petra."

Ianthe put her bottle down inside the room and attempted to heave herself over the sill.

"Use the door," Leo said rudely, not helping her.

Breathlessly, she wriggled in, falling into the muddle of books and boxes on the floor.

"Five minutes," Leo said, "and then I'm throwing you out."

She beamed at him.

"It's so lovely to see you."

"I'm in a horrid mood and I don't want to see anyone."

She made her way into the disgusting kitchen and returned with two smeary tumblers.

"It always comforts me that this house is so revolting that no woman but me could bear it. At least the mess proves to me you haven't *got* a woman."

"Who'd have me?" Leo said unwisely, pouring vodka.

"Oh, me, me, me—"

"I don't count you."

Her face grew suddenly sad and serious.

"One day you *will* count me."

He looked at her. She said, "Do you think I'm at all pretty?"

He went on looking. After a while he said reflectively, "You are good-looking, I suppose, but you look so contrived and aggressive. Why don't you let your hair just lie down like hair likes to?"

"I like looking like this."

"Then don't ask me if I think you're pretty."

She said humbly, "I sort of need to know."

If she became submissive, she always set off warning bells in Leo's head.

"I've got a cause for you to put your extra energy into."

"Oh, what, what?"

"A waif has turned up in our midst, an ex-chorister, unemployed and homeless. You talk to him and see if there's some way anyone can help him. He's becoming a slight problem and he is weighing on my conscience because it was me who found him weeping in the cathedral. I'll introduce you." Leo looked at his watch. "Time's up. Out you go."

"Oh—!"

He picked up the vodka bottle and rammed it into the pocket of her huge black cotton jacket.

"Out."

"Will you kiss me?"

"No," Leo said. "Kissing's become very dangerous. I've no idea where you've been."

"Oh, Leo—"

He took her arm and propelled her out into the hall towards the front door.

"Good night, Ianthe."

She opened her mouth very wide. He said, "If you scream, you will wake Baby Chancellor and then Cherry will come out in her dressing gown and be very, very severe with you for a long time and I shall become quite furious because I need to get back to work. Good night."

When he had shut the door, she subsided on to the step and sat there, hugging her knees and dwelling with pain and pleasure upon what a beautiful, wonderful bastard he was and her fervent hope that she would never outgrow the agony of her present feelings.

4

NICHOLAS ELLIOTT HAD TO BORROW A JACKET FROM THE SCHOOL secondhand clothes cupboard to make himself suitable for the cathedral. This was Sandra's idea. Everyone else had gradually lost interest in him for the simple reason that his problem would not seem to solve itself and he remained helpless and slightly hopeless, and so responsibility for him filtered down to Sandra, who was appalled that he proposed to attend the organ service dressed in the jeans and sweatshirt layers that seemed to compose the whole of his wardrobe. Mrs. Cavendish produced some grey cord trousers that had been given to her for Cosmo, and that Cosmo had been outraged at the thought of wearing, and in the secondhand clothes cupboard, Sandra found what she thought was a very nice Donegal tweed jacket and some black shoes and an Old King's tie. Docilely, Nicholas allowed himself to be dressed like a doll and felt a distinct comfort at being in someone else's clothes, however alien to his taste. When he reached the cathedral he even felt pleased to be wearing the tie; it became his badge of belonging.

Sally Ashworth, coming into the cathedral beside him and thinking how touching it was that an Old King's boy should wish to attend the service, found herself quite overwhelmed at the sight before her. She knew the cathedral perfectly well, could point out to visitors the massive splendour of the Norman columns with Early English clerestory arches above and then of course the Perpendicular chancel and cloisters, the glory of the place—but today, packed with people, banked with luminous pyramids of flowers, its huge holiness had such power and drama that it seemed quite unfamiliar, a new and marvellous place altogether. The afternoon sunlight was pouring, as the original builders had meant it to do, through the high south windows, raising the eye up and leading it along the great ribs of the roof to the tracery above the chancel. Everybody seemed to be looking up, from the orderly rows in the nave to those sitting on the stone steps below the font and along the ledges of tombs. The wandsmen were all wearing their medals and expressions of conspicuous responsibility and Leo, elevated in his loft, was playing a Bach fugue. Nicholas, struggling through the crowded aisles to reach his special seat—allotted to him by Alexander—below the choir screen, remembered his own organist saying before every piece of Bach he taught them, "Now, you will find this very moving." Leo was playing beautifully. The faces all down the nave, row upon row, were reflecting, whether their owners meant them to or not, the effects of the building, the music, and the occasion, full of power and excitement and peace. Nicholas ducked down into his seat and looked upward. If a dove had suddenly appeared on one of those soft, full shafts of light up there, he wouldn't have been at all surprised. The Bach ended, the congregation creaked uncertainly back to life for a moment, and then, to herald the opening of the service, Leo began triumphantly upon Widor's Toccata from the Fifth Symphony.

Halfway down the nave, Sally Ashworth, dressed in a new cream linen suit with big shoulders, wondered what he was playing. She thought he had been playing Bach, but she had no service sheet because they had run out after the first two hundred and fifty people, and the people on either side of her didn't seem to have one either. Henry had a very small solo, and although of course she would know it was him when he began, she wanted to know when to anticipate his beginning. She had asked him over breakfast if he was nervous.

"I am a bit now, but I won't be then. You don't think about it." And then he had added, "I a bit wish Dad was here."

This had shaken Sally. They didn't talk about Alan much, being so preoccupied with living their busy lives, so that Sally forgot to include him sometimes, even mentally, and then felt a mixture of guilt and defiance. Henry almost never mentioned him, except to refer occasionally to things they had done together that he had enjoyed, and Sally could not remember his ever wishing out loud that Alan was with them.

"You could write and tell him," she had said lamely.

"That wouldn't be the same."

"No." She looked intently at him. "I'm sorry, Henry."

"It's not your fault—"

"That doesn't stop me being sorry. For you, I mean."

"Other people's fathers," Henry said without particular resentment, "live at home and go to work here. They sometimes bring them to school and things."

"I suppose Dad feels he couldn't get as good a job here. Not so interesting or so well paid—"

"Hooper's father's a pilot and *he* comes home."

"Henry," Sally said gently, "there's nothing I can do about it."

He said nothing. She waited a moment and then he asked if he could take a Crunchie bar with him and thundered upstairs, leaving her with the guilty knowledge that she *could* have done something, if she had wanted to. Sitting in the cathedral now, the guilt was still there. She hadn't even written to Alan for over a fortnight; he didn't know Henry was to sing a solo, let alone be made a full chorister. She usually felt cross when she thought of Alan, which was manageable, but today she felt miserable, which wasn't manageable at all. She tried to concentrate on the building. She could hear Henry's voice chanting "Perp Perp Perp" to her after a lesson on the cathedral's architecture, because, like all his classmates, he had been enchanted by the irreverent abbreviations of architectural terms. Perp but no Dec. She had an awful feeling she was going to cry.

The organ was doing something heraldic and announcing. The huge congregation rose thunderously to its feet, and the cathedral procession headed by the great Cross of Aldminster attended by taperers and servers entered the nave. Behind the servers came the choristers and the men of the choir, called lay clerks, and the assistant organist and Alexander Troy and then a stream of clergy, honorary thises and residentiary thats, and then the verger and the dean, looking quite exalted, and then the chapter clerk and last the bishop, whose troubled conscience at the precise purpose of this service, so emphatically insisted upon by the dean, was writ large upon his face. Tears rolled down Sally's cheeks, and at the sound of her sniffs, her neighbor, a kind-looking woman in a tidy frock and a beige cardigan, turned and handed her a perfectly laundered handkerchief.

"My son is a chorister," Sally said apologetically.

The woman melted further.

"Ah—"

She whispered to her husband. He peered round her at Sally with kindly interest. Henry's neat brown head bobbed through the choir screen and vanished. Through the loudspeaker system, the dean welcomed the congregation, and with a sound like a distant drumroll, they resumed their seats.

"We thank You, Lord," Hugh Cavendish said with the particular diction he kept for the cathedral, "for revealing Yourself to men and women, and for providing them with the great gift of music, with which they may celebrate and praise You."

Crouched by the choir screen, Nicholas Elliott felt joy and despair sweep over him in wonderful waves.

"To You, O Lord," the dean said, "we the people of Your Cathedral Church of Aldminster dedicate this organ, restored to all its original glory and rebuilt with all the skills of modern organ builders. With this great instrument, O Lord, may we demonstrate to You our undying zeal for the beauty of holiness."

In his stall, the bishop winced, very faintly. The beauty of holiness meant very different things, he feared, to Hugh Cavendish and to himself. Hugh Cavendish's beauty rose wonderfully before him on the south side of the choir, its pipes rich and glowing, a tribute to man's belief in the glory of God, no doubt about that, but to the bishop's mind, a peripheral tribute, for all its splendour. For him, the beauty of holiness lay in the infinite possibilities of the human soul, constantly overlaid but never quite extinguished by the beastliness of human behavior. The bishop was capable of anger, but he was not capable of hate. The synod made him furious, with its selfish inclination towards the individual view rather than a pastoral desire to present a united and *helpful* front to its troubled flock. Divided all the way and almost *proud* of it. That was as wrong as to spend all these thousands on an organ, however historic, while the world dwelt in ignorance and want. He must not think of it now. He must think of the music. Across the aisle from him, an almost perfect boy's voice began on an anthem. "Praise the Lord," he sang, "Oh my soul. Praise the Lord."

"Henry!" Sally thought. It was an astonishing sound. All round her people had adopted that particular stillness of intent listening. Henry stopped and an alto took up the tune and then a second one. Nicholas Elliott put his head on his knees. He had been a treble. But that boy was better than he had ever been, and he was singing with a directness that was quite extraordinary and strangely dignified. Nicholas sat up. It was pathetic to feel envious nostalgia, *pathetic*. He made a resolution. After the service he would go round to the chapter house, where all the clergy and the choir were going to have tea, and he would find the boy and he would tell him he had been *great*.

"What a success," Alexander said to Leo later, in the chapter house.

Leo looked slightly shifty.

"Funny thing, all the music was sacred but the atmosphere was rather *secular*—"

"Nonsense."

"It felt more like a concert than a service."

"It was brilliant. It was all the congregation could do not to applaud."

"That's what I mean—"

A boy appeared with a laden plate.

"Sandwich, sir? Sir?"

Leo peered.

"What's in them?"

Hooper said, "Ham, I think. It's sort of pink, anyway."

"You did so well," Alexander said.

Hooper looked self-conscious.

"Thank you, sir."

"I'd rather have cucumber, Hooper," Leo said, "and I'd rather you finished notes as cleanly as you begin them."

"Sorry, sir. I'll get Ashworth. He's got the cucumber ones."

"Why are you so hard on them?" Alexander said when he had gone.

"I'm tremendously demanding. They understand that perfectly. Hooper knows when he's fluffed something as well as I do."

Henry Ashworth appeared with a huge plate in his hands, and behind him a good-looking woman in cream with her hair to her shoulders, and Nicholas Elliott.

"Sir!"

"Cucumber and a deputation—"

"Mrs. Ashworth," Alexander said quickly, smiling, "I hope you are bursting with a very proper pride."

"Oh, I am—"

"He's great," Nicholas said to Leo, "really great. It sort of hit me—"

"Hear that?" Leo said to Henry.

Henry looked intently down into the sandwiches.

"I'm pleased with you," Leo said.

Alexander put a hand on Henry's shoulder.

"Go and feed the canons, Ashworth. They are always ravenous, particularly the honorary ones. Old Canon Savile, who died last year, always came to chapter meetings on horseback and came stamping in shouting for sandwiches because his ride had made him so hungry. Would you excuse me?"

"I owe you an apology," Sally said, turning to Leo with the same directness that he had recognized in her son. "It was idiotic of me to telephone you the other night. If I had just had the patience to wait until today, I should have obtained the answer to my question." She looked at Nicholas and gave a self-deprecating smile. "I telephoned Mr. Beckford late at night to ask if he thought Henry's voice was just good or really good."

Nicholas, still full of the warmth of his determination to be generous, smiled back and said again, "He's really great."

"He's a nice chap, too," Leo said. "Very straightforward. No trouble at all."

"He's no trouble at home. Of course, he isn't yet—"

"Hello," Ianthe Cavendish said. She was wearing her black cotton jacket and a long tube skirt made of striped T-shirt material and a single huge silver earring of twisted wire and black beads.

Leo looked down at her with displeasure.

"What are you doing here?"

"I'm the dean's daughter," Ianthe said. The fingernails of one hand were painted plum colour. "Remember?" She turned to Sally. "Hello."

"I'm Sally Ashworth."

"And this," Leo said, cutting in, "is Nicholas Elliott. I told you about him."

Ianthe eyed him.

"Know anything about music?"

"I did—"

"Rock music?"

"Well, I listen to it—"

"I run a record company," Ianthe said, "rock bands. We've signed up some amazing new people. Hey"—she turned to Sally again—"was that your kid? The one with the great voice?"

"She doesn't usually talk like this," Leo said. "This is her streetwise accent for company. She can sound perfectly normal if she wants to."

"Tell you what," Ianthe said to Sally, ignoring him, "wouldn't mind signing up your kid. Course, he couldn't sing that stuff for us—"

"Go away," Leo said, suddenly really cross. "Go away and show off to someone more impressionable. Nicholas, take her away. Tell her what you want in life and see if she can help you. See if she can actually be of use for once."

A gleam of pathos softened the bravado in Ianthe's eye, but she quelled it. She took Nicholas by the arm.

"Aren't you a bit hard?" Sally said when they had gone. "She's awfully young."

"She's awfully *silly*. You are the second person to accuse me of hardness this afternoon. I must be getting cantankerous, living alone and thinking of nothing but sacred music and small boys. Heavens!" he said, breaking off and laughing. "That might have been better put—"

"Isn't it odd, that the dean's children should all be so—so unorthodox?"

"Don't you think it's inevitable?"

"Do you mean because of the Church—"

"Yes."

"You think that girl's in love with you. That's why you were so rude to her."

"She thinks she is too. I'm trying to be as unlovable as possible."

"But you make yourself very attractive if you are rude to her."

Leo looked at her.

"Do I?"

"Yes."

"Lord. But if I'm nice, *think* what would happen."

"But only briefly. Very intense, but over quickly. Then she would get bored."

"With my being nice?"

"Yes. Because it isn't so glamorous. Moody and mean is much sexier."

Leo smiled broadly.

"I haven't had a conversation like this for ages. I'd forgotten what it was like. Would you like some more chapter house tea?"

"No, thank you."

"Why did you ring me, honestly, the other night?"

Sally said without hesitation, "Loneliness."

"But Henry was in the house and he presumably has a father—"

"He's in Saudi Arabia. And Henry is a boy and is separate and he is a true musician, and I am not, and that makes him more separate. I am not complaining, I am absolutely sick with pride and pleasure, but I have noticed. And since you asked me, I am telling you."

"I never thought about mothers before."

"No. You wouldn't. That's because you are a professional—"

The dean appeared, radiant.

"Ah! The two people I most wanted to see. I can't congratulate you enough, Beckford. It was an absolute triumph. The cathedral hasn't heard such music in years, if ever. And Mrs. Ashworth, my dear Mrs. Ashworth. What a voice! We knew he was good but today he surpassed himself. Why just that solo, Beckford? Why did we not hear more?"

"Because, Dean, talented though he is, he is still only a probationer and other choristers are more experienced—"

"We are swamped with praise," the dean said, not noticing. "Mrs. Knatchbull from Croxton Manor brought, quite unbeknown to me, an expert on musical instruments from the V. and A. who is quite bowled over by the organ itself, never mind the restoration, and countless people, my dear Beckford, *countless*, have said to me that they can't name another organist with your gifts of phrasing and rhythm. The chancel is absolutely thronged with visitors looking at the organ, thronged. I only wish the lighting were better. I can't thank you enough, Beckford, or congratulate both of you sufficiently. This is a great day for Aldminster, a great day—"

When he had swirled off into the crowd, Sally said, "I mustn't keep you. And I'll do everything I can in future to be the right sort of trouble-free mother."

"Then," Leo said, surprising himself, "I shall be rather disappointed. Come to a rehearsal if you like. I mean it."

She shook her head.

"I won't do that. And I must go." She held her hand out. "Good-bye. And congratulations."

He pulled a face. "Don't you start," he said but he held her hand warmly and he smiled when he spoke.

She and Henry walked home together down the Lyng, and bought oven-ready chicken Kiev on the way, for supper, as a treat to celebrate, and a tub of chocolate-chip ice cream for Henry. When they got back, Mozart was full of complaints that his supper was late, and after they had fed him, they got their own supper ready, and ate it at one end of the pine table with the television balanced at the other end, and watched an awful game whose main purpose appeared to be the humiliation of the participants, which they both enjoyed a lot. Then Henry had two helpings of ice cream, and Sally had a cup of black coffee, and they played Trivial Pursuit, and then Henry was driven up to have a bath, and Sally read him the first terrifying chapter of *Moonfleet* with the Mohune coffins bobbing and crashing about in the darkness of the flooded vault. When she had turned his light out, she had a bath herself and went to bed for a luxurious read, not of her usual by-women-for-women clever fiction, but poetry. This was a good sign. She only ever wanted to read poetry when she was happy. She climbed into bed and picked up Brian Patten, and Mozart came in and, after a few conversational remarks, settled himself down weightily beside her and purred himself into silent sleep.

Two streets nearer the close, up the Lyng, Ianthe and Nicholas shared a pizza and a bottle of Orvieto. Ianthe said she would treat Nicholas because he must be sick of school food, and Nicholas, though he didn't fancy her at all, was pleased to be out with a girl again and relieved not to have to talk carefully and politely for a while. Actually, Ianthe did most of the talking while Nicholas ate most of the pizza, so that by the end of the evening, he knew that her elder brother was brilliant, but *brilliant*, and her sister was a weirdo, and her little brother was a real pain, and that Ikon had a really great future and that she'd like to kill Leo Beckford. She had to talk very loudly to be heard over the music of the pizza place—"Dire Straits, I ask you. Can you *believe* they can play crap like this?"—so most of the people at the adjoining tables knew about her too, and as they were very young, they became rather interested when she said, "Soon we'll be able to pay ourselves around a grand a month—"

"A *grand!*"

She lit a cigarette and drew tremendously on it.

"Something like that. What are you going to do?"

"Don't know. Keep hoping something will turn up."

"Might be able to help you," Ianthe said in the offhand voice people use when they say they'll ring you and then never do.

"Yeah," Nicholas said, understanding her tone. "Thanks."

"No. Really. I'll see about it."

"I've got a bit depressed—"

"Don't tell me," Ianthe said. "I get right down, but I mean *down*."

She ordered more wine and Nicholas told her about his mother and his father and his father's new family, and being sent down from Oxford. She became quite sympathetic and when they had, between them, finished the bowl of brown sugar that stood on the table ready for coffee, and the wine, they went out into Lydbrook Street and Ianthe said she would take Nicholas down to the dockland pubs the next morning; otherwise Sunday might really *get* to them both. Nicholas went home to his room in the infirmary quite cheerfully, for him, and Ianthe went home via Chapter Yard and observed that Leo actually appeared to be trying to clear up his sitting room. He was wearing corduroy jeans and a checked shirt and he looked so isolated and sexy that her knees nearly gave way under her, and she almost knocked on the window. But then she remembered she was furious with him for putting her down in public that afternoon, so she strode on home and woke Cosmo up because she felt like listening to music but didn't want to do it alone.

Leo had come back to Chapter Yard feeling extremely restless—no doubt the tensions and excitements of the afternoon accounted for that—and was for the first time absolutely exasperated to open the sitting-room door and find the room exactly as he had left it. It looked as if he had thrown all the contents in and then stirred them about with a giant spoon. It was so *unintelligent* to live like this, because it was exhausting and sapped creative energies. He picked up the nearest tape lying on a pile of old newspapers and colour supplements and slammed it into the cassette player and it was Vaughan Williams's *Job*, which he wasn't really in the mood for, but he couldn't bear to waste ten or twenty or forty minutes hunting for the Fauré he would have preferred.

He made himself a sandwich and a mug of coffee and took them into the very heart of the muddle to assess the situation. The first move was clearly to see what there was that he could throw out. Newspapers, of course, months' worth of flown and forgotten Sundays, easy to throw away as long as he didn't allow himself to be seduced by a single headline as he threw; and then books back in bookshelves once he had removed all the other objects from the latter, and sheet music in a box, well, several boxes, and cushions on chairs not the floor, and clothes in a heap to take upstairs, and the wires sorted out a bit so they didn't form this lethal sort of crochet over everything . . .

He started well. He went round to the Chancellors' and borrowed two dustbin bags. "I had to smile," Cherry said to her husband. "Leo clearing up!" He asked her for two bags, so she gave him precisely that, off a bargain roll. He took them back and filled one in twenty minutes, and then he came across the photograph book he and Judith had made when they were first married, and was about to throw that in too and then couldn't resist one look, and there was Judith, scowling over her flute, so he sat down with the book and turned the pages. There was Judith on their penurious honeymoon in the Quantocks, wearing jeans and gym shoes; himself up a ladder painting the window frames of the first house they had, in Lincoln, with his first proper job; Judith reading in the garden with her hair all over her face; Judith asleep in a bed that looked as if a combine harvester had been across it. It had been hopeless, his marriage to Judith. She wasn't designed by nature to live with or for anybody but herself. And yet he had pestered her to marry him, bothered the life out of her for months until she had relented at last, saying warningly that she wasn't going to change for anybody. And she didn't. When the rapture of the first months was over, it began to madden Leo that she would make no concessions to a shared life at all. All she wanted to do was to sing and to play her flute and to work, increasingly, for the women's movement. They lived in squalor and acrimony. Judith took to going to Greenham Common for weekends, and then for weeks on end, and when she was arrested and Leo went to try and prevent her from going to jail, she told him to go to hell, and she went to jail anyway. When she came out, she returned, briefly, to Rochester, where he was then assistant organist, collected her possessions, and left. They were divorced a year later, and Leo resigned his post because he was made to feel that he had to.

He moved away, right across England, and got a job teaching music in the big girls' public school in Aldminster: St. Mary's. He knew nothing about Aldminster, or girls. He had a tiny flat in the school, and some of the girls besieged him there, and there was an embarrassing, unavoidable episode with an excitable Iranian girl, who had become obsessed with him, and he was again faced with resignation or dismissal.

He was taken in, a refugee, by Martin Chancellor. Martin was a bachelor then, and assistant to the amiable, indolent, unadventurous organist who had played the organ at Aldminster for twenty-five years. Martin and Leo had met in the city's musical circles and had quite liked each other; there was, Leo deduced, at least nothing in Martin Chancellor to *dis*like. For four months, Leo gave private piano lessons in the mornings and evenings and nursed his grievances during interminable solitary afternoons, and then the organist had a heart attack, quite without warning, and Leo, in a burst of defiance against outdated values, applied for the post.

He was by far the best organist of the applicants; even Martin Chancellor, feeling keenly that Leo had bitten very hard the hand that fed him, admitted that. But he was divorced. It was a great stumbling block to the dean and chapter, and if it had not been for the bishop, Leo would never have succeeded. The bishop summoned Leo to him and talked to him in a way that seemed gentle to the point of blandness until he looked back on it and saw how probing the bishop had been. They had talked first of music.

Why cathedral music, the bishop had asked, why not organ recitals, conducting, records, instruction—no problem at all with such skills as Leo's? Why not found his own choir? He would earn only seven thousand a year at Aldminster after all, so was this not a piece of unworldly and pointless recklessness? Leo, turning a teacup round and round in his hands, said that all that really seemed to satisfy him, the only situation in which he felt, heart and soul, that he had come home, was to play and hear sacred music in a sacred place.

"Are you a Christian?" the bishop asked.

"I don't know. I struggle—"

"There are so many ways of being a Christian."

"I come closest to faith when I am playing a cathedral organ, and as that is also the time when I feel most richly fulfilled, I suppose that makes me at best a very lopsided part-time Christian."

"You are an exceptionally good organist," the bishop said.

He had sat silent then, swinging one foot under his purple cassock, until he began to ask Leo about his marriage. Leo tried to be fair and truthful.

"Do you hate her?"

"No. But I am still angry sometimes."

"Anger," the bishop said, picking up his own teacup and finding to his regret that it was empty, "is a very different matter from hate. And as to your divorce"—he paused and waved his empty cup thoughtfully—"in my view, a Christian marriage is a good one, not necessarily a first one."

Instinctively, both their gazes were drawn beyond the study windows to where Janet Young, in an old jersey of the bishop's, was cutting down spent Michaelmas daisies.

"I have been extraordinarily lucky," said the bishop. "It seems to me that you and your wife were not."

When Leo got up to go, he said, "Thank you so much for seeing me. I know there isn't any hope really but it's been a comfort to talk."

The bishop shook his hand.

"I shall pray about this a great deal, and talk in certain quarters very much less." A thought struck him. "Did you know that Bach sired twenty children? In two marriages. Extraordinary." He let Leo's hand go. "God bless you."

Three weeks later, Leo moved into the neighbouring house to Martin Chancellor's in Chapter Yard, as organist of Aldminster. Alexander Troy had come to see him at once and they had liked each other immensely and found that they shared similar ambitions for the choir. Then Felicity had come, and Leo had supposed himself in love with her, because she was so distinguished and delightful, and because, in his gratitude to the bishop or God or whoever it was, he had an overflowing heart and the overflow needed a channel.

He had been happier, those five years at Aldminster, than anywhere before. The reputation of the cathedral's music grew steadily, and so did Leo's own ability, so that if he went into the cathedral, as he often did, for the exhilarating and extraordinary release of extemporizing, he would emerge from the organ to find a considerable audience. St. Mary's had even asked him to return to run the music department once more—the new headmistress, a breezy woman who had spent most of her career in America, said that Leo was a fine musician and she didn't care about old tattle—which doubled his income. He had friends and briefly, after Felicity Troy had with great kindness told him not to be an ass, a girlfriend, head of Horsley Art School's graphic department. Leo had rather enjoyed her, and it had been a relief to have someone to go to bed with, but his great liking for her would not somehow turn itself into love. They were still friends and Leo didn't any longer want them to be more, although he did feel, increasingly, that he wasn't building the human side of his life as he was the musical side.

He closed the photograph book and put it in a dustbin bag. Then he got it out again and put it on the bottom shelf of the bookcase, underneath a pile of *National Geographic* magazines. Judith wasn't dead, after all, and they had been married. You couldn't just eliminate either her or the marriage. He looked round the room. He was suddenly immensely tired; the rest would have to wait. He turned off the lamps, picked up the heap of clothes, and trudged upstairs. In the morning, Cherry Chancellor, nipping out early to get the Sunday papers, noticed that his sitting room looked exactly the same except that the two grey dustbin bags now squatted in the chaos like a pair of begging hippopotami.

Hugh Cavendish could not sleep that night. He was filled with a kind of sober exhilaration, a feeling that he had found a mission.

He lay in bed beside the solid and slumbering Bridget, and then, after an hour of lying wakeful, he got up and put on his dressing gown, and went down to the kitchen, where Benedict, though sleepily pleased to see him, made it very plain that one in the morning was no time to stir from one's basket.

The dean made tea and a piece of toast, and found paper and a pencil and settled himself down at the kitchen table. It was very warm, thanks to the stove, and quiet. The dean drew a rough plan of the cathedral, and marked in the significant objects and then, as round black dots, the present position of the lights. The positions hadn't really changed in years—except for an attempt in the fifties to make them complement the natural light in the cathedral—not from the late nineteenth century, when the gas lamps had required the poor bedesmen to clamber eternally up and down the western staircase to light and then extinguish them.

The V. and A. man had been right. What the cathedral needed now was new lighting, concealed lighting with no dazzle, lighting that would enhance the beauty and the mystery of the building. There was no doubt too, after this afternoon, that the musical reputation of the cathedral would go from strength to strength, and there would be concerts and recitals, and, of course, musicians were always greedy for more light. As to funding it, well, there were the Friends of the Cathedral, bless them, and, of course, the Historic Churches people, and it was many years since Aldminster had applied to them for anything, so they might look quite responsively on such a request. He must see about a lighting designer, of course, and consult the cathedral architect, who had proved such an indefatigable ally over the restoration of the organ. The organ. The dean's happy and swift train of thought stopped abruptly. The organ, the glorious, renovated organ, brought with it an enormous snag, in the shape of Leo Beckford. Leo, brilliant organist though he was, pulled *against* the dean, no denying it. So, in a less aggressive way, did Alexander Troy. If Martin Chancellor had been organist, the dean thought, he would have been an ally, his aim would have been to bring both the instrument and the choir *within* the dean's benevolent sway over cathedral and close. But Beckford and Troy made the dean feel that the choir was so much *not* his that it was almost, at times, in opposition to him. He would even, he thought, go so far as to believe that they deliberately kept the choir from him. But they could not keep the organ from him, and without the organ, Leo had no future as an increasingly visible national musician. He must be delicate. He must control Leo without losing him. He must rule his beloved possessions with diplomacy as well as strength and benevolence. Pulling the paper and pencil towards him, he resolved to start with the practicalities. He made a list of people to telephone, and a second piece of toast. Of course, the interior masonry would have to be washed if it was to be better illuminated; he must see the works yard about spare scaffolding.

The cathedral clock struck two. Benedict raised his head and listened. At the table, the dean pushed away his paper and plate and cup, and folding his hands and bowing his head down on them, he began most thankfully to pray. "There is no need to say anything when you pray," the dean had heard Bishop Robert say at a recent confirmation in the city. "Just take time to look at God. And let Him look at you. That's all."

5

WHEN IT BECAME KNOWN AMONG THE COUNCILLORS OF ALD-
minster that the dean and chapter were looking for forty-five
thousand pounds to fund new lighting in the nave and aisles of
the cathedral, Frank Ashworth felt it would be a good moment
to renew his suggestion about purchasing the headmaster's house.
He found the dean in a very different mood from the one he had
been in at their last interview, very buoyant and not in the least
pliable.

"Mr. Ashworth, we are not, I am happy to tell you, in the position
that men of finance call demandeur. The Friends of the Cathedral
can raise two-thirds of the sum, and we can obtain grants for the
remainder."

"We can wait," Frank Ashworth said. "There's no hurry. No
doubt you'll need the money someday."

"I must be honest with you," the dean said in tones of the
smoothest confidentiality. "You must dismiss all hopes of the headmaster's house. The cathedral and its close will be attracting an
immensely increased number of visitors and the environment must
of course be protected for them."

"Does it not trouble you," Frank said slowly, "to be spending so
much money on new lighting when not only is the old lighting
perfectly adequate to most people's minds, but when the city needs
money so badly to help its people?"

"The cathedral belongs to the city and its people. They are very proud of it—"

"Lights in the cathedral won't help them find jobs or cure them when they're sick—"

"Mr. Ashworth," the dean said with an authoritativeness Frank knew better than to match just now, "you and your council look after housing and employment and health. We leave you to do that. We care for other vital elements in mankind. You leave us to do that. Good morning."

Frank's reply was to make an appointment to see the bishop. Robert Young opened the door of the palace himself, to a waft of baking and Radio Three from the kitchen, and led Frank into his long light study with its battered furniture and books and model airplanes on the mantelpiece.

"I can't, you know," Bishop Robert said, biting the earpiece of his spectacles, "interfere with the dean and chapter business. I serve the diocese, not the cathedral alone."

"It's the principle I've come to talk about, Bishop."

"Mm."

"It bothers me that so few people in the city use the close and the cathedral."

"It bothers *me*," the bishop said.

"To be frank with you, Bishop, the close scares them off. It's too elitist."

"You think so?"

"I know so."

The bishop put on his spectacles.

"Let me think."

After a minute or two, he said, "In a sense you are right. People are disconcerted by a ritual they have not been brought up to find familiar. In that sense, the cathedral might look like some kind of club whose rules they don't know. But not elitist in the sense I think you mean. An elite, if I understand it, is the pick, the flower of something. In God's eyes, there is in humanity no such thing."

Frank said, smiling, "I didn't come to talk theology—"

"Were we?"

"Edging that way. I came to put to you the idea that the people of the city should have a place, a building, that is their own, to help them to feel comfortable—"

"A secular place? A meeting place?"

"Yes."

"I am all in favour of encouraging people to use the cathedral. I spend a lot of time urging people I meet to do just that. And I can see that a meeting house might get them closer, although I am always opposed to anything artificial because that simply confounds the problem." He looked at Frank Ashworth and said determinedly, "You can only win people lastingly to anything, by love."

"Doesn't it seem to you wrong that the headmaster and his wife live in about a quarter of their house?"

The bishop sat up.

"*Wrong?*"

"When the people of the city could well use the house as is their right to, to feel the close is their own."

The bishop stood up.

"Mr. Ashworth, you presume too much."

"The privileged will protect their own, then—"

The bishop took a firm grip upon his temper. "Forgive me for quoting the dictionary once more. Privilege means, among other things, a freedom from burdens borne by others. The people of this city, Mr. Ashworth, are so privileged. You carry some burdens for them, I try to carry others. The headmaster of the King's School carries yet more. I support you wholly in your desire to make the close more approachable, but I will not be party to a scheme that wears an altruistic mask to cover a heart of envy." He crossed to the mantelpiece and picked up a little Spitfire and looked at it affectionately for a minute before putting it down again. Then he turned back to Frank. "I believe your grandson is now to be a full chorister. I congratulate you."

"I'm not comfortable about that either," Frank said. "It's my son's notion he should be at the King's School, not mine."

"I believe boys from the city schools have as much chance of becoming members of the choir as boys at the King's School. In fact I believe there are at least half a dozen bursaries and scholarships open to any boy from any school. And am I not right in saying that the chief education officer of the city is a governor of the King's School?"

Frank got slowly to his feet.

"It's the same problem, isn't it? The same problem as with the close. People feel they aren't welcome."

The bishop walked across to the door and laid his hand on the handle.

"In my experience, Mr. Ashworth, people believe themselves to be welcome almost anywhere unless they are deliberately instructed that they are not. It is part of the Church's teaching to extend the warmest welcome to all comers, and that welcome awaits everyone living in this city, both in the cathedral and in the heart of every member of the close, every day." He opened the door. "I will see you out, Mr. Ashworth."

When Frank had gone, the bishop sought the comfort of the kitchen.

"So right in his heart! So right! But so devious in his head. Not having God with you is like trying to walk normally on one leg; it twists you, it must. He sees everything in terms of class—"

"Did you tell him," Janet Young said, laying strips of pastry across an apple tart, "that you went to a grammar school?"

"No," the bishop said, "it didn't come up. The council has a scheme to try to buy the headmaster's house for some kind of social centre."

"What's wrong with that?"

"Nothing. It's probably right. But the motives and methods are not right. Is that for lunch?"

"Sorry. It's for the weekend. When Matthew is home."

The bishop sat on a corner of the kitchen table.

"He's a good man. He has given his life to this city, but he believes that only he knows what people want."

"Do people know what they want themselves?"

The bishop leaned sideways and kissed his wife.

"I rather want lunch. And my specs have disintegrated again."

"You shouldn't eat them. Why don't we get you a second pair? I did feel rather ashamed of that photograph of you in the *Echo* in your mitre and a large lump of Sellotape holding your glasses together."

"Bishops don't need to be *soigné*."

"Ones that sit on floury kitchen tables certainly won't be."

"Janet . . ."

"Yes."

"I wish people today weren't so *unhappy*."

She put the tart in the oven, and came back to him, and laid her warm cooking-scented hand on his.

"At least you're in the right job to help *do* something about that."

Using a Choir Schools Association meeting as a pretext, Alexander Troy went up to London to look for his wife. He noticed, as he usually did, that his entering a train with a dog collar on made fellow passengers suddenly alert—few of them sitting next to him could quite relax. Further up the carriage, two American nuns in school sandals, Crimplene frocks,and abbreviated modern veils, talking travel, were creating the same wary suppressed interest around them. Alexander looked at the young woman reading a printout and the man in a bomber jacket softly tapping a rolled-up copy of the *Sun* against the window who shared his quartet of seats, and wondered what they would do if he told them why he was going to London. He would appal them, of course. Instead, he did what they would expect him to do, and extracted from his briefcase a copy of *The Times* and a draft of his end-of-term speech. He looked up once and the young printout woman was looking at him with keen interest, an expression that changed to indignation when he smiled at her.

He got out at Paddington and went to pay the little silent tribute to Brunel's statue that he always liked to do (if he had time he went also to salute Sergeant Jagger's moving exhausted bronze soldier), and then he went down into the seething tunnels of the Underground and made his way with great complexity to Highgate and Felicity's brother, Sam. Sam led a hybrid life as a freelance book-jacket designer, cricket correspondent to a major Sunday paper, and part-time literature tutor at a crammer. He was unmarried and had the calm self-containment of one who is really interested in neither men nor women and lived in a house over which he took enormous trouble, whose floors he had painted beautifully and disconcertingly to resemble medieval maps, complete with dragons and sea beasts. Instinctively skirting a Welsh castle from whose keep a trumpeter blew a lonely blast, Alexander sat down in a director's chair slung with black leather while Sam made coffee.

"She never came here," Sam said. "I think I'd probably have told you if she was here. I *think* I would. But she did ring. She wasn't very communicative but she said she'd be perfectly safe. She will too. And she'll be back."

"It's nearly three weeks now."

Sam put two pottery mugs of coffee down on his black table.

"How long was it last time?"

"Three weeks. Sam—"

"Why does she go?"

"Yes."

Sam lit a cigarette.

"All the passion that's missing in me, old son, got walloped into her. Emotional passion, I mean. You know that. She will take life so hard. It's nothing you do. Or don't do. It's just Fliss. She was always buzzing off when we were kids, she sort of had to." He gave Alexander a narrowed glance. "You miss her, don't you?"

"Oh yes."

"I've always reckoned," Sam said, "that you're pretty good to her. Living with anyone else has always scared me witless. Can't take it. But you're so patient."

"I want to be. I don't feel *im*patient."

Sam stubbed out his cigarette.

"She gets in a state about God."

"We all do."

"But perhaps she feels she oughtn't, married to you."

"But I do myself. I think at least patches of spiritual turmoil are a hazard of the job."

"Maybe."

"Haven't you *any* idea where she might be?"

"No. And if I did, you shouldn't try to find her. She'll come back of her own accord and it'll mean a lot to her that you didn't fuss her." He looked at his watch. "Sorry, old son. I've got a tutorial in half an hour. Goon of a boy, and Gerard Manley Hopkins, God help us all three."

Alexander stood up.

"It's a comfort to see you. You make me feel her going is more ordinary than it sometimes feels in Aldminster."

"Let's face it," Sam said, "for Fliss it is. Isn't it?"

The comfort, however, did not last. Alexander sat through the meeting, rose to his feet only once to make an eloquent but not wholly relevant speech about the fragility of this unparalleled British tradition of choral singing in a hostile economic climate, and left for Paddington with a confused feeling that most of his emotional and mental lines were crossed. The train was packed and he had to stand for half the journey, being once, horrifyingly, offered a seat by a plain and trembling woman in a home-knitted jersey. Sam's calm consolation leaked away as the westward miles were eaten up, and by the time the train slid wheezing into Aldminster, Alexander was as close to the blackest misery as he had ever been. The boys were coming out of compline as he reached the school, and he was quite shaken to find what a comfort they were in their unconscious ordinariness, bursting out of the chapel with exaggerated exhilaration after the queer and particular mood of the service. He hoped Leo might be there, but Leo was not. Leo was at that moment walking down Blakeney Street to have supper with Sally Ashworth, with a bottle of Valpolicella in his pocket.

Mrs. Miles had left Alexander a pork pie and a plastic pot of fierce mustardy coleslaw on a tray for his supper. He had a heap of work to do. He had to plan the choir tour almost a year in advance and he was late already—a polite letter from the Abbé at Saint-Benoît-sur-Saône lay reproachfully on his desk, and had so lain for a fortnight. Speech Day was fast approaching, and the thrice-annual agony of reports, that eternal wrangle between compassion, accuracy, and originality, not to mention public examinations, and he could not even stop to *consider* that Felicity was he knew not where and that his house was about to become a coffee shop for the city. "Fifty-two," he thought, regarding himself without affection in the small glass he kept in his study for robing. "Fifty-two. This should be the great decade of a man's life, the *rich* decade. And I seem to have lost all interest in it. If I died now, what would I leave? What *would* I leave?" He crossed the room to his ancient record player and put on the Bach Choir singing Mathias's "Lux Aeterna," and then he went to his desk and sat down to his welter of papers. In the kitchen, Nicholas Elliott, who had come down from his lonely corner in the infirmary in search of food, found the pork pie and the coleslaw and ate both with enthusiasm.

The following afternoon, Alexander took his ancient history class across to the cathedral as an alternative to Pericles. They were very excited about this and hopped chattering round him saying Sir, Sir, Sir and not listening to his replies. Over the years, he had worked on being a good guide for small boys, and this day he took them round the half circle of past bishops in the ambulatory, from Osric, lying remote and still on his little granite tomb, to Langley Blake, who had denounced the moral laxity of the sixties in a most medieval manner, and had died in the late seventies saying "I told you so." As usual, the boys liked best the graceful cartouche put up for the eighteenth-century bishop Joshua Fielding, on account of the horses' and dogs' heads emerging from the marble scrolls, representations of the bishop's own beloved animals, which he had requested to be remembered with him. It was said that he had kept a tame hare in a basket in his study and had read his sermons aloud to the elderly sow who lived in a pen behind the palace. The humorous humanity of this never failed to strike a chord, and was an excellent prelude to taking the class into the choir stalls for a moment's quiet prayer. This was a small thrill in itself, to be kneeling where the choristers knelt, for the school was proud of its singing boys, which accounted for their being so relentlessly teased. They shot covert glances now of admiration at Ashworth and Chilworth who knew their way about these high dark pews with their interestingly carved tip-up seats and hard red plush hassocks. The seventeen boys knelt and briefly considered their hazy notions of prayer and God and their more concrete one of the pig, and then they got up with alacrity and were told not to fiddle with the psalters and the candlesticks, and were lined up in some sort of order to troop back to school for tea and, because this was Thursday, Swiss buns.

On the way out of the chancel, going past the western staircase, they met the dean, the cathedral architect, and another man coming down. All three looked gravely preoccupied. The cathedral architect was saying, "Of course, until we know the extent of the damp, or even how deeply it has penetrated the stone—" at the same time that the dean was saying, across him, to the third man, "And to think that the simple direction of the present lighting served to *obscure* all this from us." The boys halted and looked respectful. The dean, not only one of the most significant figures in the close, was, after all, a school governor, a renowned fly fisherman, and father of the legendary Cosmo, whose myth inspired the younger boys rather as Che Guevara's had fired the student revolutionaries of the sixties and seventies. The dean looked back at them from deep within his preoccupation. The architect, a childless man and consequently alarmed by anyone under twenty, began to make jocular remarks about now being able to set them a quiz on the cathedral. They regarded him stonily while Alexander explained that they should really be spending the hour on a study of the commercial rivalry between Corinth and Athens, at which the architect looked relieved and said, "Ah! The ravages of Attica."

"What ravages?" the dean said, thinking only of those vast stone ribs above him dark with the sinister damp they had just discovered.

"Spartan, sir," said Briggs, who was always, obnoxiously, both first and right in class. Somebody kicked him neatly and sharply on the anklebone. "Ow," Briggs said loudly.

The dean, his face clouded with a profound misery, drew Alexander briefly aside.

"We went up to the clerestory walkways to investigate the new lighting possibilities with Mr. Harvey here of Harvey's Electrical, and found that some of the triforium arches are running with damp, simply running, and that parts of the nave roof look suspiciously dark, which of course we have never seen because the old lighting is directed *down*, you see, into the body of the nave—"

"Does it look serious?"

"Yes," Hugh Cavendish said, "yes. It does." He looked across at the architect. "Mervyn says he isn't happy at all—"

The boys were beginning to murmur and shuffle.

"Would you forgive me? I think I ought to shepherd this lot back; otherwise it will be discovered that we have been playing truant."

"That won't do for the headmaster, will it, boys?" the architect said.

A few smiled politely. Briggs got halfway through saying that as there was no higher authority in school than the headmaster, he had nobody to answer to, but was then half-garrotted from behind by a forefinger slipped into the back of his tie and twisted hard, and went into a theatrical paroxysm of choking.

"That will *do*," Alexander said.

"But, sir—"

"You heard me."

"Ah," Hugh Cavendish said, "the desecration of routine." His eyes strayed upwards. "Ought I not to contact the clerk of works this moment?"

Outside the cathedral, Henry Ashworth detached himself from the group trying to tread Briggs's shoes off from behind and fell back beside Alexander. This was not to say anything particular but, it seemed, merely to be companionable. Alexander said, after a while, "And when are you to be presented to the dean as a full chorister?"

"In two weeks, sir. I've got my ruff now and Mrs. Ridgeway's fed up because the new ones have got Velcro, not buttons, and she doesn't believe in Velcro so she's got to take it off and put buttons on."

"We must rehearse you. Before the war, full choristers were always given a ceremonial copy of Boyce's *Cathedral Music*." He eyed Henry. "Perhaps it is as well that we don't do that anymore because the book is about as big as you and Chilworth put together."

Chilworth, who had been arguing with Briggs, dropped back now beside Henry to say, "Sing A flat."

Henry sang.

"Sing A double flat."

"There," Chilworth said, "I *told* stupid Briggs you could," and ran back to his argument.

A sudden affection for them all shook Alexander in a spasm of gratitude. He looked down at Henry with warmth.

"Fluke," Henry mumbled, and blushed. "Sir," he said.

The dean and the clerk of works, an experienced and lugubrious man who had to have the last word on everything, spent a depressing hour together in the clerestory walkways. Jim Woodcote, conscious that the responsibility for damp of this magnitude was bound to be laid at his door, was more silent than usual, even to the point of frequently ignoring the dean's anxious questions. It was apparent to both of them that the trouble spot was a long line along the edge of the south face of the nave roof towards the western end, the face most naturally exposed to the rain-laden winds from the estuary. Woodcote's powerful torch beam picked out long dark fingers of damp creeping up the vault of the nave ceiling and, most alarmingly, the odd shining trickles of wet running from the clerestory recesses at the points where the great springing ribs of the roof left the walls. As Jim Woodcote's own alarm grew, so his manner became more and more dour. Having declined to speak at all for some ten minutes, he turned at last to the dean and said he couldn't make any kind of assessment until he'd been up on the roof outside and had a look at the west and south parapets on the nave roof. He then shut his mouth tight and made sweeping movements with his torch to indicate that they should descend to the ground. Hugh Cavendish, endeavouring to remind himself what a marvellous craftsman and tireless overseer Woodcote was, had no choice but to obey.

He went home in a mood as abject as it had, earlier that afternoon, been elated. Half an hour remained to him before he must set out, forty minutes across the diocese, for a cheese-and-wine party given by the Friends of the Cathedral, a splendid body the prospect of whose zealousness, in his present frame of mind, was severely daunting. In the drawing room Bridget was having one of her clergy wives' teas, occasions which the dean knew divided far more than they united, since half the wives asked could never come on account of being full-time teachers or physiotherapists or nurses, and their absence was made much of by the regular core of Bridget's slaves, who attended punctually. From upstairs came the thump of Cosmo's reggae, unnecessarily loud on account of Cosmo's being temporarily gated, as requested by Mr. Miller, to prevent his leading his free-wheeling gang through the residential streets of Horsley after school hours, taking lids off dustbins and calling obscenities softly through letter boxes. If the dean were to go up and ask Cosmo to turn the music down, Cosmo would smile at him with immense frank warmth and indicate by dumb show that he could not hear and therefore could not oblige. If the dean attempted to touch the cassette player himself, Cosmo would wait until he had gone downstairs and then turn the noise up until the house trembled from cellar to attic. When the dean had once taken the machine away altogether, Bridget, saying "Poor Father is so tired, he isn't himself at all," had given it back to Cosmo within hours.

The dean went into his study and closed the door upon all the varied domestic defiance in the rest of the house. He crossed to the window and looked with love and something close to anguish at the cathedral, suddenly seeming, for all its majesty, so vulnerable, a great spirit dwelling precariously in a frail fabric. He could not bear the thought of giving up the lighting scheme; Mr. Harvey had fired him with visions of the nave roof illuminated with an almost theatrical magic by concealed floodlights and fluorescent tubes, the triforium arches silhouetted against a hidden glow, the choir screen standing dramatic and dark against the upflung light from the chancel beyond. And in any case, if the roof was really serious, would forty-five thousand pounds make that much difference? The clock struck five-thirty. He was due at Croxton in forty-five minutes, and he still had on his dusty shoes and old flannels from climbing about the cathedral. The journey at least would serve as thinking time; he felt instinctively that he must have some suggestions ready, some plan afoot to defend his lighting scheme against the demands the roof was bound to make, irresistibly, of the cathedral coffers. He opened the study door. They were singing "Jerusalem" in the drawing room, no doubt to emphasize, to any clergy wife who was in the least doubt, that in Bridget's eyes the Women's Institute, which she virtually commanded in the county, was a body of much greater significance than the Church. Sighing for a dozen reasons, Hugh Cavendish grasped the lovely bannister rail and began to climb the stairs wearily to change.

"Shut your eyes," Leo said, "while I put the light on and decide whether I can bear to let you look."

"I live with men," Sally said reasonably, "and work for another. I'm quite used to mess."

"But this," Leo said in a voice that had an edge of awe to it, "this is really five-star mess."

She opened her eyes.

"So it is."

"If I'd known I was going to have the impulse to ask you back here, I wouldn't have left it like this."

"Didn't you?"

"Didn't I what?"

"Know you might have the impulse to ask me back?"

"Of course I did," Leo said. "I'm as poor a liar as I am a house-keeper. I suppose it's a sort of test. If you can stand this, I might have a chance—"

"A chance?"

"Sally, don't *flirt* with me."

"Why—"

"Because I'm serious."

"You can't be. You came to supper last night and we went to the wine tasting tonight and—"

"I'm serious."

"Oh Lord," Sally said, but she was enchanted.

Leo went to the window and pulled the single curtain until it hung in a panel across the centre, and then he took an armful of books, a cardboard box of bottles, and a muddle of newspapers off the sofa and said, "Sit down. I think I've got some wine."

"I don't really want any more to drink."

"Coffee?"

"Lovely."

"It isn't. It's instant. Don't let me be serious, Sally, I'm so *useless*."

"It isn't up to me," she said dangerously.

"I said, Sally, don't flirt."

"I don't know what to do with you."

He knelt by the sofa.

"*I* know what I want to do with *you*—"

She had the same inward sliding sensation she had had when he had arrived at the wine tasting and stood in the doorway, looking round for her. She was helping her boss pull corks and pour wine, so she couldn't do much more than wave, and he came across the room and looked at her most particularly and took a glass in either hand saying, "Burgundy and Burgundy?" and went away to talk to other people. She hadn't exchanged another word with him for an hour, and then he had come back and said, "Come home with me, for half an hour, so we can talk," and here she was in this charming crooked chaotic room with Leo about to make love to her and her wanting him to, all the way.

She said, "I must think."

"Fatal."

He got off his knees and stood up.

"I'm going to find some coffee in my evil kitchen."

She followed him across the room and leaned in the doorway while he poked around finding mugs and spoons and the coffee jar.

"Leo, I really don't know *what* I'm doing. Am I just another bored wife married to a man I never see who is periodically unfaithful to me anyway? Are you just lonely?"

"It isn't like you to talk like that."

"But you don't *know* what I'm like! You can't—"

"I can and do know enough to perceive in you a coolness and a gallantry that I am bowled over by. You're also wildly attractive."

"So are you."

"That's better," Leo said.

Sally said in a much steadier voice, "I didn't mean to sound as if I was whining. But it has all rather rushed in and grabbed me when I wasn't looking."

"Hasn't it just."

He handed her a mug.

"Tell me about Alan."

"If you like. But I shan't reveal anything at all interesting. I just don't like him much anymore. We have nothing to say to each other and nothing in common except Henry."

"So?"

"So it has crossed my mind fairly frequently in the last year that I don't want my life to trail on like this much longer. I sometimes think, What if this is all there is?"

Leo steered her towards the sofa and sat down beside her.

"Have you had an affair with anyone?"

"Since I married Alan? No."

"Well," Leo said, without moving towards her, "you're going to now."

"It isn't just your decision."

He inclined his head.

"We'll go at any pace you like. Can't you see? I want to do what you want, as well as what I want."

"I've never got so far so fast with anyone in my life."

"Nor me."

"You were married though, weren't you?"

He got up and pulled the book of photographs from under the magazines on the bookshelf. Sally followed him. He opened the book and put it in her hands.

"There she is."

"What happened?"

"I was desperate for her to marry me until she did and then it was quite hopeless. I never liked her really, I was just desperate."

"Are you desperate now?"

"No," he said, "just enormously happy," and he took the book away from her and put his arms around her and was kissing her

when Alexander, who had found the front door unlatched, knocked
at the sitting room one and walked in without waiting for an answer.

Sally tried to break free, but Leo held her.

"Alexander," he said. His voice was quite level.

"Please," Sally said and Leo let go. She went quickly across the
room to Alexander, said, "Good night, Mr. Troy," and slipped past
him and out of the door.

"What are you *doing?*" Alexander demanded.

"A superfluous question."

"That," Alexander said, advancing on him, "that is the mother
of one of your choristers, do you realize? Henry Ashworth is a charge
of both yours and mine. What are you thinking of?"

"Of her, and of myself."

"Leo, Leo—"

"Why are you here?"

"I rather wanted to talk."

Leo sighed and put his hand on Alexander's arm and guided him
to the sofa.

"I'll talk all you like but not about Sally Ashworth."

"It can't go further, Leo, you must give her up—"

"No."

"How long have you known her?"

"Two days, properly."

"Then—"

"No, Alexander."

He went into the kitchen and found the bottle of wine Sally had
refused and returned with it and two glasses and a corkscrew.

"You've only just staggered through the last scandal, Leo."

"This isn't a scandal."

"Do you think you love her?"

"Do you think I am going to tell you something I haven't even
told her?" His voice became angry. "You haven't any prerogative
on love—"

Felicity's name hung unspoken in the air between them.

"I don't want to quarrel with you."

Leo held out a glass of wine.

"Very wine ordinary, I'm afraid."

They drank for a while in silence. Then Alexander began to talk about the council's designs upon the headmaster's house and the episode with the dean that afternoon, and Leo said how thankful he was to be out of the close politics.

"You might be dragged in, willy-nilly."

"Why?"

"I sense a thunderstorm rumbling away round the edges."

Leo refrained from saying that perhaps it was Alexander's own personal thunderstorm, and said instead, "Oh, it's always like this. Storms in teacups. Remember my appointment, for one."

Alexander stood up.

"I must go."

"I think you haven't said what you came to say."

"It went wrong," Alexander said, "didn't it?"

"You'd better say it. It's either now or some other time and I'd rather hear it now."

"I came," Alexander said, "for some balm for my wounds. But from your last remark, I can see that that's the last thing I'll get—"

"You mean Felicity."

"Yes."

Leo put a brief hand on Alexander's shoulder.

"I'm sorry about that. But I can't help you. I can only hope fiercely that she will come back to you."

"I shall go looking for her, if she doesn't."

"Alexander—"

"She's my wife. We are bound to each other. I can't just feebly let her drift."

"She's a person—"

"All persons are persons. But this one is my beloved wife. There's a world of difference between giving someone room and leaving them to be lonely and afraid. That's one of the things marriage is *for*."

Leo said, thinking of Sally, "And if *marriage* leaves you lonely and afraid?"

"You must signal for help."

"As Sally Ashworth is now doing."

"But not," Alexander said with emphasis, "to her husband."

"He won't listen."

"Or perhaps you will listen more easily and sympathetically."

Leo picked up his and Sally's coffee mugs.

"You love Felicity. Sally and Alan do not love each other anymore. Coffee?"

Alexander shook his head.

"Judith and I stopped loving each other. We didn't *mean* to but it happened. You are lucky to be so unhappy, you are lucky to love someone as you love Felicity."

"I know. But I don't think I should give up if I stopped—oh God, what a stupid conversation! We mean so many things by love, so many rich and various things that there must *always* be enough of something left to help a marriage to survive—"

"No," Leo said, "not necessarily. But I wish you were right."

"I believe in marriage."

Leo's voice rose.

"That isn't your prerogative!"

Alexander moved across the room and opened the door to the hall.

"For better or worse—"

"A splendid exit line," Leo said with venom.

"Don't be cheap."

They looked at each other across the disordered room.

"You're a great fellow," Leo said, "but I can't cope with you tonight."

"That makes two of us," Alexander said, and went out into the hall.

When he had gone, Leo rang Sally. She was very calm.

"He's such a nice man. I think he was horrified. Did he tick you off?"

"Not really. He asked me to stop seeing you."

"And?"

"I refused."

"Oh," she said on a breath, and then, "Did he mention Henry?"

"Yes."

"Leo—"

"Sally, I don't have any children but I spend a lot of time with them. It seems to me that you can't live your life *for* them; otherwise they can't live for themselves. If things are right for you, there is a better chance they will be right for them."

"I admire Henry, you know, as well as love him."

"I admire him. As well as like him. And I love you."

"You can't *know*—"

"I can," Leo said, "and I do," and rang off.

Three minutes later he rang back.

"I'll say the same thing after I've made love to you, too. Only more often."

"Leo, don't be so head-turning—"

"You don't *know*," he said with sudden energy, "the sheer relief of having found what I hardly knew I was looking for. Sleep well. I'll ring you tomorrow."

She put the telephone down and switched off her bedside light. In the street outside someone kicked an empty can along the pavement, and behind her knees, Mozart humped himself into a different shape and purred slumbrously. Upstairs, Henry would be as he had been when she had kissed him good night, rammed down under his duvet, oblivious of her and exclusive to himself. A vast happiness settled across her like a huge relaxing hand and drew her luxuriously into sleep.

6

THE ROOF OF THE CATHEDRAL, THE DEAN INFORMED AN EMER-gency chapter meeting, was going to cost at least a quarter of a million pounds. The parapet mullions were seriously decayed and whole sections must be removed without delay, for safety, and the rest spliced. The worst wear was at the base of the mullions, where the soft stone had worn away to allow gallons of water to lie in the angle formed by the roof and the parapet. This water had seeped its way into a large section of the south and west roofs. There was nothing for it but to strip the roof, re-line and re-lead it, and make lengths of new parapet. It would take a year to repair the roof and longer for the stonework. Cathedral funds could find perhaps fifty thousand; the rest must be found elsewhere.

One of the canons suggested an appeal. Two others at once pointed out that the appeal for the restoration of the organ was still open and the public would hardly be likely to subscribe to both. It occurred to the dean to reveal Frank Ashworth's offer to buy the headmaster's house, and then, for a reason he did not care to explore, he decided against it. It was, after all, quite out of the question that such a jewel should pass from the close to the council and therefore pointless to set such a red herring a-swimming.

A slightly fractious murmuring arose among the canons. One suggested a cut in the diocesan educational services to help pay for the roof, either because he forgot or because he wished to provoke a fellow canon who was in charge of education in the diocese. Another suggested less support for the mission for the dying in Calcutta, which was particularly dear, they all knew, to the bishop's heart; and a third, suspecting that the Historic Churches Fund had already been approached by the dean on the question of the new lighting, asked why that body should not be appealed to.

Hugh Cavendish eyed them all serenely. His drive to Croxton had indeed proved fruitful and the cheese-and-wine party soothing to his feelings, being so full of admiring praise for his loving care of the cathedral. He leaned forward and put his clasped hands in front of him on the table at which a dozen generations of chapters of Aldminster had met.

"Gentlemen. I hope you will bear with me, but I have a scheme which I need to revolve a little further in my mind before it is fit for your consideration. When we next meet, I hope to be able to lay before you my proposal for solving our present predicament."

"Old fox," Canon Ridley said later to Canon Yeats, helping him down the stone staircase to the close. "Something's up. When he gets all stately like that you can hear the cogs clicking away in his brain like Meccano."

"There's a rumour," Canon Yeats said a little breathlessly, trying to accommodate the stair rail, two sticks, and his colleague's well-meant but misdirected arm, "that we'll be selling off the headmaster's house. Fetch a tidy bit."

"Don't you believe it. The dean would never countenance selling a building, let alone a good building. He'd sell *us*, if we were worth anything, like a shot. Care for a bite of lunch before you get back?"

Frank Ashworth was not surprised when the dean wished to make an appointment with him, but he was intrigued by being asked if they might meet privately. Accordingly the dean, early one evening as an extremely pretty apricot sunset threw the cranes on the docks into dramatic stork-like relief, drove down to the block of flats in Back Street, and took the unpleasant grey plastic-lined lift to the top.

"I had no idea you had such views from here."

"I'm directly above where I lived as a boy, only sixty feet higher."

The dean walked to the windows that gave on to the sharp rise of the city up to the crown of the cathedral.

"I've never seen it from here. It's magnificent."

"I hear I'll have a fine view of scaffolding for the next year."

"I'm afraid so," the dean said easily. "Of course, we'll make all the haste we can."

"Scotch, Mr. Cavendish? I'm afraid I've no sherry."

"A small one. Thank you. I see you are a collector of books."

"Always have been. I don't seem to have passed a love of books on to my son, though. There'll be no point in leaving them to him."

"Your grandson perhaps?" He raised his glass. "Your very good health."

Frank Ashworth said in a softer tone, "Ah. Henry."

"The reason I have come to see you is in some way related to Henry."

Frank motioned him to sit down. The chairs were deep and comfortable and hideous, their sides and back covered in battered brown leather, their cushions in brown velvet. From the depths of one, the dean said, "I rather wanted to know your opinion of the choir. Knowing, that is, your feelings about what seems to you the inaccessibility of the close."

Frank eyed him suspiciously.

"My feelings about the choir are much the same. I'm proud of Henry, but I feel he had a leg-up to get in, a chance that other kids in the city don't get."

"There are bursaries—"

"Oh, I know that. But they don't get the musical training, they don't have parents who know how to help them or have the money to help them."

"Do you think the choir is important?"

"Important?"

"Do you think we need a choir?"

Frank looked uneasy.

"The cathedral'd lose something without music—"

"We have a wonderful organ. I am only referring to the choir itself."

"It would be a pity if we didn't have the choir. Part of the city's history, really."

The dean settled himself more comfortably than ever.

"If for some reason the dean and chapter couldn't keep up the choir, would the council be at all interested in funding it? It would give you a much more democratic freedom in the choice of choristers."

"I couldn't say," Frank said slowly, "that the council could or would take on any direct responsibility. I think most members would be sorry to see it go, although if asked, I should think most of them feel about it as I do. What does it cost you?"

"Between fifty and sixty thousand a year."

"So the cathedral roof could be paid for in four or five years?"

"Certainly. I am faced, you see, with a choice between the building and a musical tradition. The stronger claim of the former seems to me unquestionable."

Frank turned his glass round in his hands.

"You aren't, you know, faced with that choice at all. You could sell us the headmaster's house and pay for the roof at once."

"That might, in time, become part of the bargain. The cathedral is paramount."

"Let me make quite sure I understand you. You propose to disband the choir, thereby saving yourself fifty-five thousand a year, and you need at least outline support from the council to help fight off your critics. In return, you won't close the door on the headmaster's house."

"As you said yourself, we shall continue to need money."

"You're going to have a fight on your hands."

"I know that."

"I can't promise help."

"But you will try?"

"I'll think about it."

When the dean had gone, Frank went to his eastern window and stood looking up at the cathedral. Nothing mattered for Hugh Cavendish but that cathedral; it meant so much to him that you couldn't trust him to keep his word about anything, if it conflicted with what was best for the cathedral. But there was more to it than just love of the cathedral, which could be seen, Frank thought, as an altruistic kind of love, and that more was power. The dean wanted to rule the close; the close was his kingdom. If there were elements in that kingdom that wouldn't subject themselves to that rule, then they must go. The choir was an element like that, because of Alexander Troy and Leo Beckford and, interestingly, because of its growing quality, which would give it greater popularity and, in turn, some independence. The dean would hate that; independence would smack of subversion to him. . . . Odd that a fellow of his social standing should be so afraid of opposition and therefore react to it by ejecting it or crushing it. Frank grunted to himself. A few years in the council chamber would have taught the dean a thing or two about dealing with opposition. As to his own feelings about the choir, Frank believed most stoutly in its inequality, yet a queer chill crept into his mind at the thought of being party to its disbanding. He thought, with an undoubted inward tremor, of facing Sally over it. Even more, Henry. But if the dean were to keep his word and the house in the close were to become the realization of a cherished project, was that not a sacrifice for the greater good? Henry had been brought up just the way his wife had brought up Alan, full of illusions of privilege, but Henry had more sense than Alan, had a better character altogether, and he would see the justice of what was being done. And if the choir could be kept, for the boys of the city rather than the boys of the King's School? Would he not then be achieving everything he wanted and thought right?

He went across to pick up the dean's whisky glass and take it with his own into his small and tidy kitchen. He looked at the glass for a while and then said aloud to it, without particular rancour, "Twisty old bugger."

Two days later, after early communion, the dean cornered Alexander coming out of the Lady Chapel.

"Ah. Troy. I was hoping you'd be here. I think I've some rather good news for you."

Alexander, who had knelt during the service listening to the gulls round the tower in the summer morning and feeling intensely caught up in the sheer strength of the sense of history in the cathedral, turned a rather abstracted face towards the dean and said he was glad to hear it.

"I paid a visit to Frank Ashworth earlier in the week," the dean said, coming confidentially close, so that the folds of his robes brushed against Alexander, "and I think I have, successfully, at least postponed his interest in the headmaster's house."

"I'm immensely relieved, but how—"

"Deflecting his attention, really. Offering him another project to think about. But I thought you'd be glad to know."

"I am, dean, more than I can tell you. It's been quite unnerving wondering what might be about to happen."

"A feeling I share. You know how I value the buildings round the close. And I am also extremely concerned that if we take steps to make the close, shall we say, more accessible to the public, that they should be the right steps. Selling an architectural gem does not really seem to me to be a right step. But of course I am biased"— he smiled at Alexander—"I have to confess it."

Alexander, feeling that courtesy alone demanded some reciprocal generosity on his part, said he was so sorry to hear of the enormous cost and upheaval involved in repairing the nave roof.

"I may have solved that too," Hugh Cavendish said. "In fact it was part of a bargain I struck with Ashworth to save your house. I don't have to tell you what subsidizing the choir costs us annually, and I mooted to Ashworth the notion of the council taking the responsibility of it from us."

Alexander stopped walking. They were almost at the south door, where a knot of clergy who had also been to the communion service had gathered, before dispersing out across the close to their various lives. He put his hand on the dean's sleeve.

"Are you saying—?"

"Well, I hope it won't come to that. Believe me, I don't want to lose our young choristers, but priorities are priorities. I'm sure you agree—"

"No," Alexander said loudly. "No."

"My dear Troy—"

"Are you suggesting disbanding the choir to pay for the roof?"

"As I said, I do hope it won't come to that. Ah, there's the bishop. He's off to London today and I must catch him before he goes. Would you excuse me? Of course, I'll let you know any developments—"

Leo Beckford, arriving for choir practice five minutes later, found Alexander standing alone, like a great statue, ten feet inside the south door.

"Are you all right?"

"You keep asking me that—"

"You don't *look* all right—"

"Would you?" Alexander said wildly. "Would you? If you had just been told that the Cathedral Choir of Aldminster, instituted by the first Anglican bishop of the city to sing masses for the soul of the king in 1535, was to be disbanded by the dean and chapter to pay for building repairs and offered instead to the city council?"

Somehow, he got through assembly, an interview with a retired Aldminster manufacturer who generously wished to give the gymnasium a new all-purpose floor, a second interview with Roger Farrell, who ran the athletics and wished to make a formal complaint at the organist's obstructiveness over allowing choristers any practice in the field, half an hour's correspondence, a telephone call with the school auditor, and a period of Tacitus with the A-level Latin set, before he had time to face the dean's announcement with any collectedness of mind. "Don't worry," Leo had said, "it's only part of some old holy politicking. He can't touch the choir. It's here by royal charter. Quite safe." And he had given Alexander what seemed in retrospect an almost condescending pat, and had gone off towards the north transept with an indecently light step.

He was probably right. It needed an Act of Parliament to repeal a charter conferred by the Crown. But no royally given immunity could protect the choir from the subtle offloading and inevitable undermining that lay behind the dean's bland proposal. The council take over the funding of the choir! The council take over, as it must if it were to dig into its pockets, a uniquely precious choral tradition of which it naturally had no understanding?

"Coffee?" Sandra said in the doorway.

He shook his head.

"Nicholas is here, Headmaster. He says can he have a word and as you're free until lunch I said I thought if he was quick—"

She was looking sorry for him again and it made him want to hit her. In his view she did not have the capacity to understand his suffering, blurred as her mind was with romantic delusions and the desire to *understand* other people. With an effort he dredged up mentally a litany of her good qualities, smiled at her as broadly as he could, and said he'd be happy to see Nicholas. Nicholas was wearing jeans and a faded navy blue sweatshirt with "No Nuke" stencilled across the chest in white.

"I'm sorry to be a bother, sir, but I feel I ought to move on and I don't quite know what—"

"Sit down," Alexander said. "I'm afraid we've all rather forgotten about you. But you've been immensely useful. The games fields haven't looked so good in years and all in time for Sports Day—"

"It's the least I could do. But I can't go on really, like this, drifting. I'm getting a bit depressed and I know, I mean, I think I know, what I want to do."

"Good," Alexander said heartily.

"I want to go back into music."

"Do you? Excellent. In what way?"

"Well, that's the problem. I don't really know who I ought to talk to—"

"If you want to perform—"

"Oh no," Nicholas said, hurriedly, "I'm not good enough for that, not nearly good enough."

"Have you talked to Mr. Beckford?"

"No. He's so busy and I—"

"Shall I have a word with him?"

"Oh, would you?"

"He has a lot of contacts in the city. He might come up with an idea. I expect you're getting rather sick of the infirmary."

"Well, I am a bit."

The telephone rang. Sandra said, "Shall I come in and take him away now?"

"Thank you." He turned to Nicholas. "I'll have to throw you out, I'm afraid. But I won't forget."

In the common room after lunch, John Godwin, who was crippled and wise and had taught history at the King's School for thirty years, patted the armchair beside him to indicate that Alexander should sit down.

"I'm sorry to tell you, Headmaster, that I know why you are looking like that."

Alexander dropped heavily into the chair.

"Bush telegraph already?"

"No doubt one of the vergers was listening. Shocking old gossips, always have been—"

Alexander looked round the crowded room.

"General knowledge?"

"I'm afraid so. Discussion level dropped on your entry."

Alexander sighed.

"Can you give me some kind of advice? I imagine the Farrell brigade is behind the dean blowing whistles—"

"It'll die down when the first excitement is over and they realize that our greatest mark of universally recognized distinction vanishes with the choir. In any case, there's a royal charter. I seem to remember hearing of a nineteenth-century dean trying to sell off the choir to augment his income and being baulked by the charter. Go and look it up. It's in the archive office."

"Even so, I don't like feeling that the common room isn't behind me."

John Godwin smiled and picked up his walking stick preparatory to getting up.

"Don't lose a wink of sleep over that, Headmaster. When their bluff is called and it means siding with the school or the chapter, all this placard carrying will stop. Nothing like a threatened invasion to give a nation a dose of patriotism." He levered himself up. "Farrell's a good agitator, but he isn't on the *academic* staff, after all. Go and look at the archives, and then read the charter out in assembly."

"Thank you, John," Alexander said.

"Don't thank me, Headmaster. It's a luxury to be listened to."

When he had gone, Alexander steeled himself and crossed the room to the group round Roger Farrell, who, in an immaculate tracksuit, was talking about the junior county athletic trials. Alexander made some anodyne opening remark and Farrell said, loudly, "We hear the school's going to be dragged into the twentieth century, Headmaster. If you ask me, in the nick of time."

"All I ask of you, Farrell," Alexander said in a burst of temper, "is a little professional loyalty. As well you know."

And then the whole room went silent, and he only managed to get himself through the door by a fraction of a second before he began to shake.

It was the day for after-school choir practice. Leo would be up there in the practice room with twenty-four boys getting the descant right for evensong or whatever the problem of the moment was. The thought was of stupendous consolation. So, as ever, was the cathedral itself, mysterious in the late-afternoon light, impregnable, impersonal, yet offering sanctuary on every level. Alexander, in his gown ready for evensong, threaded his way among the remaining whispering tourists—he always caused a faint stir on account of the splendour of his appearance—and made for the door in the north transept leading up to the practice room.

"*Wooldridge*," Leo was saying angrily.

"Sorry, sir, sorry, I didn't see the change of clef—"

On the dim stair, Alexander waited. Ireland in F; notes falling as cool as glass drops.

"Soft, *soft*, on 'holy is His name . . . ' "

He laid his cheek against the cold ancient stone. The desire to weep was enormous. Saint Paul had known about music and God; join together, he had told the early Christians, join together singing and making melody to the Lord. Nothing was more powerful than music, more uniting, nothing lifted man in worship as music could, the voice of the trumpet calling out, "Come up hither, come up to Me."

"Can you make sure you get that F sharp?"

Handel had written the *Messiah* because he wished to make men better; he had said so, quite simply. He had felt that he saw Heaven while he was writing the Hallelujah chorus. And what composer, commissioned by a secular city council whose preoccupations were so alien to such vision, could hope to write music such as that? The spiritual importance of what he could hear from the room above broke over him in a wave. Salvation lay that way, the food for a man's natural religious appetite.

The last falling notes of the last Amen—

"You're tired," Leo said, "all that cricket—"

"We like it, sir."

"I like it too. I just don't like it when it makes you too dozy, Ashworth, to remember to turn over the pages of your chant book."

Alexander opened the door. The choir straightened respectfully.

"Off with you now and get ready. You've ten minutes at least." He crossed the dusty room to the piano, where Leo sat, straight-backed in a battered corduroy jacket, his hands still on the keyboard.

"I shouldn't have brushed you off this morning," Leo said. "You were quite right. It's an awful prospect."

"We must talk about it. I've been down there on the stairs listening—"

"We weren't at our best tonight. Very ragged canticles."

"Leo, the *privilege* of this music, all it can do that nothing else can do—"

"You don't need to tell me."

"I'm going to fight every inch of the way."

"Me too. Do you realize I might become a council *employee*? Imagine trying to talk choral music at city hall." He got up and began to stuff music haphazardly into his briefcase. "Look, I must go, I'm not dressed—"

"I'll walk down with you. I thought Martin was playing tonight."

"He is. I want to hear him. The 'Nunc' has got very dispirited and he was going to try something new out tonight."

"Leo, I want you to take Nicholas Elliott in for a while."

Leo paused, his briefcase open in his hand.

"Lord, I'd clean forgotten about him, poor fellow. Is he still lurking in the infirmary?"

"Yes. He thinks he wants to work in music."

"He's got an excellent ear," Leo said, snapping the briefcase shut, "and a good musical sense. If only he wasn't so wet—"

"He mightn't be, if he had some real project in hand."

Leo grinned.

"Like acting as a chaperon to me? Sure, I'll take him in. He can muck me out. But it won't make any difference, Alexander. If I could only meet Sally in the silent reading room of the public library, it wouldn't make any difference."

"Leo, I do beg you to think again. It can only lead to the most awful unhappiness all round, particularly for that boy."

"Just mind your own business," Leo said rudely, "would you?"

And then he brushed past Alexander and banged out of the door, leaving the golden dust motes whirling agitatedly in the air behind him.

The headmaster's stall in the choir had often afforded Alexander refuge, as no doubt it had also done to all his predecessors over almost five hundred years. It gave him a marvellous view of the organ and with it a sense of the music rising over him like some tidal wave. The choristers directly ahead were always, at the beginnings of services, deeply conscious of him, but in the singing they forgot him and he could watch them with the admiration and affection they always inspired in him. There was such dignity in their absorption; it struck him every time. "They love it," Leo had often said, "they love singing." Three years ago, with the reluctant sanction of the dean and chapter, Alexander had given the choir Christmas off because he had felt that they should be with their families for once, and they had, the following year, pleaded to be allowed to stay. It struck him often that they liked being expected to achieve adult standards of behaviour, just as their profound enthusiasm for their music was as natural to them as breathing. "Miraculous," a newspaper had called their dedication; they themselves considered it normal.

The archdeacon, peering through pebble lenses like an old badger, came in to the chancel to take the service. Summer evensong never had quite the magic of winter evensong, when only the lamps in the choir stalls were lit, and the voices went soaring out into the vast dark quiet of the cathedral, but it was an unearthly time all the same. Alexander rose. The boys and the lay clerks waited before him, white and blue against the dark screen below the organ pipes, the third boy from the left Henry Ashworth, whose mother was having an affair with his choirmaster and organist. If it wasn't for the music, where, Alexander wondered, could a boy like Henry turn, and yet, weirdly enough, if Henry were to discover about Leo, would not the music continue, strangely, to unite them? Unconsciously, in the intensity of his feeling, Alexander pounded his fist into his open palm and received a glare of the most stern reproof from the pebble lenses.

"If we say we have no sin we deceive ourselves, and the truth is not in us. If we confess our sins, God is faithful and just and will forgive us our sins and cleanse us from all unrighteousness."

They knelt.

"I wish," Alexander prayed, "that I did not take everything so violently to heart. I wish I had dispassion. I wish I had coolness of judgement, and reserve. But as I seem to have none of those things by nature, and have failed dismally to acquire them in half a century of life, please help me to use all the uncontrollable energies I have instead to save this choir for this cathedral, because once it is gone, a terrible poverty will afflict the people that can never be assuaged by any other means. And while You are at it, please find Felicity and send her home, because I am stronger when she is by me and I need to be strong. And do something to save Henry Ashworth from being the innocent victim of a human muddle. I'm sorry about this list of wants when I am here to glorify You, but tonight the wants are uppermost in my mind and as You know better than anyone, I am always at the mercy of what is uppermost in my mind."

He opened his eyes and rose with the others to his feet. Psalm Sixty-one. The choir was poised, calm and ready.

"From the ends of the earth I call to you, when my heart faints: O set me on a rock that is higher than I."

Alexander, shaking his head like a dog getting water out of its ears, grasped his service book with resolution. From his rock, he would defy every last one of them.

7

THE COUNTY ARCHIVIST, A GRAVE YOUNGISH WOMAN WITH A SWEET smile and huge tortoiseshell-rimmed spectacles, put a black japanned box down on the table in front of Alexander.

"I'm sorry to be so long, but even though you rang in advance, I hate taking documents like this out of the safe before I have to."

The county records office was housed in a long temporary-looking building behind Aldminster Brewery and hardly looked substantial enough to contain anything as solid as a safe. The room they were in reminded Alexander of the "hut" classrooms that had been put up at the King's School when the numbers had begun to grow on his arrival.

"I have to stay with you, I'm afraid—"

"I shall be delighted," he said gallantly.

"It's the regulations—"

"Please don't apologize."

She unlocked the box and opened the lid.

"There," she said, reverently.

They both gazed inside as if at a holy relic. The charter lay before them, greying sixteenth-century vellum, brownish sixteenth-century ink.

"May I touch it?" Alexander asked.

"I'm so sorry," she said, "but I shouldn't let you. I'll lift it out for you if you like—"

"Does that mean that if one has to produce it in court, you would have to come along too, as official bearer of Exhibit A?"

She looked startled.

"Court?"

"I hope it won't come to an actual court hearing, of course. I'm banking on the mere physical existence of the charter in this office being enough to save the choir. The wording has been printed many times."

She stared at him.

"But, Mr. Troy, you can't use the charter as evidence! Surely you realize that."

"Whyever not?"

"Because it was never ratified. It was drawn up, exactly as you see it; but it never received the royal assent. You know the story, it's in all the school histories, it's in the guidebooks—the dispute with Bishop Fisher—"

"Yes, I know that is technically the case, of course. But we have always observed the charter, in every detail. For four hundred years it has been our cornerstone—the school simply couldn't have existed unless we had done so!"

"The school has observed the charter *voluntarily*. But I'm afraid, in court, it would have no valid existence. It's exactly like a will that has been properly drawn up in every detail but never actually signed."

Alexander sat down heavily on the nearest plastic chair.

"Surely you were aware of this?"

"Of what happened at the foundation, of course. It's part of the school's history. But the legal consequences had never occurred to me . . ."

"Well, I don't suppose the existence of the school as founded has ever been questioned before. Not in the courts, at any rate. Of course, the founder's *intentions* are quite clear in his letters, but I doubt if they carry much legal weight either."

Alexander brightened a little.

"Letters?"

She bent over the box and with infinite delicacy lifted out several sheets of yellowed paper encased in clear stiff film.

"Letters between Bishop Thomas and Henry VIII. The letters that explain to the king how he is starting a choir for the king's benefit, and a school for the choristers to attend which will be named in the king's honour. And this is the king's reply. He says he is much gratified and pleased but no more. And then, look, the bishop writes again hinting at a royal charter and the king replies that he cannot give it yet for the great love he knows the bishop still bears to the pope. You see, the bishop wanted to be made an archbishop, and Henry refused because he believed him still a Catholic at heart. Isn't it fascinating?" She looked quite exalted. "These letters are unique."

Alexander touched the top letter lightly.

"They are wonderful, but they aren't what I needed. I need a proper royal charter."

She looked worried.

"There isn't one. There are only the school statutes, which do indeed state that the life of the school shall only be the life of the choir, but of course that doesn't have anything like the same legal weight."

Alexander brightened.

"It might help. Thank you. Do you have a typescript of the relevant bits?"

She nodded.

"I can get you a copy. I'd like to help. I go to choral evensong every Sunday." She gave him her pretty smile. "I'd conjure you up a valid royal charter if I could."

He grimaced.

"It's rather a blow."

"It's ironic too. I believe Aldminster is the only King's School which *isn't* protected by royal charter."

He went home in some gloom via Chapter Yard. There was no reply to his knock but when he peered through the sitting-room window, he could see Leo in an armchair with his back to him and his feet on the television, talking into the telephone. He banged on the window, but Leo didn't look round, so he propped himself against the house wall and wrote a quick résumé of his discovery on a blank page in his diary, tore it out and dropped it through Leo's letter box.

"Judith was really a genuine feminist," Leo was saying into the telephone.

"Don't talk to me about feminists," Sally exploded at the other end, "don't mention bloody feminists. They haven't a clue how ordinary women live, so they despise them and brand them as disloyal. They are a separate sex from ordinary women."

"I know. I only mentioned Judith's feminism because you are so different, thank goodness. What about women priests, then?"

"Hum," Sally said happily, thinking. She loved these conversations, she loved Leo really asking her things and being properly interested in her replies. She had said a few days ago that she couldn't bear omelettes and he had said at once, "Oh, *why*, tell me?" and she had said it was the gummy strands you might meet in the middle of them and he had listened seriously even to that. She had read somewhere that the early stages of a love affair are characterized by the ability to relish your lover's reading even a telephone directory aloud, and perhaps in three months Leo wouldn't care at all for her opinion on omelettes or women priests, but for the moment it was wonderful.

"What if you were a woman parish priest and the old and sick needed visiting but all your children had measles and you couldn't afford a nanny on your stipend?"

"How practical."

"Women are practical."

"Then they would make good parish priests."

"And leave men to preach, I suppose—"

"And be archbishops, of course."

"Of course. What's that noise?"

"Nicholas."

"Nicholas?"

"Nicholas Elliott has come to be my lodger for a bit. I told you. That was him banging the front door and all this muttering is him saying sorry about banging the front door."

"I'll ring you back later," Sally said. "I'm going to make pancakes for Henry."

"Not too much later. I've got a lot more to ask you."

"About what?"

"Oh, nuclear disarmament, the National Health Service, the philistinism of the present government, the jumble sale state of my wardrobe, things like that—"

"Leo—"

"Are you laughing?"

"Yes. I'm putting the phone down."

The line clicked and fell silent.

"Do you know," Leo said, looking at the receiver, "that even the telephone is filthy."

"I'll clean it," Nicholas said. "Here, I found this note for you."

Leo took it absently and looked round the sitting room.

"You've done an amazing job in here. How do you know how?"

"Matron."

Matron believed in Satan finding mischief for idle hands, so during Nicholas's long weeks in the infirmary she had taught him to sweep floors before washing them and how to clean windows with hot water and vinegar and crumples of old newspaper. She had been matron at the King's School when Nicholas was a schoolboy and therefore represented to him something of a rock.

"I suppose the secret is to forswear reading a single word of anything you pick up while clearing up."

"I don't read much—"

"No. I've noticed. It irritates me rather. *Why* don't you?"

"I've got out of the habit, I suppose."

"Well, get back in it. I can't share the house with an illiterate, however handy with a duster."

"I wouldn't know where to begin—"

"Do you want me to thump you?" Leo said in exasperation.

"Suggest something," Nicholas said, struggling to make an effort.

"*The Hitchhiker's Guide to the Galaxy*, and *The Collector* by John Fowles, and don't say you haven't got either, because I've got both. And don't ask me which is shorter, either."

"I wasn't going to."

"What were you going to do?"

"I'm going to see a film."

"Good. Because I'm going to work."

"I'll go and get ready."

He went upstairs and came down again five minutes later looking precisely the same. Leo was at the piano scribbling on a score.

"Shall I pick up some Chinese for supper?"

"Good idea. There's some money on the draining board."

"I feel bad I can't pay you anything."

"You will when you can."

"I like it here," Nicholas said, grateful and awkward.

"Nick—"

"OK, OK, I'm going."

Walking down the Lyng towards the cinema, Nicholas thought about Leo. He was easier to deal with than most people in Aldminster because he just came straight out with things and told you you were being a pain if he thought you were. Nicholas felt genuinely bad about the money, but Alexander had forbidden him to register for the dole if he hadn't even tried to get a job, and he hadn't, and then Alexander had found some ancient charity somewhere in the school records and was giving Nicholas a tenner a week so he wasn't utterly destitute, and the school was helping with his food. Out of the first tenner, he'd bought a tin of furniture polish he intended to use on all the furniture in Leo's sitting room. He didn't suppose Leo would notice for a moment, but it made him feel better to be planning it.

He suspected he might have a mild crush on Leo. Leo seemed so in charge of himself, so that even though he was clearly crazy about Sally Ashworth, he could switch off from her absolutely and be a musician through and through. It looked to Nicholas as if Leo knew where he was going and what he wanted; there was nothing *pathetic* about Leo. Leo would never go mooching off to a cinema alone, not knowing what he was going to see, and when he got there probably not be able to choose between Studio One or Studio Two and no doubt not go into either in the end. Leo had told him he was apathetic, and he knew he was, in a way, except that it wasn't so much general indifference as not knowing what to care about. He felt good when he had had his first assault on Leo's kitchen, really good, until Cherry Chancellor had come and said, "Now *who* did this!" and he found he didn't want to say that he had. She gave him some rubber gloves as a joke and he hated that.

There was a queue outside the Studio One entrance for a film of an E. M. Forster novel. Nicholas didn't much want to see it, but he didn't want Leo to call him illiterate again, so he joined the queue behind a middle-aged man in big glasses and a woman wearing a denim flying suit too young for her. They were talking about the cinema in a very professional-sounding way and the woman kept saying, "I simply think he knows what he's doing. Those films simply *work*." Her hair was tousled and streaked and she had huge silver earrings like swinging shields. Nicholas supposed they were married; he could imagine them shopping together in Habitat. The man said, "I know what I meant to tell you. I heard it at lunch today. They're going to axe the choir."

The woman's head jerked up.

"The cathedral choir? You don't mean it!"

"Sign of the times, I gather. Can't afford it anymore. The cathedral roof is collapsing and all the money has to go on that."

"This is *very* serious," the woman said.

"It's hardly one of the best in the country—"

"All the same—"

"And another thing. They've got planning permission for a block of loos bang in the middle of that nice medieval bit at the bottom of the Lyng."

"You don't *mean* it—"

"Ramps for wheelchairs, toddler changing room—"

"Annex for junkies?"

"Wouldn't put it past them. God, I hope this film's worth it, look at the prices—"

"It will be," the woman said, "I promise you. His films simply *work*."

Nicholas loved the film. It was optimistic and romantic and the photography of Italy particularly was beautiful. He went out of the cinema very much wanting to go to Italy and to be in love, and only when he was buying spring rolls and sweet-and-sour chicken from the Wong Kee Fish Bar did he remember about the choir. He ran back to Chapter Yard with an urgency he hadn't felt about anything for years and dumped the takeaway pots on the piano and said to Leo, "What's this about the choir?"

Leo's mind came from a long musical distance away at its own pace.

"What?"

"I heard a couple in the queue saying the choir has to go because the cathedral's falling down."

"Roughly, that's the threat."

"But they *can't!*"

"They can, I'm afraid. We thought we were protected by a royal charter but it turns out that we aren't—the choir was apparently Bishop Thomas's own idea to try and please Henry VIII because he wanted to be made an archbishop. We are going to do everything in our power to stop them. The dean proposes the council should take the choir over and save the chapter fifty thousand pounds a year."

"The council don't *know* anything about music."

"I know."

"I—I'd like to *murder* someone—"

"Good for you."

"What are you going to do?"

"Fight," Leo said, "write letters, petition, rack our brains for schemes to raise money—"

"Does the choir know?"

"Not officially."

"It makes me sick—"

Leo got up.

"If you could think of a scheme, it would mean instant canonization for you. Can we eat? Whatever's in there?"

"I'll heat it. It gets all gluey cold. I read a book this evening but I read it in the cinema."

"Good," Leo said. He looked at Nicholas. "I'm pleased to see you angry."

"I'm furious."

They ate standing up in the kitchen, using spoons for the chicken and their fingers for the rolls. Then Nicholas said he was going to turn in, and Leo let himself out of the house and walked across the close and down through the steep quiet streets to Blakeney Street. When she opened the door, Sally said, "Oh, how lovely," and then she kissed him and said, "Henry's got hold of some awful rumour about the choir."

"Mr. Dean," Alexander said sonorously, his hand on Henry's surpliced shoulder, "I present to you Henry Francis Ashworth, to be admitted chorister of this cathedral."

Henry stepped forward. The choir stalls were packed and only he and Chilworth and the dean and the headmaster were standing in the middle at the foot of the altar steps. He raised his face, framed by its new ruff, towards the dean. The dean held up his hand in a gesture of benediction.

"Henry Francis Ashworth, by the authority committed to me I install you a chorister of this cathedral church. May the Lord grant you the will to obey, the power to lead, and the grace to accomplish the various tasks of your position. The Lord watch over your going out and your coming in from this time forth for evermore. Amen."

He put his hand on Henry's head. Henry bowed it slightly and said "Amen" in response. He was greatly relieved. What Briggs told him must be wrong, because they'd never make new choristers if they were going to do away with the choir altogether. Wooldridge said Briggs was a piss artist, which Henry felt was a description that fitted him just right, whatever it meant. And the bishop had come. The bishop wouldn't have come unless the whole thing was serious. You *had* to have a choir, in Henry's opinion; otherwise the cathedral would be just like a museum. It was just the kind of rumour Briggs would invent because his voice wasn't good enough for the choir; his last thing was saying he didn't believe in God, and when everyone got bored with that, he'd started about the choir.

"Michael Anthony Roper Chilworth," the dean was saying.

Chilworth's ears were bright pink. He'd told Henry that his parents wanted him to be a chorister more than he wanted to be but he'd give it a whirl. He liked the singing, he just didn't like all the time it took away from cricket in the summer and football in the winter. Chilworth was very offhand about his own voice, but he was always very generous about Henry's. Being in the choir, Henry thought, made you get on with each other.

Back in the choir stalls they stopped being particular and were merged back into the choir itself. First the thirteenth-century hymn to Saint Magnus and then Wooldridge and Henry alone together with Lalouette's "O mysterium ineffabile." They got through it without a hitch. Then prayers and an address by the dean about the unifying glory of music that caused Leo and Alexander much need for self-control at their separate seats in the organ loft and the stalls, and then "Praise, my soul, the King of Heaven," and everyone filed out while Leo gave his all to Bach's Fantasia and Fugue in G Minor. In the choir vestry, Chilworth and Henry solemnly unbuttoned each other's ruff.

"The Vienna Boys Choir have to wear sailor suits. With shorts."

"I'm starving," Henry said.

Chilworth produced half a bar of something from his pocket.

"You can have that. I've gone off peanuts."

Henry said, "Briggs says they're going to get rid of the choir because there's no more money."

Chilworth quoted his father.

"You don't want to listen to gossip. Anyway, they're going to take us to Norway next year."

"Norway! I thought it was France."

"Yup. My father heard."

"I've never been in a plane!"

Martin Chancellor came in to chivvy them.

"Get on with it, you lot. Ruffs in the box, please, Mason."

"If you put conkers on a cello string, you can really *whack* with them—"

"Harrison, pick up that surplice, don't *stand* on it—"

"I've got the video of *Superman III*—"

"Botham's *brilliant*—"

"Harrison, did you hear me?"

"You do have to go in a plane to Norway, don't you?"

"Sir, sir, Briggs says they're going to disband the choir—"

A sudden silence.

"It's—been suggested," Martin Chancellor said. He and Cherry had worked out their reply to such questions over supper the night before. "But nobody should worry. There is a strong chance that someone else may take it over if the dean and chapter decide to let it go."

"But would we still sing in the cathedral?"

"There wouldn't be much point in you singing anywhere else, now would there?"

"But if the dean isn't in charge—"

"We don't know he won't be."

Harrison said defiantly, "I'm not singing anywhere that *isn't* the cathedral. There's no point."

"I'm afraid it isn't our decision."

"Mr. Beckford will be livid."

From the doorway to the vestry Leo said, "Mr. Beckford already is."

They turned to him.

"I hope," he said to Martin, "that you've been whipping up a little youthful support?"

Martin said, "It's hardly my place—"

Leo took a breath. He looked round at the boys.

"Hands up," he said, "all those in favour of keeping the choir as a fundamental part of the Cathedral of Aldminster."

Twenty-four hands went up. Chilworth said, "What's fundamental?"

"Right. Hands down. I'll let you know when I'm issuing rifles to defend the choir stalls. I should get in a bit of target practice."

Martin thought how Cherry would disapprove of jokes about firearms. He said, "I don't think we should listen to rumours. Nothing is decided, after all."

"All I'm doing is trying to stop the *wrong* decision being made."

"My father's got a twelve-bore—"

"I've got an air gun—"

"We've got a really *brilliant* catapult—"

"Now look what you've started," Martin said quietly.

"It's only talk. But it'll ginger them all up and their opinion *counts.*"

Martin opened his mouth to say that, choristers or not, they were only children, but closed it again. That would be Cherry's opinion, he knew, but for once, he realized that Cherry was wrong.

"Now," said Bridget Cavendish playfully to Janet Young, meeting her in the post office, "are we going to mention The Subject or are we not?"

Janet Young, who had had an unwanted letter that morning from a consortium of village WIs complaining that Mrs. Cavendish was allowing them less and less autonomy, smiled as warmly as she could and said, "Not."

"Hugh's having sleepless nights," Bridget said, taking no notice but managing to observe that the bishop's wife's feet were bare inside her sandals, which, even if they were nice feet and brown, which they were, and even if the day was hot, which it was, was really appalling. "It's so unjust. He's trying to preserve the city's heritage, the *nation's* heritage and all he gets is the vilest abuse. I knew we were wrong to appoint Leo Beckford as organist. He's wholly unsuitable and his attitude is absolutely *secular.* And the poor headmaster doesn't know if he's coming or going with that wife of his, so one really can't hope for a sensible opinion from him."

"Six first-class stamps," Janet Young said through the grille, "and this parcel second class, please, and a passport renewal form."

"I must say, I don't blame you wanting to get away from it all for a bit—"

"It's for Matthew. He isn't very organized—"

"Don't talk to me about children. Or rather schools. If only Hugh had listened to me about Cosmo and sent him to Marlborough, where my family have always gone. Have you spoken to Rachel Frost?"

Janet had spent an hour on the telephone listening to what the archdeacon's wife had to say about the choir.

"She's spoken to me."

"She supports us, of course."

Janet picked up her stamps and change.

"I don't think she's very musical."

Bridget put a hand on Janet's arm.

"Do tell me what the bishop thinks. In perfect confidence, of course."

"Robert and I are trying very hard not to talk about it just now."

"But you must have an opinion."

"Oh yes," Janet said, and smiled again, "we have an opinion, but we are holding on to it for the moment until the air clears a little."

"It won't clear, you know, unless people speak up."

Janet's smile grew enormous.

"Do forgive me. I've simply got to run. Robert's got a confirmation over at Handley and I've promised to drive him so he can work on his talk on the way. Isn't this heat lovely?"

"Lovely," Bridget said and then turned to be commanding to the post office clerk to relieve her feelings. Heaven knows what the Youngs' position on this business was. What support could you expect from a bishop who plainly preferred his parish priests to his senior clergy and the laity to them? When she had challenged him recently about his support for sanctions against South Africa in the synod, he had given her a twinkling look and said, "Don't you think bishops *ought* to be pink?" and she had been much disconcerted to realize he was teasing her. When he had then relented and told her that he had voted for sanctions because he believed firmly that the synod should present a united front, she had become very confused and not known what to think because he seemed to elude her every pigeonhole. And now here was Janet Young being secretive and walking about the cathedral city with bare legs. At least, she wouldn't be doing any lobbying among clergy wives, which left the coast clear for Bridget; Huffo was going to get massive support, she'd certainly see to that. She'd made two lists, one for the close and one for the diocese, and she was thankful that Felicity Troy was out of the way for the moment, because you could never rely on Felicity to do anything orthodox or to refrain from winning people over just by *looking* at them, it seemed.

"Two pounds sixty-four," the post office girl said.

"Tell me," Bridget said in her particularly encouraging voice, "tell me what *you* think about the cathedral choir."

The girl stared.

"I don't really care," she said, "not one way or the other."

Hugh Cavendish thought Napoleon must have felt like this before Waterloo, not really trusting new allies who had been enemies only months before and rather uncertain as to the size of the opposition. His own assessment was complicated by the fact that he did not wish to play quite straight by his biggest ally, the city council, because he had no intention at all of selling them the headmaster's house, but every intention of using it as a carrot. He thought privately that they would make a fearful horlicks of running the choir but could see at present no other way of achieving his various goals, both overt and covert, without disbanding the choir altogether, which he shrank from. He had not shrunk at all at the beginning, but to his irritation Ianthe had started him off during an enraged telephone call when she said she not only had a philistine for a father but a butcher of history to boot. The last phrase she had once overheard Leo using about someone quite different, but the dean was not to know that and was much wounded by her eloquence. The chapter at least was behind him, except Canon Yeats, whom everyone else talked down into miserable silence—"They wouldn't let me *speak*," he told his wife in despair that night—and all the canons seemed relieved at the possible prospect of no longer having to be governors of the King's School, which they appeared to find a chore, particularly as there was no remuneration.

"The plain truth is," Canon Ridley said, "we are all flat-out with work as it is. Everything conflicts. We simply can't make the school the priority it ought to be."

Hugh Cavendish had let a small silence fall and then he had said, "Quite."

As to the choral music, again only Canon Yeats had seemed anguished.

"There's still our organ," everyone had said encouragingly.

"But it isn't the *same*. Spiritually speaking. Nothing uplifts like the perfect treble."

"Only because that is what we are used to. Anyway I disagree. To me the organ is the king of instruments."

Canon Yeats had been disentangled from his sticks and helped down the stairs with particular assiduousness and assisted very tenderly into his car.

"A good man," Hugh Cavendish said, looking after him as the car jerked its way towards the city, "a good priest. But oh he does hate change."

Canon Yeats represented only a small and ineffectual part of the opposition, however. The dean knew that he could count on his organist as an enemy, possibly his assistant organist too, although he was a much meeker character, the headmaster, and such local support as they could rally. The issue was unlikely to attract national attention because Aldminster was not a famous choir, and the need to save the fabric of the cathedral would attract the huge national pro-restoration lobby in any case. He would use the next chapter meeting to draw up a formal proposal, and invite an equally formal offer from the council for the headmaster's house. In the meantime he proposed to get estimates and schedules of works to confront the opposition, who would, he was quite confident, have nothing so efficient to counter him with.

When Ianthe Cavendish got off the train at Aldminster on a grey June Friday evening, the first thing she did was to buy a copy of the *Echo* from the stall outside the station. The headline said, CHOIR MUST GO TO SAVE CATHEDRAL, and then, underneath, CLOSE HOUSE TO BE BOUGHT FOR THE PEOPLE. It was rather under a mile from the station to the close, so Ianthe bought a packet of cigarettes and a fudge bar from the nearest sweet-shop to sustain her, hitched her black canvas bag onto her back, and walked along, chewing and smoking and reading the paper. Her father had told the *Echo*, it seemed, that in only a decade over half a million pounds would be saved by not maintaining the choir, money that could be spent on the cathedral. There was a photograph of her father and Benedict outside the south door of the cathedral, and below it one of the choir in procession with AXED printed in heavy type underneath it. There were indignant remarks from several of the choristers' parents, including a quotation from Sally Ashworth, who had said, seemingly, "It's appalling and we are going to fight every inch of the way." The headmaster and the organist had apparently declined to comment, but for all that, the paper's leader described the close as being in an uproar, with people either at one another's throats or refusing to speak to one another. Ianthe, dislodging bits of fudge from her back teeth with her tongue, thought the weekend promised to be rather fun.

She hadn't meant to come down to Aldminster again, not for months. She had meant to stay right away from Leo after he had been so awful to her, and she had attempted very hard to fall in love with a journalist on a rock magazine who seemed really keen on her and had even, to her amazement and no doubt to his own as well, sent her flowers. Nobody had ever sent Ianthe flowers. It made her feel temporarily very romantically inclined towards the journalist, but only, it seemed, when he wasn't there. When she saw him, she thought about Leo almost all the time, which hardly gave the journalist a chance. She'd tried to talk to Petra about it, but Petra was in the middle of making a pretty marvellous enormous metal horse, rather Greek somehow, and couldn't concentrate on anything else. It was a commission, too, which was exciting, and in any case Petra, grown weary of her lover's wife's depredations in the studio, had thrown him out and was trying not to miss him, so she wasn't in a very sympathetic mood about love. Fergus's beautiful Minna wasn't much help either, because she'd been brought up in America and she believed you must never let a man kick you around. If Fergus treated her, just *once*, the way Leo had behaved to Ianthe, she said, she'd have been out that door like lightning. Ianthe had tried to explain that she had never, unfortunately, been *in* Leo's door, so to speak, but Minna was much more interested in her own point of view than in Ianthe's predicament anyway, so she was not a satisfactory confidante either.

Ianthe had thought and thought about what she should do to change things with Leo. One thing was clear: she mustn't beg him for anything else; she really had to play it as cool as she could. She also had to show him that she wasn't yobbish, which he seemed to think. She had a new haircut which was certainly more becoming, though pretty square, and had bought some less aggressive makeup and, because Ikon had, to its own astonishment, signed up a group whose second record was actually in the top fifty, a few new clothes. She also concocted a plan designed to show Leo that she was a responsible human being, as well as to provide Ikon with a dogsbody, which it badly needed. They had all agreed they needed a sympathetic and musical dogsbody, instead of a girl called Sharon, who was only interested in getting back to Brentford on time each night and filed her nails between phone calls. Ianthe had had her brainwave then and said she thought she could fix it.

When she got to the deanery she found her mother in the kitchen making a salad and Cosmo sitting on the edge of the table picking the bits out of it that he liked.

"Don't," Bridget was saying.

"Tomatoes are good for me."

"They can be good for you at supper."

Ianthe said, "Hi," and slung her bag on to the floor and the paper onto the table.

"What a fight seems to be going on around here!"

"You've had your hair cut, dear. Very pretty."

"It's *not* pretty."

"No," Cosmo said, "it's not."

"You haven't been down for weeks," Bridget said fondly. "Naughty girl."

"*Work*, Mum."

"There's no such thing," Cosmo said.

Bridget patted his bony black-clad knee.

"Bad boy."

She came round the table and kissed Ianthe and looked her over.

"You do look nice, dear. What pretty earrings."

"Mum . . ." Ianthe pleaded.

"You go and have a wash and I'll make you a cup of coffee. You smell of trains."

"I've been on one. And I'd rather have whisky."

"Don't show off, dear."

Cosmo cackled.

"I've got some duty-free in my room. Brent got it when he went on the hovercraft to France for the day."

"Cosmo!"

"I haven't drunk it *all*—"

"Too stupid," Bridget said. "I don't know whether you are worse apart or together."

The telephone rang from the hall. Alert instantly, Bridget put her knife down and went to answer it.

"You've come down to see Leo," Cosmo said.

"No, I haven't."

"You're wasting your time."

"What do you know about it? You're only a kid. Anyway, it isn't him I've come to see."

"Who then?"

"Not telling. Where's your whisky?"

"In a welly in my room. Who are you seeing?"

"Nick Elliott."

"Nick Elliott!"

"Not like that, idiot. Business."

Cosmo got off the table.

"If I give you some whisky can I borrow your black T-shirt with the bat on it?"

"OK."

They went out into the hall and as they passed their mother, Bridget was saying, "Actually, Rachel, we're quite pleased with the coverage in the *Echo*. Hardly a voice raised in protest, my dear. Hugh really comes into his own over this sort of business."

"What do you think?" Ianthe asked Cosmo as they began to climb the stairs. He grinned at her.

"I like the fight," he said.

Ianthe waited until after Saturday-afternoon choir practice before she went round to Chapter Yard. She washed her hair and put on new black pedal pushers and a big clean white sweatshirt, and when Nicholas opened the door he said, "Wow. Hi," which was pleasing.

In the sitting room, which she could hardly recognize, Leo was in an armchair with his feet on the piano stool, and he looked at her for quite some time before he said, "How *very* nice."

Then he got up and kissed her and offered her a chair and said, amazingly, "How very good to see you."

"I've been flat-out," Ianthe said. "I really think we're beginning to make it. Who's been at this room?"

"Mrs. Mop here, alias Nick. I'm scared to dent cushions these days."

"Then I know I was right to come," Ianthe said.

"What, what—"

"I'm going to offer your cleaning lady a job."

"What!"

"We're expanding. We need a dogsbody, messenger, telephone answerer, someone who knows about music. You said Nick wanted an opening in music—"

"Nick?"

"Oh I do, oh great, *great*—"

"Who's going to clean the ring off my bath?"

"You are."

"Perhaps I'll just have a ring. Ianthe, are you serious?"

"Sure am. We've discussed it. Sixty quid a week, free doss on my partner's sofa—that's Mike—use of the bike we all share for messages. Can you ride a bike?"

"I can learn!" Nicholas said. He spun a cushion in the air. "This is *great*."

"What," said Leo to Ianthe, "has made you so businesslike?"

"I always was. You just never noticed."

"You *look* different."

Ianthe wanted to say did he like it but she thought from his expression that he probably did and anyway he was being so amazingly nice she thought she wouldn't provoke him.

"When can I start?" Nicholas said.

"A week Monday."

"This is so good!"

"Yes," Leo said, "it is. It's the one good thing that *is* happening. Have you heard about the choir?"

Ianthe rolled her eyes heavenwards.

"Makes me sick."

"In removing Nick, you aren't only removing my nanny but my lieutenant into the bargain, I hope you know. We're planning a siege in the choir stalls. Poor Alexander is beside himself."

"I can come back," Nicholas said excitedly, "any time you need me."

Leo got up and went across the room to the kitchen.

"Let's celebrate with a drink. I've even got some wine and these days the odd clean glass—"

"I say, *thanks*," Nicholas said with energy to Ianthe. "Are you sure?"

She looked airy.

"Company decision."

"Where *is* the company?"

"One room, seven floors up, the wrong end of the Charing Cross Road. Well, a room and a half really but the kettle lives in the half."

"London," Nick said.

"Sure thing. Want a smoke?"

"No thanks. And don't here. Leo'll go bananas."

Ianthe considered bravado and decided the atmosphere was too good to waste, so contented herself with chucking the cigarette packet onto the hearthrug to show that she *could* have smoked if she'd chosen to. Leo came in with the bottle and a handful of glasses and trod on the packet on his passage to his armchair. Nicholas, elated as he couldn't recall being ever in his life before, got tremendous giggles and began to chuck cushions about.

"Are you sure you want him?" Leo said to Ianthe.

She grinned and raised her glass to him.

"Here's to the choir."

He looked at her.

"Thank you. And here's to a glorious future for you two. May you become millionaires."

She felt terribly happy, so she got up and kissed Nicholas and then she kissed Leo, and he kissed her back and everything seemed, all of a sudden, just too bloody good to be true.

8

SANDRA NOTICED THAT THE HEADMASTER HAD LOST WEIGHT; QUITE a lot, really, for such a big man. It was unfair for him to do it just now, to do something poignant like lose weight out of unhappiness, because Sandra's boyfriend had recently proposed to her, and although she knew that she and a man like Alexander Troy lived in different worlds and that she would be much happier and more natural with Colin, she could not help her yearning. She liked Colin, loved him even, and certainly approved of his decently acquisitive way of life, but Colin wasn't admirable or uplifting and certainly never gave her heady seconds of excitement at the set of his shoulders or with particular gestures or inflexions. She had known the proposal was coming for weeks and so, playing the game by the same rules of proper delicacy, had said she would think about it and tell him on Friday. That meant that on Saturday they could buy a ring and announce the engagement ten days later on Sandra's mother's birthday. What she must not do, she told herself, was to spend the time until Friday in fruitless anguish for what could not be, nor in bringing in homemade prawn mayonnaise sandwiches— which she knew Alexander loved—to try and persuade him to eat. She was, instead, very businesslike all week, thereby earning from Alexander the warmest gratitude, which did her resolve no good at all.

It was Sandra who suggested he should go and see the bishop.

"Remember Mr. Beckford. He'd never be here if it wasn't for Bishop Robert. My mother disapproves of him because she says you never know which way he's going to jump, but I think that makes him modern. And he's really keen on music."

She rang the palace and spoke to Janet Young, who said the bishop was free about five. Then Janet said that if the school had any boys who needed to do something for the good of their souls, the palace herbaceous border would be pleased to see them, and Sandra laughed and said she was welcome to the whole of the fifth year at that rate. At five to five, accompanied by three boys who had been caught smoking with unnecessary defiance in the common room garden under a lilac bush, Alexander crossed the close to the palace and despatched his charges to the border and the bishop's wife, who, though universally known to be kind, was also universally known to be intolerant of skimped work. From the bishop's study window, the bishop and the headmaster could watch the culprits weeding away under an eagle eye.

"She terrifies me in the garden," the bishop said. "It's like being a very small boat commanded by a ferocious skipper. Perfectionists can never understand that the rest of us are mere mortals."

"They are very lucky to get away so lightly. It exasperates me how much they *must* show off. As day boys, they have hours and hours in which to misbehave when we have no power to prevent them, but they have to break the rules not only in school but as close to the seat of authority and as publicly as they can."

"Perhaps a spell of gardening at the command of a woman is a rather fitting retribution for a display of macho swaggering. Ah, look. They've seen us. Poor fellows, spied upon from all sides. Are any of those choristers?"

"No. Too old. Our oldest is fourteen and that's about the top limit, really."

"I imagine," the bishop said, guiding Alexander away from the window and towards an elderly chair upholstered in much-washed linen union, "I imagine that the fate of our poor choir is why you have come."

"I would only say this to you," Alexander said, casting himself into the chair, "and in fact it is a huge relief to have someone to say it *to*, but really I am rather in despair. I don't quite know where to turn for support. The dean and chapter are apparently five to one in favour of the plan, my common room are twenty-seven to four in favour because it does away with the choir practice priority they all hate so much, and I fear the next governors' meeting, where the dean and chapter will be present, and so will three city councillors, including Frank Ashworth. It seems to me that unless we make the choir financially self-supporting, we must lose it, and if we lose it, we lose something so precious with it that it hardly bears thinking of."

"Is the notion of its being self-supporting impossible?"

"We aren't a first-rate choir, we aren't a Wells; we can't command the national and international attention they do. Give Leo Beckford enough time and we might be first-rate, I think, although he will always be a better organist than he is a choirmaster, and he is a marvellous organist. But we haven't got any time. If the choir goes, we will never get it back, certainly never in this ancient, irreplaceable form."

He looked across at the bishop, who was swinging his spectacles by one earpiece.

"Could I—what I want to do is to ask you if you will lend your support to our cause to defend the choir. It would make all the difference."

There was a long pause and the bishop put on his spectacles. Then he took them off again and said gently, "I'm afraid I can't do that."

"Can't—"

"No. I can't. I would like to—this is in the strictest confidence—but I can't. Like you, I believe in the unique power of choral music in our cathedrals, but you see, my prime duty and desire is not to this cathedral or to the form of worship in it. It is to the Church. I cannot, you see, provide the spectacle of a divided close at Aldminster for the press to fall eagerly upon. To come out in open opposition to the dean would be the selfish gratification of personal opinion, and would undermine the Church as a whole. We must stand united, for the sake of the people we serve. We diminish the Church in the public eye if we are seen to squabble and wrangle."

"But are those very people not diminished if we lose the *effect* of choral singing in our cathedrals?"

"They are indeed," the bishop said, "but less so. Nothing is as damaging as a visibly divided Church, nothing shakes people's faith so badly."

Alexander got up and walked back to the window. Hargreaves, a hugely grown fifteen-year-old exploding out of his uniform, was apparently having a lesson on dead-heading roses. The pruning shears in his hand looked like nail scissors.

Alexander turned round.

"It will fall apart. And what about the headmaster's house?"

"Now there," the bishop said with relief, "I am very clear in my mind. It should indeed belong to the city but under the influence of the close. Let it be a meeting place by all means, but a Christian meeting place."

"It seems that you agree with me about most aspects of this whole business but you won't support me."

"Can't as well as won't. But that doesn't stop me praying for you. In fact, as old Canon Savile used to say, I'll pray like blazes." He stood up. "Alexander, what news of your wife?"

"None."

"How long—"

"Five weeks."

The bishop put the earpiece of his spectacles between his teeth.

"And will you just wait?"

"Until the end of term. Then I think I've fulfilled my side of our unspoken bargain to allow each other room, and I shall go to look for her."

"Women," the bishop said thoughtfully, "have an extraordinary power, don't they. It seems to me very real and excellent but not visionary. Is it?"

"No. Because they aren't romantic on the whole."

"Not romantic?"

"No. That's something I learned from Felicity."

The bishop said mournfully, "They would make wonderful priests."

"But a choir of girls would not have the same almost extravagantly uplifting effect as a choir of boys."

The bishop took Alexander's arm.

"That particular manifestation of purity, something quite platonic and unearthly, will certainly vanish with the choir."

"Don't *speak* of it—"

"All is far from lost, Alexander."

"It seems to me at the moment that the opposition to me grows larger every day and I correspondingly shrink."

"Nonsense. You are an enormous figure, I often think far too large for Aldminster. Janet says she can see you as a missionary captain of industry and I know exactly what she means. You, with a little help from above, could move mountains and I am not in the least without hope that you will. Do you want to take Janet's convicts with you or shall we keep them until she's finished with them?"

"Oh, keep them, please. This is probably the most constructive hour of Hargreaves's entire life. He has no idea whatsoever what to do with his ferocious energies and appetites except break things. Furniture simply disintegrates at his approach. Thank you for seeing me."

"I shan't forget any of the things we have talked about."

On the doorstep of the palace Alexander turned.

"Do you think all human endeavour springs from the need to be particular, visible—?"

"Psychologically speaking, probably. Spiritually speaking, it isn't necessary." He glanced up. "There is Bridget Cavendish. Our encounter will not now go unrecorded."

Alexander caught Bridget up twenty yards short of the deanery gate. She was wearing an expensive print frock and carrying a wicker basket full of neat paper bags.

"Just a few salad things," she said to Alexander. "I can *never* manage to remember everything at one time."

"I don't think I ever want to see salad again, just now. It's Mrs.

Monk's sole culinary idea at the moment because it's June, never mind the actual *weather*."

Bridget beamed.

"My dear Alexander, you must come in and have supper with the dean and me."

"I don't think—I should, just now."

"Nonsense. You ought to hear Hugh's excellent arguments and we could have a sensible discussion in civilized surroundings."

Alexander took a step away.

"I'm not the best of company at the moment—"

"No, no. I do understand. So wise of you to go and see the bishop."

He regarded her with something little short of loathing, bowed, muttered goodbye, and walked rapidly away. She watched him go for a few seconds, then she hurried into the deanery and opened the study door, without knocking.

"Huffo, I've just met Alexander Troy coming out of the palace and he has declined to come and dine with us. He can *only* have been to see the bishop about his wretched choir—"

The dean, seated at his desk and writing, did not look up.

"Not necessarily."

"But, Huffo, why else—"

"Plenty of reasons."

"And to refuse my invitation!"

"Would you expect him to *accept* it at such a time?"

"Huffo, I am doing everything in my power to be of service to you in this difficult time—"

The dean turned round and looked at her over his half-moon spectacles.

"Then would you be very kind and bring me a cup of tea?"

Sally worked through the third consecutive lunch hour so as to postpone writing to Alan. Her boss, who was wooing the new young barman in the wine bar in Lydbrook Street, was extravagantly grateful about this and promised to reward her amply in her Friday wage envelope. She was a better salesman than he, in any case, and usually managed to persuade someone who had come in bent upon a copy of Lytton Strachey's *Pope*—very rare—to take *Elizabeth and Essex*—not rare at all—instead and probably a case of unclassified burgundy as well. She also did housewifely things like beeswaxing the backs of the leather-bound books and putting plants about, and old plates picked up in the Thursday antique market, to make the shop alluring to people to whom second-hand book dealers did not normally appeal. Twice she wrote "Dear Alan" on pieces of scrap paper, and the third time, "My dear Alan, even if I were not in love with someone else, I don't want to be married to you anymore," and tore them all up. It struck her that Alan might be quite relieved to get such a letter, but then she wondered if she just *hoped* he would be because that would make everything so much easier.

Her one aim was not to cheat on anybody if she could possibly help it, and of course she was cheating on Alan by every day she didn't write her letter. It was only difficult to write because she didn't quite know clearly, apart from leaving him, what she was going to do. Leo wanted her to marry him, but she thought she should get used to the idea of not being married to Alan before she thought seriously of marrying anyone else. She was wild about Leo, no doubt of that, and wilder still since he had taken her to bed in his lopsided bedroom in Chapter Yard and delighted her by making love to her rather than just having sex with her, which was what she was used to. To be investigated all over with immense approving interest was as seductive as having her opinions seriously considered. It gave her amazing confidence in herself.

"It'll wear off," she said to Leo, "it can't last, this gigantic enthusiasm."

"You forget that I really like your character. Be yourself and you'll find you're stuck with me. When will you learn? I want what you are, not what I wish you were. Except for married. I wish you weren't married."

She didn't *feel* married. She felt very much Henry's mother but not at all Alan's wife. That was the prime thing she must write and say, and then she must say that it was another man who had, so to speak, given her back to herself. Alan wouldn't have a clue what she meant, but she didn't know how else to put it without sounding women's-libbish, which wasn't what she felt at all. Alan was likely to become very sentimental about Henry, but she had to steel herself for that and try to refrain from pointing out what a fair-weather father he had always been. She was going, she told herself, to be *fair*.

As to Frank, she was so furious with him over the choir, she was going to let him stew in ignorance over Alan. He hadn't come to tell her, face to face and honestly, about his deal with the dean over the choir and the headmaster's house, he had just left her to find out by rumour, and so she had stormed down to the flat in Back Street and confronted him.

"And where does your loyalty lie," she had shouted, "with your grandson or your politics, I'd like to know! You're not just a cheat but a coward too. You left Henry and me to discover this as best we might. No wonder you haven't been to Blakeney Street in weeks! Well, this is where we part company, Frank, Henry or no Henry. What do you think it's like for him to have a grandfather, a public figure, acting like this and trying to get rid of the very body his grandson has just been chosen to join? And all behind our backs!"

A tide of ancient chauvinism rose redly in Frank; his father would have hit his mother if she had spoken to him in such a way. He held his door open for Sally.

"Get out," he said, "get out before I throw you out."

They hadn't spoken since. Henry said once or twice, "Is Grandpa coming?" and Sally had said, absently, to try and indicate that there was nothing significant in his not coming, "He's up to his ears in work just now. You know what he's like." He didn't go to the cathedral to see Henry enrolled as a full chorister, but if Henry noticed, he made no comment; he was used, after all, to not having a full parental complement in attendance anyway.

Leo said Sally might be misjudging Frank.

"You don't know what the dean's like, Sal. Frank may well have found himself in a far more entrenched position than he meant, and because he isn't used to being outmanoeuvred he doesn't know how to recover himself. He's made a mistake and pride won't let him say so. I rather admire him. He's the last of the old city fathers, in essence."

But Frank was Alan's father, and in her present frame of mind, Sally did not want to make things up with him. She would tell him when she judged the moment right, just as she would tell Henry. Henry must know nothing until Sally could tell him exactly what was going to happen.

One thing she did feel very bad about, and that was the friendship between Leo and Alexander Troy. They were so angry with each other over Sally that they were scarcely speaking, and this at a time when they needed to speak, because of the choir. Sally had thought of either going away for a while or not seeing Leo but neither idea was really practicable, and in any case Leo had declared often to Alexander that he wouldn't give up his pursuit of Sally, wherever she was. She liked Alexander so much, and so did Henry, and she wished very hard for Felicity to come home so that he would have someone to confide in. She once suggested to Leo that she should go and see Alexander and try and sort things out, but she chose a poor moment, a moment when Leo was absorbed in thinking about work, and he turned on her the impersonal gaze of an absolute stranger and said there was no point in going, no point at all.

She had so much energy these days, felt so certain of herself, that she thought she could do anything. She cleaned the house throughout, even behind things, and cooked quite complicated food for her and Henry's suppers, to which his only reaction was to say with mild reproach that he hoped they'd be able to have spaghetti again soon. She took him swimming after school, and went to watch him and Chilworth practise in the nets, and offered herself for spells of duty in the school second-hand shop, which was run by just the committee-minded kind of mother she most disliked. On Thursday afternoons, when the bookshop shut, and late most evenings she saw Leo, and he would sit in the downstairs room with his lap overflowing with Mozart, who approved of him possessively, while they talked and drank wine and he played the piano for her. Only once did Henry come down, in a midnight panic about some French prep he hadn't done, and although he seemed mildly surprised to see Leo, his surprise was overtaken by relief that Leo seemed prepared to test him on his vocabulary, there and then, even if it was twenty past twelve.

"And now you can sleep with a quiet mind. *Qu'est-ce que c'est* to sleep *en* Frog?"

"*Dormir.*"

"And to sleep well?"

"*Dormir bien.*"

"Right, then. Nightmare over. Are you going to take this fat fur character upstairs with you?"

Henry gathered Mozart up.

"Thanks, sir."

"Sleep well. I'll see you eight-thirty tomorrow sharp in *very* fine voice."

Henry grinned. In the morning he said, "Why'd Mr. Beckford come?"

"To talk to me."

"About me?"

"No, old vanity pots. Just conversation. Friendly conversation."

"Is he a friend?"

"Yes. A very good one."

Henry squirmed.

"It's a bit funny to be friends with a *master*—"

"Oh? Aren't masters allowed to be people too? Anyway he isn't a master."

"He's like one," Henry said and then added, "He's OK, though."

"Gracious of you."

Henry had a letter from Alan that morning, the first to him alone for over three months. He seemed oddly indifferent to it, didn't want to open it, and when Sally slit the envelope and handed it to him, he looked at the first line or two and said rather vaguely that he'd read it later. When he came downstairs after brushing his teeth, ready for choir practice, he tore off a corner of the envelope to take the Saudi stamps to Hooper. Sally said, "Go on, take the letter to read in break," but she found it later on the little table in the hall, which they both used as a kind of pending tray. She read it. It was a breezy account of camel racing and said at the end, "Take care of Mum, old son, and I'll see you in the holidays." August, he meant. Six weeks away. In six weeks she must have made up her mind, told him, told Henry, and told Frank. It was the first chill draught of reality. She went back into the downstairs room to make another cup of coffee and to review her state of mind, and found Mozart on the table contentedly eating the butter.

The *Aldminster Echo* reporter arriving at the council chambers to interview Frank Ashworth about the city's interesting intention to take over the twenty-four singing boys of the cathedral choir was told that unfortunately Mr. Ashworth couldn't see him after all. He was quite used to being told this kind of thing and grinned cheerfully and said he'd wait. Frank's secretary said she hadn't made herself clear, obviously, Mr. Ashworth had no interview to give the *Echo*, and that was final.

The reporter made a note of this and said could he suppose that the proposal had been thrown out, and the secretary, typing away and not looking up, said she hadn't the first idea. "Very interesting," the reporter said annoyingly and then he said, "Keep cheerful, darlin'," and went down to the Lamb and Flag three doors away, where council gossip was given away free with pints of Protheroe's real ale. He knew several of the regulars in there and in half an hour had elicited the information he sought, that Frank's proposal that the city should adopt the choir had been thrown out resoundingly.

It had been the worst council meeting Frank could remember. Three of the younger members—including the one who wanted grief leave awarded to gays and lesbians in council employ who lost their lovers—had actually jeered at Frank, laughing at him with open-mouthed incredulity, in a way he found unbearably insolent. The general opinion was that the cathedral choir was outdated, elitist, and irrelevant to a modern world that did not need superstitious props like religion any longer. The gay supporter then pointed out with smiling malice that Frank had a grandson in the choir and therefore his proposal was blatantly nepotistic. The education officer, whose ineffectuality in the teachers' strike Frank had exposed, said with some satisfaction he thought fifty thousand pounds was on the steep side for Frank to suggest as a family favour.

To be gibed at was one thing; to be gibed at cheaply and ignorantly in public in this chamber, which Frank held in more respectful awe than any other room in his life, was intolerable. He had entered it first as a junior councillor just before his thirtieth birthday, and its weighty magnificence of red mahogany soberly gilded here and there with the city and county arms, the memorials to the fallen of two wars, the lettered "1888" above the great clock to date the building itself, had impressed upon him the size and the honour of his responsibility to Aldminster. In thirty years, of course, he had seen rows and heard abuse around that immense horseshoe-shaped table or from the banked seats on either side, but he had seldom, except in the last five years, seen the council lose its sense of decorum. Proclaiming themselves progressives, people had invaded the council merely to abuse, in Frank's view, their power there, to advance minority obsessions that did nothing to promote the greater good of the greatest number of people in Aldminster. Frank had come to realize with dull horror that many of them actually despised the poor and ordinary they had been elected to defend. And debate had become personal. Frank was ashamed to listen to some of the unprofessional squabbling that now masqueraded as public discussion, and now here he was in the pillory himself, at his accustomed seat halfway down one leg of the horseshoe, being accused, with grinning sneers, of attempting to line his own pocket and advance his grandson's career.

He could not even make a clean breast of it, and declare that he had allowed the dean to make assumptions about the future of the choir, had allowed the dean to extract his own acquiescence to those assumptions, because he was so eager to break into the charmed circle of the close by buying the headmaster's house. He had admitted to himself that the headmaster's house would be a kind of fifth column for the council in the close, but he was not going to admit that in the chamber now, to an audience sniffing for the underhand like rats among garbage. And yet if he did not admit it, the deduction would be made that he was somehow in cahoots with the dean; indeed that charge was already being levelled at him by a handsome young woman in a scarlet shirt, who was saying loudly from the benches that a man who was happy to entertain Hugh Cavendish in his own home was the kind of two-faced socialist the party could well do without. She had black hair and a bold, rude face and a party of devotees in the chamber roared with approval for her. Frank tried to say something about the city's heritage inherent in the choir, and she rose to her feet and shouted that "tradition" was a dirty word because it meant no more than the preservation of social inequalities, of which the choir was just one disgusting example. She said "disgusting" several times over, and it was then that Frank, who had always claimed walking out of a meeting was self-defeating, rose slowly and heavily to his feet and walked to the door. As he shut it behind him, someone said, overexcitedly, "There goes the last of the mastodons," and there was a burst of laughter.

He could have wept. Not for the insult but because of the depths to which the council could plunge, had plunged. It was not only not a great institution anymore, it was hardly an institution at all, presiding incoherently over a city in which too often the young went untaught and the sick un-nursed. He went into his office and stared at his blank blotter and knew himself to be, temporarily at least, both discouraged and bitter. Worst of all, he felt deeply disappointed in himself.

His secretary, a tired, experienced woman who had worked for councils of all political colours over the years, and whom he shared with another senior councillor, came in and asked, would he like coffee?

"No thanks."

She didn't ask how the meeting had gone; she never did. Frank had never seen her interest roused by anything at all except the January sales, when she always wanted inconvenient amounts of time off, and royal weddings. She put two buff files away in the steel cabinet beside Frank's desk and then said surprisingly, "Why don't you go up to the school, then, and see your grandson. They're free around lunch, aren't they?" and went out. When he passed her three minutes later she was typing as usual and she said, without stopping, "I'll deal with the chap from the *Echo*."

"Thanks," Frank said.

He was puzzled and annoyed to find he would like to have dropped in at Blakeney Street. Heaven knows why, or what he'd say when he got there, and Sally would be at work now in any case. He even walked past the house and noticed that there was a big jar of iris in the front window, with Mozart beside it, keeping an eye on the street, and that the knocker shaped like a dolphin that Sally and Alan had brought back from their Maltese honeymoon, and which he had always told them would get nicked, was spectacularly well polished. On an impulse he wrote, "1:15. Just passing. Frank" on a paying-in slip at the back of his cheque book, and tore it out and folded it up and pushed it through the letter box. Mozart left his windowsill at once to investigate.

He walked on, zigzagging up the streets to the edge of the close, soothing himself with the familiarity of buildings and railings and prospects down alleys. It was cool and grey and still, and all the wine-and-sandwich bars were full and the doors of pubs were open to the pavement, belching beery gusts out into the street. The close was quite full too, with people asleep on the grass or eating out of bags and packets, with knots of teenagers smoking here and there and dogs and toddlers and people on benches reading newspapers trying not to sit too close to each other. The grass was spattered with litter, and the bins were overflowing. The cathedral rose out of it all with a truly superb indifference.

Frank crossed the close by the path that ran directly under the great west window and led on to the Victorian Gothic bulk of the main building of the King's School. It passed, on its way, the headmaster's house, at which Frank glanced only briefly, and then stopped at the stone gateway that opened into the school's impressive courtyard. It was empty, but the windows of the refectory that formed one side were open, releasing a terrific clatter of knives and forks and a blast of institutional cookery. Frank intercepted a boy running towards it and asked where the junior school had lunch.

"Oh, they've had it," the boy said, breathless and eager to push on. "They're out on the fields now. They eat at twelve-thirty."

The school playing fields sloped slightly down from the close, away from the city and the estuary. When first laid out, they had been planted with beech and horse chestnut trees and bordered with fields that stretched eastwards to the then village of Horsley. Now houses and low factories and shopping precincts covered the fields, and cricket and football were played against a backdrop of brick. The trees still stood magnificently, and under one particularly tremendous horse chestnut, Henry and half a dozen others were practising back flips.

"Should you be doing that straight after your dinner?" Frank said.

Henry came across to him with unselfconscious pleasure and said, "We didn't eat it, it was hamburger, *awful*—"

Another boy said importantly, "My mother says it's all soya anyway."

"Supposed to taste the same."

"Well, it doesn't and we just flick it about—"

"Care for a short walk?" Frank said to Henry.

Henry beamed.

"OK."

They moved away down the slope.

"Sorry I haven't been to see you and your mother lately."

"She said you were busy."

"Well, that's always true. But we had a bit of a barney, your mother and me, about the choir. Did she say anything to you?"

Henry stooped for a stick.

"No."

"What do you feel about the choir? Do you think it's important?"

Henry swished his stick from side to side like a windscreen wiper.

"Course I do."

"Why?"

Henry shrugged.

"Because—of the cathedral. And the music. And—and because of God."

"Do you believe in God?" Frank said.

"Yes."

"Why do you?"

Henry sighed. This was an awful sort of conversation and not a bit like Frank was usually.

"It's obvious," Henry said and his voice had an edge of contempt. "There wouldn't be any of this"—he waved his stick—"without God, and the cathedral wouldn't be there in the first place."

"What about," Frank said, noticing the contempt and changing tack, "the boys from the state schools in the city who can't get into the choir like you can?"

Henry gave him a clear glance.

"They can. Harrison was at Horsley Junior and his parents don't pay fees."

Frank stopped walking. He was not in the mood, he discovered, for a second defeat within hours.

"How's your mother?"

"Fine."

"I saw the cat in the window today."

"He's in disgrace. He ate the butter yesterday and this morning he brought in a baby rat and let it go in the big room. We caught it in the dustpan."

Frank moved on again.

"Sometimes there have to be changes, you know, and you don't like the look of them. But in the end, you see that they were for the best."

Henry said nothing. He was thinking of the young rat's savage little face glaring up at him out of the dustpan.

"Any news from your father?"

Henry said casually, "He might come back in August for a bit."

"I'd best be getting back," Frank said. "Just wanted to have a word. Give my love to your mother and tell her I'll be round soon."

Henry grinned.

"I called her old girl last night and, oh boy, fireworks—"

"You're a cheeky monkey."

"She said 'Oh *hooray*, Henry'—"

"Come on, monkey, back to your antics."

Henry reached up and kissed his cheek.

"Bye, Grandpa. Thanks for coming."

Frank watched him racing back up towards the chestnut tree. He'd a softer spot for Henry than for anyone else in his life, no doubt about that, but right was right, and Henry couldn't grow up in a society that refused to move. From the common room window a hundred yards away Roger Farrell observed his unmistakable figure coming slowly up towards the school and turned to say with satisfaction to his colleagues, "Here comes our great ally. Shall we all go out and chair him in?"

9

LONDON LIFE WAS NOT AS NICHOLAS HAD IMAGINED IT WOULD BE. To begin with, everyone—Ianthe, Mike, Steven, and Jon—was always out, seeing people. Nicholas had thought that a stream of rock bands would come through the office and his days would be interestingly taken up with making them coffee and soothing them when Ikon turned them down, but it seemed that deals were done elsewhere and outside recording sessions took up twenty-four hours of each week's seven days. The office was where the mail came and where Nicholas answered the telephone. When people rang, they usually said, "Is Mike there?" or Steve or Jon or Ianthe, and when Nicholas said he was sorry, they weren't, but could he take a message, they usually said not to worry, they knew where he'd be most likely, and rang off. Sometimes one of the partners came in and gave Nicholas a master tape, which he had to take off to a studio in Wardour Street to have a lacquer cut. He liked that. He liked watching the cutting head on the lathe at work; it made him feel that something in his life was really happening. When he spent whole days in the office longing to be sent to the cutting studio, or even better the pressing plant in Wimbledon, he felt that nothing was happening at all.

The office was a single room about sixteen feet square with a tiny alcove off it, a lavatory two floors down, and a view of yellow brick walls and fire escapes. The partners had furnished it, in their initial enthusiasm, with two dark brown tubular desks, cubes of foam furniture upholstered in corduroy, huge plants, and self-conscious lighting. Then they had realized about the need to earn back their investment, and had simply left it to silt up with the disorganized clutter of their business. There were full ashtrays and burn marks on everything, the dark brown carpet was scuffed and gritty, and the leaves of the plants had begun to rattle from drought.

Sighing, Nicholas began to put his matron-taught skills to work. There was nothing to clean with, and a first foray into the Charing Cross Road showed a complete dearth of the kind of shop that sold brushes or buckets. He approached the black woman he met sloshing water on the interminable stairs in the building, who immediately stopped sloshing and gave him all her equipment to clean with and came to watch him while he did it because, she said, she'd never seen a man do such a thing before. He cleaned for a whole day and Jon came in at six o'clock, scattering ash, and sniffed and said, "Weird smell. Any messages?"

The evenings were a bit better if he managed to sort of grab one of the partners and get taken with them wherever they were going. They were quite nice to him in an absentminded way but he still felt very much that he was living on the edges of other people's lives rather than in the centre of his own. The money was great, though, and so were the cast-off clothes Mike gave him from a shop in Covent Garden—Nicholas went, dressed in them, to gaze in awe at the window—and sleeping on Mike's sofa was a lot better than the infirmary, though not as good as Leo's second bedroom. Mike had a distinct taste for the Gothic, and a tailor's dummy dressed as a cowled monk stood at one end of the sofa, and a vast black paper bat crouched on a hat stand at the other. The sofa itself was covered in harsh dark velvet, and Nicholas was given a duvet striped in scarlet and black. He had to keep his clothes in a series of carrier bags behind the sofa. There wasn't anywhere else to keep them because most of Mike's little sitting room was taken up with all his stuff for editing, reel-to-reel recording machines, and mixing desks; you had to be careful about razor blades on the floor because if he got really carried away editing, he just dropped them. Ianthe told

Nicholas he was a brilliant editor. Mike didn't seem to want any rent beyond being reimbursed for food and given a weekly bottle of vodka, so Nicholas felt he should clean up a bit and this really bugged him, not because he resented Mike, but because he felt himself to be so bloody feeble; he *always* seemed to end up mucking out the lives of people who were having a much better time than he was.

In his pleat-top tweed trousers and buttoned-up shirt, he went down to Aldminster after a month and stayed with Leo. It wasn't a great success. Leo was in a funny mood and wouldn't talk about anything. Nicholas asked him about the choir.

"Doomed."

"You mean the council won't take it on and the dean won't change his mind?"

"Yes."

"What are you going to do?"

"It doesn't appear to be up to me."

Nicholas tried something else.

"How's Sally?"

"Fine."

"Will I see her this weekend?"

"No. She's gone to her mother."

"Her mother!"

"She has to think, she says."

He went over to the school and everyone was out playing games and the place had the odd suspended air it usually did on Saturdays. He saw Alexander in the distance and he looked awful, and then he went into the kitchen to see Mrs. Monk, who was getting cricket teas and gave him a ham sandwich. She said, "How's London suiting you, then?"

"It's great."

"You look a lot tidier, I will say that."

He smiled. No one else had noticed.

"How's everything here?"

"Same as usual. Mrs. Troy's not back and the choir's going at Christmas. Mr. Troy ran a petition and got two thousand signatures but it doesn't seem to have got him anywhere. Shame, really. Now you can help me slice these Swiss rolls. Half an inch only or they don't go nowhere."

Nicholas went to choral evensong on the Sunday, and could have wept. They sang part of a Tallis motet and he thought, If the time comes when nobody can hear this sound anymore, it will be the end. Totally awful. When the service ended he would have liked to follow the choir back into their vestry but of course he couldn't, so he hung about until Alexander came out of his stall and down the steps to the nave, and noticed him.

"How good to see you back. How is everything?"

"Great, sir."

"Are they keeping you busy?"

"Flat-out."

"I'm so glad."

Nicholas said hesitantly, "Mrs. Monk said the choir has to go at Christmas."

"I'm afraid it looks like it. There's plenty of support for it vocally but no money at all. And the repairs to the roof start the first week in August. Nobody in the close seems quite to think as I do."

"Mr. Beckford does."

Alexander looked away.

"It's—quite complicated for him. Going back tonight?"

"Yes. Got to—"

"Good luck," Alexander said and smiled. "Keep your fingers crossed for all of us here."

When he got back to London, Mike wasn't in his flat but, surprisingly, Ianthe was. She said the shower at her place had bust so she'd come to use Mike's. She was sitting on Nicholas's sofa wearing a black dress like an elongated T-shirt, and fish-net tights, and her hair was wound up in a towel turban. She and Nicholas had by tacit agreement steered clear of each other since he came to work for Ikon, in case his employment should look unprofessional to the others, and this was the first time they had seen each other alone. She was very nice to him about his work at the office and then she asked him with elaborate casualness, flicking through a magazine as she spoke, if he'd seen Leo that weekend.

"Yeah. I stayed with him."

"And?"

"He's fine. Not very talkative this time. The choir's going at Christmas. I guess he's pretty upset."

Ianthe dropped the magazine.

"Going? You mean my father's won?"

"The council's turned it down and the cathedral lot can't afford it anymore. I'm upset too. I know you don't like it but it's great music—"

"I didn't say I didn't like it. What did Leo say?"

"Not much. I *said*."

"Will he be out of a job?"

"They aren't doing away with the organ. It's just the choir."

Ianthe looked at the ceiling.

"Anyone else there? At Leo's?"

Nicholas opened his mouth to mention Sally and out of pure instinct shut it again. However much he owed Ianthe for his job— and by early afternoon each day, he felt he owed her nothing—his first and fundamental loyalty was to Leo. He knew Ianthe had this thing about Leo, and he also knew she could be pretty vicious if she wanted to be. To tell her about Sally might expose Leo to attack. He said, "He was working all weekend. I went to the school and saw a few people. I think the choir's really on his mind."

"Can't anyone *do* something?"

"Seems not."

"Make us a coffee, Nick. I had a really heavy session last night. But we might be signing up those people who make the Jesus and Mary Chain look like yesterday's school dinner."

Nicholas obediently went out into the tiny scarlet-painted kitchen and made Ianthe a mug of coffee, and then he carried it back to her and said suddenly, "*We* could help."

She stared.

"What d'you mean—"

"We could make a record. We could make a record with Leo on the B side and Henry Ashworth on the A side and market it through the rock channels. Something unusual—"

"Don't be daft," Ianthe said.

"I'm not daft. Think about it."

"I think you're daft. We're not in the choirboy business."

"That's why people'd listen."

Ianthe took a swallow of coffee and said wearily, "Pack it in, Nick. It's cracked, your idea."

"It's not cracked, it's really cool—"

She shouted, "Shut up, will you?" and Nicholas waited for a few minutes and then he said, "It'd help Leo," and went off to the bathroom.

When he came back, Ianthe didn't say any more, but she had recovered her temper. Nicholas made some bacon sandwiches for them both, and she told him about her weekend and this guy Gerry who would not, I mean *not*, leave her alone. It was such a drag. She'd get back tonight, she betted Nicholas anything, and there'd be more flowers outside and he'd have had to go to a hospital, for Christ's sake, to get them because it was a Sunday. Nice car, though. A black MG. When she got up to go, she said, "It's a screwball idea, but I'll think about it. Don't say anything to Mike."

When Mike came in around midnight he'd got a girl with him and wasn't about to say anything to Nicholas. They went straight into the bedroom and Nicholas put some music on pretty loud because there was nothing worse than hearing them through the wall together when he was alone with the bat and the monk and the red duvet Ianthe had spilled ash on. Funny though, he didn't feel as depressed as he usually did when Mike brought a girl back. He felt a bit excited in fact, not by what they were doing in the bedroom, but about his idea. If he could think of something really unusual for Henry to sing . . .

Hugh Cavendish gave a long interview to the *Echo*. He had planned what he would say carefully, and how he would emphasize what was no more than the truth, that the cathedral choir cost the chapter about a third of its annual income. He would be very detailed about the repairs to the roof, and he would not mention the new lighting scheme unless he was asked. It was scheduled to go ahead in the new year, and he had found all the money it would cost, bar three thousand, which he rather hoped the lord lieutenant might give in memory of his mother—who always complained the cathedral was too dark—in return for a commemorative plaque in her favourite chapel. On the domestic front, there was at least a temporary, if frail, truce between himself and Bridget and Cosmo, and as far as the close was concerned, he had the tacit support of everyone and the vociferous support of several, including the archdeacon, who, at ten years his junior, very much hoped for his own decade as dean when Hugh Cavendish retired.

The reporter wanted to know what he felt about the council's turning down the choir.

"I have to confess that I understand their reasons. Of course I am sorry, very sorry. We all regret so much that we have, like too many other cathedrals, fallen victim to our times. We must just rejoice that we possess one of the finest organs in England and an organist who can do it full justice."

"Creep," Leo said when he read the report of the interview. He was feeling sore and angry himself, uneasy that Sally might decide for freedom rather than for him, unable to make his way back to Alexander, who was battling quite alone, it seemed, and looking careworn and haggard.

Frank Ashworth, reading the same report, felt very similar. The dean's "understanding" of the council wasn't, to him, worth the breath it was uttered with, and if he really understood the present council, he had no business to be dean. He was just planning his next move, that's all. He was just softening the council up so that when Frank proposed the purchase of the headmaster's house, he'd get another ignominious defeat. The dean was, in Frank's view, going to put the council in his pocket if he could, and paying them compliments was only the beginning. If Frank had anything to do with it, the dean wasn't going to find everything going his way. Frank did not intend to be outsmarted twice, nor divided from his rightful allies on the council by clever ecclesiastical manoeuvrings. The dean had asked Frank to submit a very detailed proposal about the council's plans for the headmaster's house; that request was just a feint on the dean's part, Frank was sure, but he was going to devise a scheme no council could possibly reject. A small and unpleasant inner voice asked him if he were not confusing socialist aims with personal revenge, and it took some time to silence it. That small voice was one of the penalties, he had come to know, of living alone.

The governors' meeting of the King's School took place in the seldom-used dining room of the headmaster's house. It was a beautiful room, with an intricately plastered coffined ceiling and a massive fireplace, in which the few pieces of furniture Felicity and Alexander had managed to spare for it looked rather forlorn. There was a battered old Victorian expanding table, which they had bought years ago for fifteen pounds for Daniel to set up his trains on, and which Felicity had shrouded in an immense tablecloth that reached the floor all round; ten eccentric chairs that bore no relation to one another; a small bookcase; and, sprouting from one wall, a vast black iron bracket from which hung several bunches of dull gilded metal grapes that Felicity had found when they were first married and that she was sure would one day find its perfect place. The governors eyed it nervously as they came in. The chair directly beneath it fell to the lastcomer, Canon Yeats, who could never hurry because of his sticks. He gave it a beseeching glance as he sat down.

There were twenty-two governors, a huge turnout. Alexander had to rustle up a dozen more chairs and ended up sitting next to the dean, who was the chairman, which he would have preferred not to do. They went smoothly through all the usual business, the plans for the new sports hall, the report from the finance and general purposes committee, the extension of places for girls from the sixth form to lower down the school, and then the dean said with no change in his voice, "And now gentlemen, the choir."

The atmosphere froze. Alexander looked round the room, at the canons and councillors, at Frank Ashworth, at the admirals and lawyers and magistrates and educators who made up the governing body, and only in Canon Yeats's eyes did he meet with a gleam of sympathy.

"We are faced with an ineluctable decision. I fear it is no longer even a matter of choice. Above a third of the chapter's income is consumed by the choir, and modern economic circumstances simply do not permit us the continuation of such a luxury—"

"It is not a luxury," Alexander said loudly.

The dean half turned in his chair.

"Mr. Troy."

"The choral tradition of England is the finest in the world, and unique in its particular form. It is not simply a vital part of our heritage, it is something so important to humankind that we have no business to deny it to future generations—"

"I think it might be said," the archdeacon almost shouted from the far end of the room, "that we have no right to deny future generations the intact fabric of our cathedral either! The house of God must take priority!"

The chief education officer of Aldminster, who had come to regret his attack on Frank in the council chamber and wished to make amends, quoted as nearly as he could remember what Frank had said to him.

"It's quite wrong to favour some children of this city above others. Our policy must be to discourage the rank injustice of privilege."

Frank looked at him coolly. He would never have used an emotional word like "rank" himself but he knew an olive branch when he saw one. He gave the education officer the smallest nod and said, "The council much regrets it cannot see its way to taking the choir up. Our feeling is not simply that the money is more needed elsewhere, but that social distinctions in our city only make for trouble, which it is our job, as councillors, to avoid."

The theme was taken up eagerly. It was intolerable to encourage twenty-four children to believe themselves in any way superior to any others; choirs were an anachronism, and our heritage was far better represented by the cathedral itself, anyway; religious music was in any case irrelevant in a scientific world and the reality of that had to be confronted. The lay governors pointed out that there was plenty of good music in Aldminster, that there was a first-rate organist, and that the headmaster's case seemed to be more than a little tenuous.

"Spiritual!" Canon Yeats cried, helping Alexander not at all.

"The headmaster is of course musical himself," the dean said unctuously, "which must needs affect his opinion."

"I am a clergyman too—"

"Should the worship of God be dependent upon *music?*" the archdeacon asked spitefully.

Alexander stood up.

"One of the things I most regret about the debate over the choir which has raged these last months is that it has become personal. We have all become divided from one another because clearly some deep personal chord has been touched in us all, which ironically gives me my only glimmer of hope, namely, that the choir *does* matter to all of you in some way. All I ask is a reprieve for one year while I try to devise some scheme to save what I earnestly believe we all *need.*"

The room erupted. The dean let the hubbub swell and bellow for a minute before he called everyone to order.

"A year! Fifty thousand he's asking for!"

The dean raised his hand.

"Might I suggest a compromise? We do indeed grant a reprieve but not for a year. If Mr. Troy wishes to explore avenues towards making the choir self-financing, I suggest we allow him to produce a viable scheme by the next governors' meeting. That will be in October, four months away. A fair suggestion, gentlemen, do you not think?"

Alexander sat down again, heavily, and bowed his head.

"Four months is no use at all, and you know it."

"I think, Mr. Troy, you forget yourself. May I put my proposal to the vote? Those in favour—"

Hands shot up all round the room, twenty of them.

"And against."

Canon Yeats and Alexander, their hands alone upraised, gazed at each other in despair across the table.

"You should listen to him," Canon Yeats said fretfully to the meeting at large, "really you should. It is gravely shortsighted not to." He looked at Alexander. "' . . . I am coming to that holy room/ Where, with Thy quire of Saints for evermore,/I shall be made Thy Music . . . '"

"Herbert," said the archdeacon know-it-allishly.

Canon Yeats turned his head.

"Donne, actually."

"Gentlemen—"

"One moment, Mr. Dean—Mr. Chairman," Canon Yeats said. "Mr. Troy and myself are about to be heavily outvoted and"—he shot Alexander a glance—"we are not, if Mr. Troy will forgive me, political men, and thus unskilled at, shall we say, manoeuvres, but before we are submerged I must make one thing plain and public and I won't be talked out of it. And it is this. Ours is the truly Christian point of view and therefore we are right and you may all outvote us until you are blue in the face but you can't change *that*."

There was a small and embarrassed silence and then, too loudly, "Bravo," Alexander said.

After the meeting—concluding with a prayer for unity in which Alexander could not bring himself to join—he went round the table to help Canon Yeats to his feet.

"Dear me, Mr. Troy, what a den of self-motivated men we have fallen in to be sure."

"You did wonderfully."

Canon Yeats disentangled his sticks from the chair legs.

"But it got us nowhere, did it, nowhere at all. It's all so wrong. I said to my wife only yesterday, you should not run a cathedral as if it were a parish church with the close as its parish. The spiritual responsibility of a cathedral is *infinite*. Decisions like the choir are not ours to take."

Alexander walked slowly beside him out to his waiting car, with its huge orange DISABLED stickers.

"And don't you believe them about the money," Canon Yeats said, at last settled in among his orthopaedic cushions. "That's just a bluff. Money is *always* to be found if you put your mind to it." He looked at Alexander. "Four months, Mr. Troy. Improbable but not impossible. I'm not much use for anything but prayer and addressing envelopes but I'll do those with a will. Just you say the word."

Alexander watched the car hiccup away along the close and then he went slowly back to his office in the school and there, sitting on the edge of Sandra Miles's desk with both hands round a mug of coffee, was Felicity.

"It was by the sea," Felicity said, "not far from Southwold, a tiny community, associated with the one I went to before. Only six nuns and four lay workers running a hospice for dying alcoholics, people picked up in the east coast ports, mostly women. I've worked really hard." She held her hands out. "You wouldn't believe how much scrubbing there was."

They were alone in the sitting room, in the dusk, in chairs Alexander had dragged to the window for the last of the light.

"I had two hours off each afternoon, and sometimes I went to the sea and walked and sometimes I tried to write and sometimes I found somebody to talk to. I slept in an attic room with another volunteer, which was the worst part, because she had lost a baby not long ago and had come to try and heal herself and she cried terribly in her sleep. And the patients cried and cried too. It isn't at all a tranquil way to die, even among nuns and Suffolk dunes."

Alexander had spent the afternoon with his breath held. He had not dared to ask her anything, had hardly even touched her, in case she either fled again or melted before the intensity of his feeling, like Eurydice. He had, with swimming head, gone through an ordinary afternoon, restraining himself every other minute from leaping up from Livy, Book XXX, with the Lower Sixth to rush and discover if she was still there. She seemed to be, miraculously. He could hear her talking to Sandra, to Mrs. Monk, to Roger Farrell, who had clearly come in to say that yet again Wooldridge had been prevented from turning up for hurdling, and who was being irresistibly deflected from his resentment. Alexander went on with his afternoon with superhuman self-control until Felicity put her head round his study door and said she was going over to the house and she would see him there when he was ready. He managed not to be ready for ten whole minutes.

"There doesn't seem to be anything to drink," she said.

"There isn't. I daren't let there be; otherwise I drank it."

"The Cavendishes always have a bursting cellar. I shall go and ask them for a bottle of wine."

"Felicity—"

She smiled at him.

"Oh, I must. Just *think*—"

So she had gone across the close in her flowing black cotton skirt and her fringed shawl and when the dean opened the door she said, "Hugh, I'm afraid it isn't a cup of sugar I want, but a bottle of wine."

The dean quite forgot himself and put his arms round her and said with warmth, "My *dear* girl—"

"There isn't a drop at home. And I've been in a little convent where there wasn't a drop either."

The kitchen door opened.

"Huffo, I heard the knocker—"

The dean spun round.

"Look, my dear, look who it is!"

Bridget came forward battling with a hundred conflicting feelings.

"My dear Felicity, how perfectly extraordinary—"

"That I should come back?"

The dean, beaming, wagged a finger.

"Now you mustn't *start* by calling Bridget's bluff."

"Huffo, I can't think what you mean—"

"I'm afraid," Felicity said, "that I've come to scrounge a bottle of wine."

"A white burgundy? A blanc de blanc? A hock?"

"Something very ordinary. You are very kind, Hugh."

Bridget was nearly exploding with questions.

"Are you newly back, Felicity?"

"Lunchtime. Very travel-stained still. And find you all at each other's throats."

"There have been *grave* misunderstandings. And some severe overreactions."

"I will get your wine," the dean said hastily, backing away.

"You must come and see me," Bridget said. "We must talk it all over sensibly over a cup of coffee. I always feel women are so much better at sorting things out. So much less emotional."

"I've spent the last six weeks with women. I should say they were very emotional indeed." She looked clearly at Bridget. "I've been helping to nurse dying drunks in Suffolk. Women drunks. I didn't intend to." She paused. "I thought you would like to know."

"My *dear*—"

"Here," said the dean, returning, "a bottle of nice white burgundy. A present from me—us. To celebrate your return."

"I didn't mean it to be a present."

"But I do."

When she had gone, Bridget said furiously, "You are such a *fool*, Huffo. And you make such a fool of *me*."

He regarded her.

"Do I now, my dear."

"There," Felicity said, holding the bottle out to Alexander.

"But that's *good!*"

"I know. Hugh gave it to us."

"But Bridget—"

They laughed, for the first time.

"As you can imagine."

She came up to him and laid her cheek against his chest. He did not touch her. Then she said, "Shall we drink it? In the sitting room without putting the lights on?" And when they were there, she told him what she had already told Bridget Cavendish. He said at the end, quite openly, "And why did you leave it and come back?"

"To be with you."

She held her glass up to the dying light.

"I don't go away to be perverse."

"Then why?"

"I feel compelled."

"Are you sure it is not just a test? A test of yourself? To see if you really do still want to live with me?"

"If that is so, then every time I find I do. This time more strongly than usual." She looked directly at him. "I can't promise it won't happen again, any more than one can promise never to let another row start, but I will try. I don't want it to happen again."

"And if I were to leave you?"

"I should not be as forbearing as you are with me. Do you want to leave?"

He swallowed.

"No. I never have. I—"

She said quickly, "*Don't* mention God."

He waited.

"There is so much to reconcile," Felicity said. "I never thought living could be so hard, wherever you do it. At least I think I'm learning that no other place is less hard and that if I am with you, it's easier. But it doesn't stop the pressures, all the demands like a Henry James novel, all the oughts and the wants. I am a rotten wife."

"Only in the clean-sock, marmalade-making sense, and I don't mind about that anyway. I only mind about separation and exclusion."

"I know." She paused. "I will try. I want to try. I am going to write so much down. And read. Sister Winifred at the convent said I should start with Saint Benedict."

"Perhaps—"

"Are you hungry?"

He thought about it.

"Not really."

"I expect there are eggs—"

"Later."

She got up and filled their glasses.

"Tell me what has been happening. Sandra told me about the choir and that you are beleaguered alone because for some reason even Leo won't speak to you. Poor Sandra. She showed me her ring so sadly. You've taught her the ultimate dreariness of good sense."

"Come here," he said.

She folded herself up on the floor by his chair and leaned against his knees.

"You remember little Henry Ashworth?"

"Yes. A dear, straightforward fellow, lovely voice—"

"Leo is besotted with his mother and planning to marry her. As yet not even Henry's father knows."

"Frank Ashworth's son—"

"Yes. And Frank Ashworth is pushing to buy this house from the dean and chapter to make into a social centre."

"*This* house?"

"This house. I have been given four months to make the choir financially self-supporting. I ran a petition in the city which raised nearly two thousand signatures, but no-one was prepared to give any money. I suppose I must now appeal nationally."

"Heavens," Felicity said. "*Heavens*. I think I should go back to my drunks."

"Not funny."

She got up.

"How right you are. They weren't. I know Sally Ashworth."

"You do?"

"I've bought lots of books from Quentin Small—"

"Will you talk to her?"

"I might think she was right."

"But Henry—"

"I might still think it. But I'll talk to her. And Leo has sent you to Coventry because you disapprove."

"Coventry became sort of mutual. And as Canon Yeats so rightly said, I'm no politician, I don't know how to manoeuvre people."

"You're honest."

"And clumsy?"

She put out a hand to pull him to his feet.

"Any squeak from Daniel?"

"None."

"Oh dear," she said, putting her arm through his, "how unstraight-forward everything about us is—"

He smiled down.

"You're a fine one to talk."

She smiled back.

"Hello," she said.

He stooped to give her a quick kiss.

"Come on," he said, "eggs."

10

SALLY BELIEVED HER VISIT TO HER MOTHER HAD CLEARED HER
mind. Jean Jefferies was a widow and lived in the village she had
lived in all her married life. She had a dog, a garden, a bridge four,
and an old schoolfriend to go on holiday with to the Scilly Isles.
She was a keen patron of the mobile library, kept binoculars on
the sitting-room windowsill for bird watching, and, having voiced
her objection to Alan as Sally's husband just once, on grounds of
class, she had never mentioned it again nor held it against him.
She had been brought up not to hold personal opinions about people
and her term of highest approbation was "sensible." Sally's proposal
to leave Alan and all he could provide her with for a bohemian
organist earning rather under thirteen thousand all told was not
sensible at all.

"It isn't *about* money," Sally said.

When she talked like that, Sally reminded Jean of her dead father.
They had married at the end of the war and too late discovered
that they had nothing in common outside the set of friends that
had brought them together. Graham had always gone on about
communication being so important, but in Jean's view, communication was the exchange of reasonable opinion and pieces of information and no more. Graham used to tell her often—and not
pleasantly—that she had no imagination, but she never minded.
Imagination, as far as she could see, only led its possessors into

terrible pointless labyrinths of talk and feeling that were a pure waste of time. It was stupid to let yourself get upset, as Graham always was, because then you became paralysed and could do nothing for hours. Many a weekend afternoon, she could recall, she had weeded an entire border while Graham fumed about uselessly indoors after some silly tiff they'd had at lunchtime. And now here was Sally all agitated because she couldn't for the moment fix her mind on the obvious and the prudent.

"It will pass," Jean said. "Everyone gets the fidgets. It's usually about forty but perhaps you are having them early. Don't give him biscuit, dear, or he asks all visitors."

"He'd better have that bit, he's licked it—"

Jean shooed the terrier into his basket and came back to say, "You know me, dear. I'll speak my mind just once. If you've come to get my approval, you can't have it. Your father and I were very poorly suited and we managed thirty very decent years. I am sure Alan's been silly, men often are and it means nothing, but he's your husband and that's that. It's time he came home and you lived together as a proper family. And you have Henry. What would have become of you if I had decided to pack up and walk out because I didn't like the argy-bargy?"

"I expect I'd have had a much more relaxed childhood."

"Thank you very much."

"Oh, Mum—"

"I don't want this to become personal, Sally, but people don't marry musicians."

"Presumably Lady Elgar did, and several Frau Bachs—"

"You know exactly what I mean. Being an organist is arty, Sally, it isn't reliable. What kind of home would you have?"

"A very crooked cottage in Chapter Yard."

"And Henry?"

"Things wouldn't change for Henry except he'd have a stepfather he saw all the time rather than an absent father."

"So your mind's made up."

"Almost—"

"You would have to get more than a fiddling-around job."

"It would be good for me."

"Well," Jean said, "you're my daughter and always will be, whatever we do or don't agree about. If you go ahead, you'll know what my opinion is, but no-one else will. You'd better send Henry here for a bit of fishing with his granny. It'll do him more good to talk fish than feelings."

"And Leo? Will you meet Leo?"

"Of course. But I'm not turning my back on Alan either. Now that's enough of that. You can come out and help me tie up the delphiniums. Poor things, this wind has knocked them flat."

Driving back to Aldminster, Sally considered her feelings; it had recently become something of a habit, rather like taking her temperature. She had never valued her mother's opinion on anything from morals to curtain fabric, so why she should have troubled to ask for it now, particularly when she knew exactly what her mother would say, she couldn't think. Perhaps it was habit, perhaps it was—and this was a very seductive thought indeed—yet another proof that she didn't have to ask anyone for anything anymore, that a real independence might be beginning to be hers. Perhaps she'd used her mother as a kind of test to herself. And the test had worked, because they had tied up the broken delphiniums together in the most equable way and Sally had felt she had scored a tiny victory, in the process of growing through being just a daughter into being a person as well. Growing through, growing up, perhaps, at last. She drove through the sloping city centre with much more than her usual dash, and because there was still an hour before she need collect Henry from the Hoopers, she parked the car in the close and went in to Chapter Yard.

Leo was in the kitchen, standing over a whining kettle. He didn't turn round when she came in but simply banged a second mug on the table and dropped a tea bag in it and said childishly, "And do I have my future mother-in-law's approval?"

Sally's elation and pride withered in an instant.

"That's not why I went and you know it. I don't want any tea."

Leo poured boiling water into both mugs.

"I don't know it. I don't see that you need to talk to anybody but me."

"It's more complicated for me," Sally said. "I have a husband and child. It's going to be more of a battle for me."

He dredged the sodden tea bags out of the mugs and flung them inaccurately towards the sink.

"And whose side will your mother fight on?"

"She doesn't think I'm right but she'll support me."

"And where does that get you?"

Sally sighed.

"Oh, Leo, don't be *cross*—"

"I'm not cross. I'm tense as hell and I've had a rotten weekend. You won't let me anywhere near you. You insist on the battles you will have to fight but you won't let me share them with you." His voice rose. "Do you wonder I'm tense?"

Her throat bunched with incipient tears, not for the row they were heading for but with rage, rage at Leo for ruining the singing free spirits in which she had come to Chapter Yard. She was blind with fury. He was making her feel just as Alan did when she objected to his selfish pleasure-seeking and he treated her with a bland uncomprehending indifference in return. She wasn't going to be beholden to anybody, man or woman, she wasn't going to stagger about under her burden of gratitude and guilt anymore, *owing* the sacrifice of herself to someone in return for any gift, emotional or material. She thumped her fists down on the kitchen table so hard that the tea leaped in brown tongues out of the mugs and splashed across the surface.

"These are *my* decisions!" she yelled at Leo. "Do you hear me? Mine! I'll take them myself, by myself, when I'm good and ready, and I don't have to account to anybody for them, not my mother, not Alan, not Henry, not you. Sit here and sulk if you want to. I don't care. It's just blackmail, the same old masculine blackmail. Well, I'm proof against that now and you can go to hell with the rest of them if you don't like it!"

She slammed the front door behind her so violently that Cherry Chancellor, cleaning her front windows, felt the glass tremble under her duster.

"Fireworks next door," she said to Martin. "Of course I wouldn't say anything—"

"No."

"But it doesn't really seem right in a cathedral close. It's like living next door to some student hostel."

"He's a brilliant organist—"

Cherry polished ever more vigorously.

"Well, *that's* not everything."

Martin let a small pause fall and then he said, "No. But it's a very great deal. And you've missed a bit in the top left corner."

At breakfast next morning Henry said could they have a puppy, the Hoopers had two, called Mack and Tosh, did she get it, Mackintosh. Sally said no, who'd look after it and Henry said Hooper's mum was at home all day doing the cooking and things, and Sally burst into tears. This was puzzling and distressing, but it was also ten past eight so Henry put his books into his sports bag and gave Sally a hurried kiss and went off to choir practice, where instead of Dyson's "Magnificat in D," which they were were all expecting, Mr. Beckford made them go through some of Vaughan Williams's "Mystical Songs" and nobody could get the mood right and he got furious and shouted at Henry, who hated being ticked off at the best of times and went white. They trooped over to school in a subdued straggle after this, and Leo caught up with Henry, who was trailing dismally at the rear, temporarily outlawed by the others because they did not know what to do about him, and said, "Sorry to bark at you, old fellow." This was altogether too much for Henry, who dissolved into tears of humiliation and had to be walked up and down the cloisters until he was sufficiently composed to bolt, late, into assembly and receive a look of the sternest reproof from Roger Farrell, who was his form master. Farrell took him aside after assembly to admonish him and Leo arrived in the middle of this to say it was he who had detained Henry and tempers flared publicly in the main corridor, so that Felicity, coming in to look at the week's engagements in Sandra's diary, remarked that some things didn't seem to have changed at all.

"Mr. Farrell's thrilled the choir is going," Sandra said. "I'm afraid most of the common room are. You can't persuade Mr. Farrell that anything's any good unless you have to run about to do it."

"And Leo?"

Sandra looked prim.

"Well, between you and me, I think Mr. Beckford's just being a bit temperamental. I mean, I know his job's safe at least, but it would only be half a job without the choir and he knows that really."

"I feel as if everyone is playing musical statues on the whole issue. And the cathedral is humming with lighting engineers; there's a Harvey's van outside this morning. It looks like a dozen splinter groups to me, all refusing to speak to one another."

"Oh, Mrs. Troy, you know what people are like—"

Felicity went in search of Leo but found he had fled to the organ loft and was extemporizing thunderously. Coming out of the resounding cathedral, she met Bridget Cavendish with her well-ordered shopping basket, all forgiving smiles.

"Now don't forget, my dear, the invitation is always open. You have only to pick up the telephone. Supper any day this week except Thursday or next week except Wednesday and Friday."

Felicity said, "Bridget, don't be obtuse. And don't patronize us either."

"This is a very unfortunate attitude to take I must say—"

"Thank Hugh for the wine, would you? It was delicious. Much more delicious than we're used to. But unless you want a full-scale row in your dining room, supper is out of the question just now and I think you know it."

Bridget went back to the deanery and comforted herself by saying indiscreetly to Mrs. Ray, who was washing the kitchen floor, that Mrs. Troy clearly hadn't had much of a homecoming, poor dear, she was in *such* a strange mood this morning. Mrs. Ray, who travelled in to work on the same bus as Mrs. Monk, merely remarked that it took all sorts and saved Bridget's indignation up to tell Mrs. Monk the following day. Felicity went across the close towards the Lyng, and was briefly intercepted by Janet Young, who embraced her warmly and said she was so thankful to see her.

"Robert and I simply cannot discuss it, so of course we have been sent to a kind of Coventry. I think you are exactly what the close needs. It's like having a window opened to let good fresh air in on a particularly quarrelsome party—"

Felicity looked at Janet's worn attractive face and thought, as she so often had before, that being a bishop's wife must be one of the loneliest jobs in the world, since there was an unavoidable and unwanted elevation above other mortals, coupled with an equally unavoidable isolation in the heart of the very community you were forced to inhabit, the close being the kingdom of the dean and his wife. She kissed Janet Young with enthusiasm, and walked down the Lyng amidst the morning shoppers and the strollers and the green litter bins to Brewer Street and Quentin Small's bookshop. Sally Ashworth, in a big blue skirt and a T-shirt, with her hair tied back with a ribbon and no makeup, was standing on a stool with a duster in her hand not dusting. She looked round when Felicity came in.

"Goodness," she said, and then, clumsily, "Henry said you were back. I think the whole school knows."

She got off her stool.

"I don't suppose you've come to buy a book."

"No."

Sally said, "It's such a relief you're back, we've all got so stuck. Do—do you know about everything?"

Felicity sighed.

"Yes. I wasn't going to come so soon and then there was a complication in school this morning and Leo and Roger Farrell were bellowing at each other and Henry was crying—"

"*Henry*—"

"Leo shouted at him and then said sorry."

"And I cried at breakfast because he wanted a puppy and a homey mother."

"He doesn't really."

"I screamed my head off at Leo last night. I can't bear to climb out of one box and into another."

"You don't have to climb into another—"

Sally said defiantly, "He wants me to tell him everything."

Felicity looked calmly at her.

"That isn't the same thing at all."

A young man came in off the street and asked very quietly if there was an ancient-history section. Sally took him upstairs and when she came down, Felicity was sitting in Quentin's desk chair and holding an airmail letter addressed to Alan Ashworth in Jeddah, Saudi Arabia.

"I wrote it last night and twice more this morning," Sally said. "This is a very peculiar conversation! I ought to be asking you if you're all right."

"Oh yes," Felicity said, putting the letter down.

"You want to mend things between Leo and Alexander. I can't help just now. I'd like to but I can't. I expect I'll see Leo in a few days." She gathered up four stray books on the desk into a pile. "I have to see Alan's father next."

Felicity looked up.

"Have you any money?"

"No. Not serious money."

"Could you find somewhere to live alone for a while?"

"I might manage something."

"The only person one is really stuck with all life long is oneself—"

"I've only just realized that. Was Henry all right?"

"I think so." She stood up. "I shall go and see Leo."

"Please do."

Felicity moved to the door.

"I don't mean to be churlish," Sally said, "but I have to have some space."

"Oh yes. I know about space—"

The young man came elaborately quietly down the stairs.

"Is there no cheaper Gibbon than the ten-pound one?"

"Yes, yes, there's an Everyman I think, hold on—"

"I'll see you soon," Felicity said.

She went out into the street and the unenthusiastic sunshine. She hadn't gone more than a few steps before Sally came running after her.

"Look, I haven't mentioned Leo in my letter to Alan. Leaving Alan is something quite separate, that's very important. That's what I shall tell his father, too. It's the truth."

"I know," Felicity said.

There were people pushing on the pavement round them.

"Leo made me wake up to what was so wrong, not by anything he said but by his attitude. I knew it inside all along, I'd known for ages—"

"You don't have to tell me."

"I do," Sally said. "I must be realistic."

"If it's true, you don't have to tell anyone."

"I don't want to be misunderstood."

"It's inevitable. People interpret actions as they wish to. Just *don't* apologize for anything."

"Thank you for coming."

Felicity smiled.

"Good luck. As long as you know what you want—"

"Oh," Sally said, laughing, "oh—" and shaking her head, she retreated back towards the shop, where the young man waited politely by the empty desk to pay.

"Look," Mike said. "Frankly, old son, I'm not in the business of doing favours."

They were in Mike's sitting room, Nicholas on the sofa, Mike behind his barrage of equipment, Ianthe on the floor with an ashtray and a bottle of mineral water in front of her.

"It isn't a favour," Nicholas said, "it's a business proposition—"

"You're not going to sell a single one, I'll tell you that for free. It's a no-win gamble."

"What'd it cost?"

Mike screwed up his eyes and sighed a lot and did a great many calculations on a piece of paper. Ianthe kept Nicholas fixed with a gaze that dared him to open his mouth again at this delicate juncture and put his foot in it. After five minutes of scribbling and muttering, Mike said that it wasn't economic, even with a no-hoper like this, to make less than a thousand albums, so they were looking at a bottom line of three thousand pounds and a top one of five.

"Christ," Nicholas said.

Mike shrugged.

"It's what it costs."

Ianthe said with infinite nonchalance from the floor, "S'pose we found the money? I don't say we can, but if, you know—would you help? I mean would you produce it for us. Just an idea—"

Mike got up and tried to prowl around in the tiny spaces left by furniture in the room. He was loosely made and dressed with throw-away carefulness and hated anyone to know that his parents lived in Sunningdale. He said, "Let me think. I'd be giving up most of a week, because I imagine you could only record at night, three three-hour sessions, a weekend's editing. It's a lot to ask, frankly. And I don't know about Ikon's name. I don't know at all. We have our credibility to think of."

Ianthe said, "You should come down and hear them. They're cool."

Mike shook his head.

"It's just not my kind of sound."

"If we could raise the money," Nicholas said, with far too much earnestness, "would you come then? Can we do a deal? If we can raise three thousand pounds, will you at least come down to Aldminster?"

Mike squatted down to take a cigarette from Ianthe's pack. Usually she would have jumped on him. He said, "OK. But no messing. It's got to be for real."

"Yes," Nicholas said. His heart was pounding. When Mike got up and turned away, Ianthe grabbed his hand and squeezed it hard. Mike turned back.

"It isn't going to work. You know that, don't you. It can't. Who's gonna buy it? A bunch of old ladies, and they don't buy from us. Three grand doesn't grow on trees either."

The next weekend, Ianthe and Nicholas went down to Aldminster. They were both going to stay at the deanery—Nicholas was extremely apprehensive about this—and they were going round to see Leo. Bridget put Nicholas in Fergus's room—the walls were hung with immense fierce posters of the drawings of William Blake—and terrified him with hostessy instructions about bathwater and which lavatory to use. Ianthe had sworn him to secrecy about their mission and said he was particularly not to tell Cosmo, who would reveal it to his father out of sheer bloody-mindedness. Cosmo was back on form, having been found out distributing a pamphlet he had concocted inciting the Asian boys at Horsley Comprehensive, of whom there were many, to wage covert war on the West Indians, of whom there were few. Cosmo's greatest friend for years had been West Indian, which left the exhausted Mr. Miller with his usual difficulties in pinning down Cosmo's undoubted but elusive malice.

It did not promise well, as a weekend. Meals were a fearful strain, though Nicholas was weak with gratitude for Bridget's robust cooking, and Leo was beastly when they telephoned and said he could only see them for half an hour on Saturday evening because he was going out. He sounded really cross. Ianthe bravely said take no notice and put on her new tiny skirt and a drenching of scent, and she was quite right, because when they got there, Leo opened the door, looking exhausted, and said he was so sorry he'd been a bear but the strain was really getting to him.

"That's why we've come," Ianthe said.

It took a bit of time to explain but he really loved the idea. He smiled properly for the first time. He even said he thought he could put a couple of hundred into the record fund and when they said heavens, two *hundred*, he just said he was sorry there wasn't more. Then he said, "Have you suggested this to the headmaster?"

"No—"

"Go over now. Go on. There's always a lull after cricket on Saturdays. And Felicity's home—"

"Felicity!"

"She's been working in some hospice. She's raring to help over the choir."

"My parents never said—"

Ianthe and Leo exchanged glances and laughed.

"To coin an immortal phrase, she *wouldn't*, would she—"

"Watch it, Leo, *my* mother—"

"All yours, honey child. And that's a very fetching little attempt at a skirt you're wearing."

Ianthe towed Nicholas across the close at high speed. She wanted to sing. It was *working* and Leo'd been—oh, she'd save that up to think about later. And it went on working, because the Troys were thrilled with them and Felicity rang her brother in London then and there and he promised them five hundred. He said he'd had a tax rebate.

"You might not get it back," Felicity said.

"That's what I thought when the tax man had it. At least I don't begrudge it to the choir."

They made a list of who else they could ask. Felicity said she would try shops and banks and the legion of building societies on the Lyng who owed them money morally, she said, for filling precious ground floor windows with insufferable yellow-and-blue placards about interest rates. And she would put an appeal in the paper. Ianthe said, embarrassedly, that her father would have to know.

"There's a facility fee. The dean and chapter would charge one, Leo says—"

"But he says he'll waive his own fees and if we don't need the whole choir, only Henry—"

"What about the Musicians' Union?"

"Henry doesn't belong and I suppose it's up to Leo what he does with his fee—"

"I can design the sleeve," Ianthe said. "That would save a couple of hundred—"

"And the royalty?"

"Ten or fifteen per cent—"

Nicholas said sadly, "My dears, ten per cent of a thousand records selling for six pounds can't save the choir."

"But it's a beginning! It might get them known!"

"If it's promoted as a save-this-choir record, if we really wham in on the publicity—"

"Do you know about publicity?"

"A bit—"

"Look," Alexander said. "I don't want to be an old killjoy, but I really think you are going to be badly disappointed. I've got an appointment to see a King's old boy next week who is reputed to be musical and wealthy, and dull though it may sound, I think that sort of chance is our only real one for the money we need."

Nicholas's face was contorted with the effort of making Alexander *see*.

"We've *got* to try—"

Alexander smiled.

"Oh, what a bunch of amateur enthusiasts—"

"Steady on," Ianthe said, but her indignation was mock. "Some of us round here are in the business." She stopped. "I suppose my father could just refuse to let us use the cathedral?"

Alexander began to laugh.

"Ianthe, I think we look such a hopeless star-gazing crew that he'd think himself perfectly safe."

"Great oaks—" Felicity said. She looked round at them all and smiled hugely.

"Hadn't someone better ask little Henry?"

Back Street depressed Sally. There was no humanity left in it now, where once there had been so much—strings of washing and prize leeks and doorstep natters and pay-night feuds. Only four little terraced houses were left, clinging together, dwarfed by the blocks of flats and offices with alarming leggy car-park spaces underneath, and they looked toothless and seedy. The new buildings had made a wind tunnel, and grimy blasts from the docks blew the litter about waist high. Sally thought that if one of the little houses still standing had been Frank's birthplace, he would be living in it still, with his books and his refrigerator and his record player all crammed into rooms still wearing the last coat of distemper his father had slapped on to them. Traditional, tough, soft-hearted, and progressive—in all, Sally considered, riding up in the lift, twice the man his son would ever be.

When he opened his front door, Sally said, "Shall we both apologize or shall neither of us?"

"You ought to know better than to ask me that."

"Can I come in?"

He made way for her. The big table in his sitting room was strewn with papers and the "Anvil Chorus" was thumping out of the record player. He turned it off and said, "Did Henry give you my message?"

"He said you'd been up to the school—"

Sally sat down at the table and put her elbows on it.

"Frank, I've come to tell you something. I'm leaving Alan."

He said nothing.

"I can't live like this anymore, on the coat tails of someone else's life. We hardly know each other anymore and I don't think I'm interested, either. I don't trust him and even if I'm quite fond of him, I don't love him. He isn't my companion." She was on the verge of saying, "I'm sorry, Frank," but she quelled it and said instead, "I wrote to him yesterday."

Frank went over to the imitation Jacobean sideboard that he had given his mother ten years before she died because she had craved it so, and poured brandy into glasses. He put one in front of Sally.

"I can't drink it without soda—"

He went back silently and shot soda into the tumbler; then he gave it to Sally and sat down opposite her.

"Now then. What's brought all this on?"

"It's been coming on a long while."

"He's not much of a husband," Frank said, "and he's never been good enough for you. But I don't think he's any worse than he's ever been—"

"It isn't him, it's me."

Frank looked at her.

"What's happened to you?"

"I've changed. Things have come to a head—"

"Another fellow?"

"A friend has made me see clearly. That's all."

Frank grunted.

"Girls like me," Sally said, "got married because that was the next thing we did. Our mothers didn't work; we weren't brought up to think long-term. But I can't mark time like this for the rest of my life. I'm only thirty-four."

"What do you want to do?"

"Live by myself for a bit and work seriously."

"How are you going to manage that?"

"I don't know yet."

He looked up.

"Did you think I'd help you?"

"No."

"I might."

"Frank—"

"Women have to earn their way same as any man now. Their choice. What about Henry?"

"He doesn't know anything yet."

Frank got up and walked to the window to look up with reluctant admiration at the cathedral. When Gwen had come to him saying she was going off with Peter Mason and she'd like to dare to see him try and stop her, he hadn't wanted to stop her at all. He believed that secretly she had wanted a scene, had wanted to see two huge men hurling punches at each other over her like some Hollywood movie, because she grew even angrier with him when he took it calmly, and clutched little Alan passionately against her and made silly and extravagant declarations that served no purpose except to frighten the child. The last thing Gwen wanted was her own life; she wanted to be at the cosy and cosseted centre of someone else's, and that's what she insisted on with Peter Mason, chocolates and dinner dances and champagne, and sprays of mauve orchids on their numerous sentimental little anniversaries. She was light-years away from Sally, gazing with distaste at her brandy and talking about freedom and making it alone. Whether Gwen had really wanted to take Alan with her was doubtful too, apart from the image of sweet motherhood he allowed her to convey; probably a poodle puppy would have served much the same purpose. Frank was sure no-one ever tried to explain things to Alan—not Gwen or him or Peter Mason, who proved a kindly, indulgent stepfather. They just let these things happen to Alan and he got on with the results. He turned round.

"What will you say to him?"

"I'll say I don't want to live as his father's wife anymore because we never see each other and we are too far apart. I'll tell him he won't understand now but he will later. I'll tell him I'll answer any question he wants to ask me. I won't say anything until I've seen Alan."

"Have you asked him to come back?"

"I haven't asked him anything."

Frank let out a long sigh. He moved behind Sally's chair and gave her shoulder the lightest touch as he passed.

"I'm sorry, Sally. I'm in no position to offer advice and I wouldn't anyhow. But don't rush into anything. And if you need help, you know where I am."

"Damn," Sally said, "I'm going to cry—"

"No, you're not. Not in here."

She flung her head up.

"I'm so full of my own problems I never asked you about yours."

He said from the far side of the room, "Mine? Well, I've been sitting here recovering from being made a public fool of."

"Frank!"

"I was led by the nose by the dean. I believed I was trading a chance to buy the headmaster's house for supporting him in abolishing the choir. No such thing. He's been supported all round the houses by close and council and school, and thus I end up with egg on my face in the chamber and a chance in a thousand now of getting their support on the house. So the dean gets rid of the choir and keeps the house. I lose the reputation of thirty years."

Sally got up and crossed the room to him.

"Frank, no, you haven't, it's too big a reputation for that—"

"Size makes no difference. You can lose the biggest reputation in the world in three seconds if your enemies have a mind to it. I know I sound bitter. I am bitter. But I'll pull up." He looked at Sally. "You've a lot to learn about being alone."

She went down in the lift to the street and found a parking ticket on her windscreen, which filled her with rage because the street was empty, unused at this time of day, and she had been in nobody's way. She wrote furiously on the ticket, "Use our money to fine people who are really at fault," shoved it back into its plastic envelope and drove back past the council offices to push it through the public letter box. This was partially soothing, although she would really have liked to scream at a traffic warden as well. Then she drove on to Blakeney Street and parked the car, and let herself into the house to find Henry, who had been brought home by Mrs. Chilworth, sitting on the floor watching television and eating spaghetti hoops out of a tin with a fork.

11

THE PROPOSITION TO MAKE A RECORD IN AN ATTEMPT TO RESCUE the choir filled Hugh Cavendish with a quite disproportionate fury. He disliked open defiance in his close; he abhorred the giant and ill-controlled passions of men like Alexander Troy; he was offended by the crude amateurishness of the scheme and saw the cathedral's own sacred dignity as being affronted by it too. Felicity's return—and the dean was particularly annoyed with her because he knew himself to be susceptible to her personality—had given the whole business a new lease of life at precisely the moment when it had seemed that all vital controls were slipping comfortably into his hands. The business of the choir had successfully deflected public attention from the new lighting scheme, and support for the immense repairs was almost unquestioned; they had even taken on a new apprentice in the cathedral works yard on the strength of donations pouring in and the promise of substantial grants. Then the council had laughed at the notion of taking on the choir, which was precisely what was wanted, as the dean wished it to go but also needed to have been seen to attempt to save it. And then Felicity Troy had come back.

He told himself that he did not care for her opinion any more than he cared for the organist's or the singing boys' and men's or even the bishop's, for that matter. Ancient English dioceses were poorly served, in his view, by men like Robert Young, who, however good, had had their view of the pure and ancient doctrinal tradition of the Church damaged by long service overseas. Hugh Cavendish knew the bishop privately did not support him, and even though he had expected this, it was more disturbing when it happened than he would have liked. As for Leo, the frail camaraderie that they had built up over the restoration of the organ seemed to have disintegrated entirely, and, what was worse, the animosity between Leo and the headmaster, whatever its cause, which had looked so very promising to his purpose, seemed to be much diminished.

To have, in the midst of all this, Ianthe and that hopeless boy they had all put themselves out for, so far to no avail, coming to him to ask him to waive the customary facility fee for recording in the cathedral was the last straw. He had lost his temper. No, he had said, he would waive nothing. He would require a fee of three hundred pounds to be put into the lighting fund, and in any case he very much doubted that in the busy summer months, three consecutive evenings could be found for recording. The engineers were all working late in the light season, and they could not possibly be halted; they were the priority. Ianthe had been very rude to him. She had called him a hypocrite and a dog in the manger. When they left him after this disagreeable interview, he found that he was trembling.

He looked down at his desk. Nicholas had left a list there of the music Henry Ashworth was going to sing. "Greensleeves" of course, and some Florentine carnival song and a shepherd boy's song from the Auvergne and a whole lot of other sentimental rubbish. They proposed to make a single, whatever that was, of the shepherd's song. It was a scheme quite mortifying in its silliness and doomed to disaster by the sheer incompetent inexperience of the promoters. Why then, he pondered, did it make him so angry, if indeed it could not possibly represent a threat? What was there in the sheer energy of their enthusiasm that nauseated him so much? He roamed up and down his study while Benedict watched him uneasily from the hearth rug. He must not lose control, either of the close or his temper; he must never forget for one moment that he owed, rightly, everything he could give to the sustaining and enrichment of the cathedral. He picked up the telephone and dialled the cathedral architect.

"Mervyn?"

"Ah! Dean, good morning—"

"Can I trouble you for something?"

Mervyn always made a spinsterish fuss about his busyness.

"Of course, Dean, I'm only too pleased but of course I am simply rushed off my feet just now—"

"Only a valuation—"

"A valuation?"

"Could you organize it for me? For the headmaster's house. There is no need to say anything to anyone of this. If you see Mr. or Mrs. Troy, you might say it was routine."

There was a pause.

"Dean, I shouldn't like not to be open—"

"My dear fellow, it is your estimates that are giving us these financial headaches. Three years' worth of stone-masonry for the parapets alone! I am merely exploring every avenue, you understand. Of course I should always prefer to beg and borrow than sell, but people eventually get to the bottom of their pockets, you know."

"Quite—"

"Could you do it in the next week?"

"I can't promise, Dean, though naturally I will do my best—"

"Thank you, Mervyn. Thank you."

"Dean, I think I should tell you that I met your daughter and a friend talking to John—in the works yard. They were apparently in search of a platform of some kind to stand a chorister on for a recording. I wonder if you—"

"I know all about it," the dean said. "It's some childish scheme. Please don't give them any help."

"Oh, Dean, I shouldn't, but I think John—"

"I will speak to John."

At lunch Bridget was in a strange and noble mood. She helped out his quiche and salad and filled his water glass with a kind of high-minded solicitude, and only when they were peeling apples for dessert afterwards did she make a stately speech about feeling herself to be torn between a wife's natural duty and a mother's love.

"I suppose," the dean said, "you mean Ianthe's nonsense over this record."

"Her heart is in it, Huffo."

"My name is Hugh. If her head were in it, the scheme might have the smallest chance of succeeding. As it is, she will make a great fool of herself, and of the close too, if we are not careful. You cannot possibly think she is right."

"She talked to me in the kitchen. She talked to me of the soul of the cathedral."

The dean put down his apple.

"I too have talked to you of the soul of the cathedral. The difference between us is that I am very clear as to what I mean by it. Ianthe is blown hither and thither by her emotions. No doubt this current silliness is an attempt to ingratiate herself with Leo Beckford."

"At least," Bridget cried, "I can say I know my children! You are so hard, Huffo, so unforgiving—"

"No doubt," the dean said, "no doubt that is how you wish to see it." He got up. "If you will forgive me, I must get on. I will leave you to contemplate the anguish of your position."

Alexander travelled up to London in a very different mood from the one in which he had gone to seek Felicity. He could not precisely justify his buoyancy, but the mood in the close had so lifted since her return, and the tide of opinion had so swung in the choir's favor, that he felt it only right to trust in his confident instincts. He wore his dog collar for psychological reasons—a banker in a bronze glass eyrie in Bishopsgate would find him difficult to refuse, thus dressed—but he bought a *Private Eye* to read on the train and treated himself to a taxi to take him to the City.

The old King's boy, new director of the corporate banking division of a huge Anglo-American conglomerate, greeted him on the sixth floor in a panelled reception area hushed by the depth of its carpet. The receptionist looked like someone's extremely expensive but reliable wife, and brought them coffee in bone china cups. They sat in a room lined with prints of ships in pewter frames, furnished with the kind of impeccable reproduction furniture Alexander associated with the third floor of Harrods, and looking over the City's curious cubist horizon to the consoling dome of St. Paul's.

Paul Downey made benign small talk about his time at King's. No, he had not been a chorister, too interested in chasing balls of various sorts, he was afraid, and no, he hadn't been back to Aldminster since he left, though of course he'd always meant to . . .

"School mythology claims you as musical," Alexander said, smiling.

Paul Downey looked abruptly portentous and said, "Opera."

So Felicity was right. "You'll find it's opera he claims to love," she had said when she heard he was a banker. "It goes with backgammon and skiing in Verbier and handmade shoes. It's part of proving they aren't only obsessed with money. It's terribly *chic* to love opera."

He had been amazed.

"How do you *know* such things?"

"Malicious observation and reading Mrs. Monk's newspaper."

"I love opera too," Alexander said now, to Paul Downey. "I just wish that *our* wonderful strain of music attracted the money that opera does."

"Cathedrals do a wonderful job."

Alexander leaned forward.

"If I can't raise at least the promise of fifty thousand by October, our choir won't have a job to do at all, wonderful or not."

Paul Downey slid a stiff white envelope from the inside pocket of his admirable suit.

"I rather gathered that from your letter. I have worked out some figures because, as you surmised, we do have a charitable fund to draw upon. Let me explain it to you. Our aim is philanthropic and most of our interest is in medical research. We are major contributors to research into heart disease—"

Alexander's eyes dropped involuntarily to the prosperous curve of Paul Downey's waistcoat. With difficulty he restrained himself from saying that such support seemed to him hardly altruistic.

"—and cancer of course, and naturally our Third World lending carries an impressive programme of aid projects with it. I am in a rather delicate position, as I am sure you will appreciate, as the claims of the choir at Aldminster must seem a very *personal* request to my fellow board members. But they have reacted very well, I think. A loan was considered too complicated to arrange on account of its security, but they are pleased to make a *gift*—of five thousand pounds."

Alexander got up quickly to take his dismay to the window and the prospect of St. Paul's. Behind him, Paul Downey said in his even, reasonable voice, "You see, it was felt that your choir, however valid to its city, has a very *local* claim. We feel it very much our duty to put money into schemes of at least national and at best international significance. You were most eloquent in your letter about cathedral music, but that is of course your personal enthusiasm. I should feel the same if they tried to axe the chorus at Covent Garden. I do hope you appreciate our point of view."

There was a silence while Alexander wrestled with himself and then he turned and said with a clumsiness he could not help and much regretted, "Could you not, as an old boy, help us privately, even just to help us raise a loan?"

Paul Downey looked extremely serious.

"Oh no, Mr. Troy. I couldn't do that."

"Then I must thank you sincerely for your gift and return to Aldminster."

Paul Downey rose.

"I wish we could have done more but our responsibilities are—global."

"Are there any other old boys you can think of who might feel less—detached, shall we say?"

Paul shook his head.

"I'm afraid I have lost touch with almost all of my contemporaries. Regrettable I know, but the pressures of life simply don't allow me the time any longer."

In the silent lift dropping him down to street level, Alexander gazed with loathing at the blond suede with which it was lined. Above him and walking swiftly back to his office, Paul Downey reflected for two minutes upon the calibre of Church of England clergymen, and upon how easy it apparently was to lose one's sense of proportion living in a provincial town, before his secretary met him and said his call to Tokyo was on the line and waiting.

Alexander's journey home was in some ways quite as depressing as the last one. That brief brush with the huge, impersonal outside world had only served to make his own cause the more hopeless. However insulated in his own world, Paul Downey's view of the cathedral close at Aldminster—admirable, excellent, worthy, but *small*, a spot of local bother—was perfectly genuine. He could, he supposed, trail round from company to company, cap in hand, but he would never raise enough to *secure* the choir's future, and he would half kill himself in self-abasement to achieve it. It was salutary but profoundly discouraging to see his cause as others saw it, and he must make use of the lesson, if he possibly could. If the outside world couldn't, with the best will in the world, see the size of the problem, then the inside world of Aldminster must be made to.

Speech Day at the King's School dawned dull but dry. By noon the classrooms, laboratories, studios, and workshops were filled with parents stooping dutifully to admire Metalwork Job One and violent graphics for the covers of imaginary magazines. The tradition was for picnic lunches to be brought and eaten beneath the trees of the playing fields—an immense gastronomic competitiveness had arisen over this in recent years—while Roger Farrell's gymnastic squad performed in the centre of the field, and the school military band oompahed from the terrace below the main building. After lunch, parents were herded into the vast Victorian Gothic school hall and seated in obedient rows beneath the massive red timbers of the vaulted roof. On the dais, a table bearing all the books to be given as prizes stood in front of the phalanx of governors, the headmaster, and the guest of honour, an old boy who had become a nationally known hero of the Falklands war. The boys, and the sixth form girls, sat unnaturally subdued among their parents, gazing ahead at the extravagant pedestal of orange and yellow flowers that Sandra Miles had ordered for the dais and had known to be a mistake the moment it arrived. Alexander had told her it looked very jolly and Felicity had very kindly not mentioned it at all.

The headmaster, it was apparent to everyone in the hall, was in a mood of exaltation. He was always big; today he seemed immense. He exuded a huge vitality and benevolence. For most of the parents this was extremely promising, since, living locally, they were well aware of the schism in the Close, and their opinion was almost exclusively divided depending on their own children's aptitudes. The parents of musicians and arts-oriented pupils smiled upon Alexander; those with sons and daughters who were gifted athletes and physicists scowled. Alexander, oblivious of everything except his passionate belief in what he was going to say and the optimism that had been swelling in him since Felicity's return, rose to give his annual address. The audience, well trained, waited for the traditional recital of the school's achievements over the year.

"The cathedrals of France," Alexander said unexpectedly, "some of the most beautiful of the cathedrals in the Western world, are silent."

The faint rustlings in the hall died abruptly away.

"There are organs, to be sure, and piped music. But there are no choirs. In twenty-seven English cathedrals, on between four and six occasions every week, you may hear sung offices, a sound not just unique in itself, but one that takes us back down an unbroken musical line to Thomas à Becket, to Saint Augustine."

Mr. Vigors, the deputy headmaster, leaned forward slightly to give the smallest recollecting nudge to the sheet of school statistics he had, as in every other year, prepared meticulously for the head-master. Alexander gave Mr. Vigors a warm smile and returned the paper exactly to its original position.

"Without the choir of boys' voices, that particular sound, a sound of unrivalled beauty and power, would not be possible. For five hundred years, music has been composed to that top line of extraordi-nary sound, and it is in English cathedrals alone that it remains still uncorrupted, strong and free, with a higher standard of voice being recruited every year."

From the twelfth row, Sally observed Hugh Cavendish, two seats away from the headmaster, recross his legs with tremendous delibera-tion. She looked down at Henry. He didn't look back; he was listening.

"If there is privilege in the subject of English choral music, it is ours, the listeners'. No boy is barred from this choir in Aldminster because he cannot pay the fees. But if we lose the choir, we not only damage our souls, our inner selves, call it what you will, but we also deprive the future both of something so precious and ancient it is not ours to destroy, and of something the future may long, quite justifiably, to preserve. What we lose in breaking a hitherto unbroken tradition we may never have again. And yet"—his voice rose—"and yet in this cathedral close there is at present a proposal to do exactly that."

There was by now a distinct agitation on the platform. Alexander turned to either side, his gown swirling, as if to still a swelling storm. His voice grew stronger.

"This threat is just the beginning. A change of government may well pose a much greater danger. But if we do not begin fighting now, we will be unprepared when the battle becomes a war. May I remind you that the first protocol of the European Convention of Human Rights declares that the State must respect the right of all parents to ensure that the education and training of their children conforms to their own religious and philosophical convictions. Many of you, when asked off-the-cuff, might declare you think choral music irrelevant, but I believe that upon reflection almost every one of you would defend to the last the pure clear atmosphere of educational choice and opportunity. Music is one of those choices. I am not alone in believing it to be a vital one."

He glanced at Mr. Vigors and smiled again.

"I am almost done. I must be plain with you. To save this choir for a year alone, this choir which comprises twenty-four boys from this school and twelve lay clerks, of whom three were once pupils here and all of whom live in or near this city, we need fifty thousand pounds by next October. We are making a record and we need three thousand pounds to launch that alone. We are organizing summer concerts in the city. We are holding a sponsored hymn-singing marathon in the hall here two days before the end of term. We need your help. We need donations, we need fund-raising events. We need publicity. Every year one or two of our thirty-seven choirs and choir schools goes to the wall, but Aldminster shall not be among them. Together we will ensure that for as long as we are alive to achieve it, the King's School shall send its singing boys to the cathedral as it has done these four hundred years."

He stopped. Hugh Cavendish had his eyes closed. The archdeacon's face was working furiously. Alexander picked up Mr. Vigors's sheet of paper.

"Now then. To the school's other triumphs. An unprecedented enthusiasm for further education has, I am delighted to say, resulted in an equally unprecedented number of university places—"

Sally looked down at Henry again. She whispered, "What did you think of that?"

"Superb," he said. *"Brilliant,"* and he swiveled in his seat to catch Chilworth's eye four rows behind him. Together, they jabbed their thumbs jubilantly into the air.

"I could of course say nothing this afternoon in public," Hugh Cavendish wrote to Alexander Troy that evening in a hand-delivered note, "but in my view and in that of most of the governors to whom I have spoken since, your speech today was no more than the grossest abuse of your position. Nobody knows better than you that the decision over the abolition of the choir was taken with the most profound regret and solely—this I must emphasize—for the sake of the preservation of the cathedral, whose maintenance must be of paramount importance. The intemperance of your speech serves only to create disunity in a school and city where everyone else is striving to achieve an essential harmony. I am grieved beyond measure that you should have taken the arbitrary decision to speak without even the courtesy of consulting the governing body first. In the governors' opinion, the only reparation possible for today's damaging episode is for you to issue an apology to all parents, to be sent out with the school reports, in which you pledge your loyalty to the governing body. Without that, I can only fear that the certainty of your remaining headmaster at the King's School becomes doubtful."

"Read that," Alexander said, tossing the letter across to Felicity. He had taken his dog collar off and was sitting in an open-necked shirt in the garden of the headmaster's house with her, while the blue dusk thickened round them.

She held the letter up to the light spilling out of the sitting-room window.

"Silly man," she said. "You should never write letters in such a temper."

"I frequently do—"

"He's threatening you with dismissal unless you climb down. He seems to forget that the school thrives under you. I wonder what has touched him so very much on the raw?"

Alexander yawned.

"*His* close. *His* cathedral."

"You seem awfully calm. Usually a letter like that has you spinning about in a bellowing fury."

"Well," Alexander said, "five fathers wrote us cheques there and then. I couldn't count the number of mothers offering to hold things and sell things. And the choir themselves were being chaired round the cricket pitch—"

"And the common room," Felicity said. "I can't get over it. The Farrell faction dwindled to a handful in tracksuits—"

"That's John Godwin's doing."

"Nonsense. It was your speech."

"It was self-interest. They don't want to see the school lose face or status, because it's catching."

"*Nonsense.* It was your speech—"

"Am I interrupting?" Leo said from the garden door.

"My dear fellow. Not at all. Did you hear—"

Leo stooped to kiss Felicity.

"Did I hear! The close is absolutely humming and the *Echo* wants to print your speech. You aren't answering your telephone so they rang me. That's why I've come."

"Excellent."

"And the dean?"

Felicity held out the letter.

"See for yourself."

"I'm going to get us all a drink," Alexander said. "At least I am going to see if there is something *to* drink and if there is, we'll drink it."

"I'm glad to see you here," Felicity said to Leo.

He looked up from the letter.

"You went to see Sally."

She nodded.

"Have you made it up?"

"No. That's another reason I'm here. I can't be on non-speaks with everyone. I began to feel like some kind of pariah."

"Sally *must* take it all seriously. For everyone's sake. You must see that."

"Are you suggesting that *I'm* not serious? That I'm just flirting? For Christ's sake, I want to *marry* the woman. She says no-one has ever given her the belief in herself that I have. And what does she do with that self-confidence? Brandish it at me and say she isn't at all sure she wants *any* husband, just her own life."

Felicity said, "You must wait."

Alexander came jubilantly out into the garden.

"Will you look at this?"

He dropped a bottle of whisky in Felicity's lap.

"It was on the kitchen table. There was a note saying, 'To Mr. Troy with all good wishes from M. and B. Harrison.' Their boy is a chorister. They run an off-licence in Horsley. What a lovely tribute."

"You shouldn't drink it," Felicity said teasingly. "It's another seven pounds for the cause—"

"If it wasn't for tomorrow," Alexander said, "and assembly and an A-level Greek set before nine o'clock, I should drink every last drop."

"And this letter?"

Alexander plucked the bottle out of Felicity's lap and brandished it.

"I shall leave that," he said grandly, "to assume its proper perspective."

The junior chamber of commerce of Aldminster, meeting for its regular luncheon session in a private room at the Stag's Head— renowned in the eighteenth and nineteenth centuries for the Stag's Head Flyer, the fastest post-chaise to London from the west country—found that every one of its members but three had been ap-proached for money for the choir fund and had succumbed. The three who had not, discovered that they felt rather aggrieved at being omitted, and two resolved there and then to send unsolicited cheques that afternoon. They were nearly all small private enter-prises and chafed under the rule of a Labour council—at least a new-style Labour council, since admiration for Frank Ashworth remained almost universal—and their generosity had something of a political edge, as well as a sympathetic understanding of David's relation to Goliath. It appeared too that the dean was not much liked. His rods, his wine, his manner, his wife, were all stumbling blocks. He was, someone said, too grand for Aldminster.

The article from the *Echo* on Alexander's speech had been read by almost all of them. Even if most of them would instinctively have preferred to listen to Frankie Vaughan or Sir Harry Secombe, they felt a swelling of civic pride that a record should be made of a boy chorister who had been born in the city hospital and who had lived and been educated in the city ever since. Felicity had traded heavily on that on her vast circle of visits, telling her potential donors that the money was going into a three-thousand-pound fund for an immediate use, rather than a fifty-thousand-pound one for a less identifiable future. It had taken her only a week to raise the money for the record.

"The funny thing is," she said to the wine bar owner in Lydbrook Street who had, to her surprise and delight, written out a cheque for a hundred pounds, "that I simply detest organizing and asking people for things. I can't believe how good you are all being."

He was not a man who cared much for women, but he knew when gallantry was called for.

"Depends how we're asked, doesn't it—"

Sally helped her on half days, and a surge of parents appeared burning with a kind of missionary zeal. A mother with the adminis-trative appetites of Bridget Cavendish made a list of parishes, housing estates, industrial estates, and schools and allotted each one its fund-raising representative. Two girls from the sixth form produced a campaign poster, which the father of a third ran off on his commer-cial copier two hundred times. Volunteers from the fourth and fifth years were given batches of these to pin up. Bridget Cavendish, opening the door to let Benedict out before breakfast one morning, found that a poster had been tied to the bars of the deanery gate in the night. She took it in at once and waved it in outrage at the dean, and quite failed to notice, in the energy of her own reaction, that he looked not so much angry as full of profoundest misery.

"Just—take it away."

"But, Huffo, will you not *do* something?"

"I shall do nothing."

"It is open defiance and disloyalty."

"Confrontation is not the answer."

"Huffo, what is the *matter* with you?"

He could not look at her, he could hardly bear, at this moment, to be in the same room with this life's companion who understood *nothing* of the articles of faith by which he lived. His isolation was very terrible, so terrible that at times just now he could not even look at his God, let alone pray to Him. He raised a hand in a strange helpless gesture and let it fall again.

"Nothing is the matter. Nothing in the least. I fight my battles, Bridget, by diplomacy, not cannonades."

"I think you need a holiday. You are not in the least yourself, poor tired Huffo—"

He said nothing. She put the poster down and went briskly about the room patting cushions and adjusting vases and pictures. Then she said in a voice of stifling motherliness, "Breakfast in two ticks, dear," and went out.

He went, as usual, to the window. It was a pearly morning and the close wore the ancient, mysterious sanctity that was its own, late and early each day. In the soft light the cathedral seemed to float a little on its vast green cushion. Hugh Cavendish gripped the windowsill.

"Dean," he said to himself. "Dean of the Cathedral Church of Aldminster. *Dean*."

"Heavens," Felicity Troy said, "I'd no idea there was anyone here. Who are you?"

The young man in a fawn suit with a surveyor's rule in his hand said that he was from the cathedral architect's office and that Mrs. Troy's lady in the kitchen had let him in, seeing as it was official.

"Official?"

"Mr. Mount was coming himself, Mrs. Troy. He particularly wanted me to explain to you. But he has a migraine, he suffers dreadfully from migraines—"

"I don't want to be unsympathetic," Felicity said, "at least, my better self doesn't. But I wonder if Mr. Mount's headache has any connection with having to survey this house?"

The young man looked shocked.

"Indeed it hasn't. He's confined to his bed. He had a terrible night and could hardly speak to me over the telephone."

"And why did he not telephone me? And why did he not telephone to make an appointment in the first place?"

"I believe he tried several times but could get no reply. He was very short of time, you see. The dean wanted the house looked at *urgently*."

"The *dean*?"

They were standing on the extraordinary staircase, with its heavy Baroque newel posts and shallow, generous treads, at the point where a vast window on the half landing, filled with luminous old glass, gave a wide green view down into the garden.

"The dean's ordered a survey of all close property," the young man said. He looked anxious. "It's purely routine."

"Then why do you need to measure anything?"

"The dean wanted a particularly detailed survey of this house."

There was a huge blue-and-white bowl on a chest in the window, filled with potpourri. The young man gave it a nervous stir with the end of his pencil.

"I tried to telephone too, Mrs. Troy, but there still was no answer, and my instructions were to come today."

"Where have you been?"

"The ground floor only, and I was just going up—"

"But now you are not."

"I'm afraid my instructions are—"

"I don't like your instructions," Felicity said. "I suspect them.

And I don't like the way a detailed survey has suddenly been bounced on us without warning. I want to know what's going on."

The young man said desperately, "I must see the roof—"

Felicity moved very slightly so that he could not climb higher without barging past her.

"I'm aware this visit isn't your fault, but I'm afraid you can't go any further. I'm sure your visit is really a valuation, and if my suspicions are correct, we should have proper notice. You go away, like a good boy, and tell Mervyn that."

He blushed rose pink.

"But Mr. Mount sent me."

"Tell him that I sent you back."

He began to retreat down the stairs. He looked wretched. She followed him, two steps higher all the time.

"Just off-the-cuff, what do you think it is worth?"

He stared at her.

"I couldn't tell you that!"

"A quarter of a million?"

His eyes bulged.

"I don't know."

She stepped past him and opened the front door. Sunlight fell in across the flagstones. He hurried out.

"Goodbye, Mrs. Troy."

"Goodbye," she said; then she shut the door on him and the sunlight.

She felt sick. The hall, with its painted panelling, its benign and beloved proportions, square and welcoming, seemed to sway and bulge at her. Keeping close to the walls, she crept round to the staircase and crouched on the bottom step. Lose the house. Alexander had said something lightly of it but they had both known that Hugh Cavendish would sell his children before he'd sell a single building in the close. But if the unthinkable happened, if some weird change of the dean's heart had taken place to do with nothing at all logical or predictable, they would have no power to stay. The headmaster had to be housed, certainly, and to a certain standard, beyond doubt, but not necessarily in the most lovely of the domestic buildings round the close. That had been such unbelievable luck, when they had come to Aldminster, to find that traditionally the headmaster had always lived in the house. It had been an unspeakable solace to her, exuding charm and tolerance. Was the loss of it the price they might have to pay for the choir?

She got up slowly and went into the sitting room. She had written poetry here. She hadn't written any in months, and of course her recent exuberance was the worst possible state of mind for poetry. She sat down in the spoon-back chair she had rescued off a skip one day and gazed at the garden. If the choir *was* going to require the price of the house, did she want to pay it? What was she fighting for? For the music, for history, for God, for Alexander, all of them, none of them . . .

She closed her eyes. She was fighting the darkness, the undreamed-of darks within herself, the black dishonesties without. Her lips moved.

"For we wrestle not against flesh and blood, but against principalities, against powers, against the rulers of the darkness of this world, against spiritual wickedness in high places."

Her lashes were wet. Saint Paul would not have cared for her tears at all, being something of a misogynist, relentless, illumined, one of the most single-minded men in all history. She blew her nose. It was perhaps absurd to sit here on a Thursday morning and lament the fate either of her house or of the world's soul. She went purposefully over to the telephone, an instrument she feared, and dialled the number of Ikon's offices in the Charing Cross Road.

12

"IT WOBBLES," HENRY ASHWORTH SAID.

"Not if you don't fidget."

"He can't sing if he's got to think about not fidgeting—"

"Does he have to be that high?"

"Yes. Definitely. I want the sound to go *out* into the building—"

Henry experimented with his weight all on one foot and then the other. The pile of wooden boxes rocked smartly.

"Wedges," Mike said to Nicholas over the intercom from the choir vestry, where all the equipment was set up. Mike fascinated Henry. He was wearing dark glasses even in the cathedral and he treated Henry as if he were an adult.

"I want space in the sound," Mike said. "OK? And move those mikes out a bit. The space mikes. We've got to get presence into this. OK? Now, Henry, give us a note."

Henry sang F sharp.

"It's weird in here," Mike said. "The usual levels are chronic. Perhaps we'll have to move you down the place a bit, down those steps into the—"

"Nave," Henry said helpfully, "the sanctuary steps."

"OK," Mike said, waving his hands at Ianthe, whom he disliked to see his ignorance of anything. "OK, OK! The nave—"

He was amazed to find himself here, and even more amazed to find himself charmed by it. He'd never recorded outside a studio before; he hadn't come across professionals like Leo and Henry since school, professionals who were strangely impersonal after the rock musicians he was used to. He supposed it was a different kind of identification really; he'd have to think about that. Ianthe had brought him a tape she'd made of Henry singing George Harrison's "My Sweet Lord" and he'd been really impressed. It wasn't just the voice, it was the phrasing. He heard it at the end of a bad week, a week in which he'd had to tell Jon that Ikon couldn't just *carry* him any more and Jon had taken it really badly and Steven had threatened to go too and he'd given them three days to think things over. So on impulse, he'd said to Ianthe that he'd come down to Aldminster, and here he was, with all the equipment installed with her in the choir vestry and Nick with a stop watch and him with the score and this nice kid who seemed to be able to do almost anything with his voice that you asked him and this *cathedral*. He thought it was sensational, but it spooked him, too.

"OK up there?" Nicholas said to Henry.

Henry beamed at him.

"Yes," he said.

The cathedral was dim but not dark, and to be alone up there in the great shadowy space was quite exalting. He wished, though, that it was full; he would have liked packed rows of people to sing to. They started with the Handel. He was very excited, he could feel his lungs filling and filling, and his arms rose involuntarily from his sides like wings. Then he made a mistake.

"Mr. Beckford, I keep getting this wrong, third line down, second bar, 'and preach the gospel of peace'—"

It took take after take. Then "Greensleeves," which he and Leo had rehearsed over and over, and then the French song, which he loved, sending his voice down the cascade of notes like a waterfall. He began to pull violent faces between takes.

"He's getting bored," Leo said. "We must give him a break—"

Henry jumped up and down experimentally on his tower for a bit.

"Oh I like it, I really do, but there's no-one to look at—"

"Once more," Mike said from the choir vestry, "once more. Hold each note back till the last minute. Get it?"

Henry closed one eye and snapped his fingers.

"Yeah, man," he said to himself, alone on his box. "Yeah, *man*."

Sally imagined that during these evenings while Henry was at the cathedral she would have the time and peace to think things out. She had made a few plans already. Quentin Small had agreed to take her on full-time as long as she would also do his books for him for less than his accountant, and she had looked at three flats and been alarmed by all of them. She had decided not to see Leo for the moment, in case the effect he had on her clouded her thinking, but then of course she thought about him in the time she should have given to thinking about her future. And then Alan rang. It was perfectly logical that he should, having received her letter, but somehow she had wanted to trust to the usual difficulty of telephoning from Saudi Arabia, and so she got a tremendous fright when she picked up the telephone and it was him. He sounded exasperatingly calm, almost jovial.

"What's all this then, Sal?"

"Didn't you read my letter?"

"Sure, but—"

"Then you know. I'm sick of being shackled to a man who doesn't give a damn for anyone but himself."

Alan said, "I know I've been away for a long time but you know that it's all for *us*—"

"Don't give me that *stuff*—"

There was a tiny pause.

"Look here," Alan said, "we can't discuss this at x pounds a minute. I can't come back just *right now*; we're actually installing and I can't take my eye off them for a minute. But I'll be back in a month. We'll talk then."

"I might not be *here* in a month."

Alan said, as if it were a well-known fact, "You won't leave Blakeney Street. What kind of position would that put you in?"

"What have you rung *for*?" Sally demanded.

"You sounded wound up, in your letter—"

"Wound up?"

"Yes. I feel bad I've been away so long."

She felt feverish with temper.

"I don't want to talk to you any more, Alan. I'm going to put the telephone down—"

"Don't push me, Sal, don't push me—"

"Is that a threat?"

His voice changed.

"How's Henry?"

She gave a wild squeal and flung the receiver at the wall. It bounced once or twice to the length of its curly cable and then clattered to the floor. When she picked it up, the line was dead; Alan must have put his end down almost at once. She was absolutely consumed with fury and loathing, shaking with them, whole degrees of passion beyond being able to cry. She lay face down on the rush matting of the big-room floor and just yelled and yelled. It seemed to her so disgusting that a person like Alan should be in her life at all, let alone Henry's father; it was utterly offensive, revolting, violating. His indifference, his complacency, his hypocrisy, his phoney sentimentality . . . She remembered his saying to her, eyes wide with incredulity, when she had taxed him with using call girls and he had admitted it, "But, Sal, *that's* not cheating on you!" Her whole existence seemed insulted by having to share it with such a man.

She stopped screaming and sat up. Mozart, asleep in the basket of clothes waiting to be ironed, had not stirred. The old blue plates still rolled along the dresser shelves, the lamplight fell on the newspaper where she had cast it on the floor, the loaf sat decoratively in its trail of crumbs on the wooden board, left over from making Henry a sandwich. Even the telephone, back on its cradle on the wall, was pretending nothing had happened. She began to cry then, noisily and messily, roaring with her mouth open like a cross child. Self-pity Mozart could *not* take; he rose measuredly from the ironing basket, paced across the floor, and let himself out through the cat flap into the little garden behind. It was horribly lonely when he had gone.

She got up from the floor and went over to the sink and ran cold water into her cupped hands to splash on to her face. Then she tore yards off a roll of paper towel and dried her face and blew her nose; her skin felt as if it were several sizes too small. One of Henry's jerseys lay on a rush-seated chair by the table. She picked it up and held it against her as she went up the stairs and then, repulsed by her own sentimentality, folded it with rigorous precision and put it away in his cupboard. She had hardly finished making up her face when the front door banged thunderously and Henry was stampeding into the big room shouting, "Mum, Mum, it was *brill*—"

She went down to him. He was wildly excited.

"He said empty your pockets and I said why, and he said otherwise you'll jangle and I had to take my watch off and I coughed by mistake in the Ave waiting for my note and the tuning suddenly went adrift and I had to do a million re-takes and they built me this sort of tower, I'm *miles* high, and Mr. Beckford had to play the organ so I couldn't see him and the mike cost five thousand pounds Mike said. It was *fantastic*."

She made him scrambled eggs, and Mozart, reassured by Henry's return that there would be no more unpleasant emotional displays, came back in and cried for milk.

"Can't wait till tomorrow," Henry said, "it was so superb."

"You mustn't get too excited. It might not sell at all, you know, it's a tiny company, hardly anybody knows about it."

"But it'll be in the cathedral shop," Henry said, "and Ianthe's going to take my photo for the cover and then do a mad drawing all round it—"

"In your ruff?"

"No, casuals." He looked longing. "She said had I got a baseball jacket."

"And?"

"*Couldn't* I?"

"But they're so awful—"

"They're *brilliant*."

"Shall we talk about it tomorrow, when you're less over-the-moon and I've adjusted my prejudices?"

He grinned.

"You sound like Mr. Troy. He came in to watch us. He said I was great."

She got up and picked up his plate.

"Mozart and I think you're a bighead."

He was delighted. He went capering upstairs doo-dahing loudly to himself, and then she heard the taps being turned on full blast and through the rush of water the eerie, haunting notes of the shepherd boy's song from Auvergne.

He fell plumb from the summit of excitement into oblivion. She sat on the edge of his bed until he slept, then she went downstairs, and because he had made her feel so much more normal, she dialled Leo's number. A girl answered.

"Could I speak to Leo?"

"Sorry," Ianthe said, "he's not here. He was, but he's gone off again—"

"It's Sally Ashworth—"

"Hi!" Ianthe said with warmth. "Henry tell you how it went? It was really great—"

Sally said untruthfully, "That's why I rang."

"Henry's such a performer. I mean, Mike doesn't usually say much, but he's mad on Henry. He and Leo've gone to the pub. I'll say you rang."

"No," Sally said, "don't bother. I just wanted to know if you were all as excited as Henry is."

"You bet."

"Night," Sally said.

She put the telephone down with immense care to compensate it for earlier manhandling. She was so exhausted she couldn't bring herself to do all the tidying, preparing things she usually did at night. She pulled herself upstairs by the bannisters, tread by tread, washed with a clumsy staggeringness, and fell into bed. She lay there for a few minutes, almost stunned. Then she dragged herself up again, crossed unsteadily to the mantelpiece, tugged off her wedding ring and dropped it into the Chinese jar where hair-grips and stray buttons and safety pins from the dry cleaners seemed to accumulate. She stood for a moment, head bowed, and then she turned and toppled back into bed to sleep as if she had been felled.

"I should have rung," Frank Ashworth said, "but I found myself in the close, so I thought I'd drop by."

Felicity, holding the front door half open between them, regarded him without welcome.

"Is your husband in?"

"He's just come over from the school, as a matter of fact."

Frank peered at her. She had bare feet and was wearing the kind of skirt he associated with gypsy fortune-tellers, who used to come with the travelling fairs to Horsley Common when he was a boy. The common was a housing estate now with silly street names like Primrose Way and Cowslip Close.

"Could I see him for five minutes?"

Alexander came out of the sitting room, saying he thought he had heard the doorbell.

"Mr. Ashworth—"

"I wonder if I might have five minutes—"

"Of course," Alexander said. His voice was matter-of-fact.

Frank stepped in saying, "It concerns Mrs. Troy too, so if you'd join us—"

The sitting-room floor was spread with new curtains for their bedroom that Felicity had suddenly decided to make as a hostage to fortune against their having to leave the house. Almost the entire room was covered with rough cream Indian cotton that gave off a strong smell of sunburned grass. She made no reference at all to this, so the three of them took chairs twelve feet from one another around the edge and Frank felt himself disadvantaged. Alexander appeared to notice nothing; both he and Felicity sat and watched their visitor.

"I believe a valuation has recently been carried out on this house," Frank said.

Alexander nodded.

"I expect you know that it has long been my wish to provide the people of the city, the ordinary people, with somewhere of their own in the close—"

Alexander burst in. "The principle of course—"

"Sh," Felicity said.

Frank turned his head slowly from one to another. He looked tired beyond measure.

"My wish hasn't changed. But the times have. The timing too.

This isn't the moment, because such a house wouldn't be used for the proper purpose, for the people of the city. I fear that just now it would be used for minority interests, so"—he paused, as if he needed to summon up the energy to go on—"at the next council meeting I'm going to withdraw my proposal that we should buy this house."

There was a silence. Felicity and Alexander did not look at each other. Then Alexander said soberly, "Thank you for telling us, Mr. Ashworth."

"You'd a right to know." He gave Alexander a sideways glance. "You don't always hear from the proper quarter."

He stood up. Alexander and Felicity rose too and the three of them processed in silence around the edge of the curtain fabric and into the hall.

"Your Henry has done us all proud this week," Alexander said.

Frank smiled for the first time.

"Cocky little monkey," he said and went out in to the close.

Behind the closed door of the headmaster's house Alexander said, "What *is* going on?"

Only fifteen governors could attend the emergency meeting summoned by the dean, but the necessary three clerical members were present in the dean, the archdeacon, and Canon Yeats. Bridget had taken enormous trouble to arrange the dining room like a boardroom with notepads and pencils and carafes of water, and she had made a batch of shortbread for Mrs. Ray to take in with the coffee. The dean had refused to discuss the matter with her—she tried to tell herself that this was perfectly proper of him—but she knew that what he was seeking was a vote from the governors of no confidence in Alexander Troy.

Alexander's crime, in Bridget's eyes, was not this nonsense over the choir, or even his use of school Speech Day as a personal platform, but his defiance of the dean. The only small ameliorating factor was that he was, undeniably, a gentleman. But the prestige of the high officers of the Church was to Bridget something sacred, something hardly to be subjected to the finger-snapping of lesser men. To her, such insolence was outrageous, and although she believed sincerely that Alexander should be punished, she was also afraid that if he were dismissed, his replacement might well not be what she would care for at all. Hugh's own stature would be diminished if he was entirely surrounded by men—here even Bridget hesitated in her mind over the words—men not of his own *sort*. Heaven knows, there were enough of them in the Church as it was.

When she had shut the last governor into the dining room, she went to her bureau to sort out the cathedral guides muddle which she had, ex officio, taken over from the chapter office. The chapter steward had not been in the least pleased about this, but as the guides rota had become terribly confused, with far too many unreliable members, he had not been in much of a position to refuse when Mrs. Cavendish had swept away the files, saying that she would sort them out. She had done just the same thing to the cathedral bookshop two years before and reorganized it to perfection and found a new manageress and aroused resentment and indignation all round. At least the Mistress of Embroideries, a fierce old academic doctor with an immense knowledge of historic fabrics and embroidery skills, had the strength of character to defend her own patch, and the voluntary team who cleaned the monuments had always had the discretion to lie very low indeed. The Friends of the Cathedral were slowly massing together for strength; as the bishop said with ironic regret to his wife, Bridget Cavendish was wonderful for *uniting* the diocese.

For an hour and a half she sat and made lists and rotas and telephone calls. Mrs. Ray went in with the coffee tray at precisely eleven, but in the seconds that the dining-room door was open, nothing could be heard but polite murmurs at the sight of biscuits. At noon, the door opened again and the governors began to surge into the hall. She sprang to show them out, bright with enquiring smiles. They thanked her gravely. Canon Yeats was the last, heaving himself on his sticks. She was most solicitous with him but he seemed not to notice her much, being preoccupied, it appeared, not so much with the deanery steps as with his thoughts. Huffo did not come out at all. Bridget assisted Canon Yeats down to the level of the close, and as she held the gate for him, she could not resist saying vivaciously, "I *do* hope the meeting went well!"

Canon Yeats stopped to look at her. He had never liked her. Her big handsomeness always reminded him of those dreadful bossy voluntary army women who had made his wartime army chaplaincy such a nightmare. "I should have liked," he said to his wife later, "to have planted the end of my stick on her great bust and *pushed her over*." He gave her a glimmering little glance before turning away.

"It went well, Mrs. Cavendish, but it should never have been called in the first place. The ways we have fallen into are very wrong."

She went back up the steps to the deanery. The dean was not in his study or in the dining room. Mrs. Ray met her in the hall between the two and said the dean had said not to wait lunch for him because he would be out until three and would pick up a sandwich. Mrs. Ray must have invented the last phrase because it was never one the dean would use. Bridget went out through the back door to the garage; the car was gone. She returned to the house, told Mrs. Ray that that would be all for today, thank you, and then climbed heavily up the staircase to the nobly windowed bedroom she had curtained and draped in convolvulus chintz, and where she and Hugh had now slept, side by side, for sixteen years. She sat down at her dressing table and looked at herself without the smallest atom of pleasure. Hugh had been defeated by the governors and had not felt that he could, or wanted to, come to her for comfort. She leaned her elbows on the glass surface, under which tens of photographs of her children lay imprisoned, and lowered her head into her hands, covering her eyes. The house was very quiet. In its silence, her elbows numbing on the cold glass, Bridget Cavendish went down, for the first time in her life, into the pain of love.

When the dean walked into the council offices, the receptionist, who knew everybody and everything, said that Mr. Ashworth wasn't in today. The dean said in that case, he would be grateful to have a word with any senior councillor who could spare him a quarter of an hour. The receptionist said she would see what she could do, and showed him into a small waiting room with a cactus on the table and racks around the walls full of public health leaflets. "Nobody will bother you in here," she said to him, and shut him in.

He went, inevitably, to the window. It looked on to the car park and beyond that to a well-worn corner of the Lyng Gardens, where the grass had been rubbed off the earth around flower beds planted with the municipal favourites, scarlet salvias and orange African marigolds. There was a stout and gloomy girl slumped on a bench with a toddler strapped in a folding stroller by her, and beyond her two men lying flat out on the grassless earth with their heads covered by the same newspaper. It was one-thirty. The dean had driven about for over an hour, debating to himself. For once, he had not gone to the cathedral—he had vowed he would not go in except to services until the record makers had removed all their rubbish—but had instead made for the ring road and driven round that, mindlessly, like a donkey on a treadmill. At one point, he had turned off and gone down to the estuary and listened to the gulls, and bought a pork pie from a little corner shop, which he ate ravenously in the car. It had heartened him. He had turned the car back to the city and headed for the council offices.

They kept him waiting twenty minutes. He read about heroin addiction, whooping cough, dental care, and sexually transmitted diseases; then he found a batch on legal aid and citizens' rights, and read those too. When the door opened and a different girl came in to say Mr. Thornton could see him now, he was reading the in-case-of-fire instructions on the back of the door and she nearly knocked him over. She was embarrassed by his dog collar and addressed him as "you" because she did not know what else to call him. He followed her into a lift, and up two floors to a long corridor covered in carpet tiles, which echoed to the intermittent clack of typewriters.

Halfway down, she opened a half-glazed door and showed him in to a small room with two modern tweed-covered armchairs and a low table bearing only an ashtray. She went over to an inner door, knocked, and then opened it to say, "Your gentleman, Mr. Thornton." She turned back to Hugh. "You can go in."

"It is usual," the dean said with as little heat as he could manage, "to call me Dean."

She goggled at him. He went past her into the inner office and found Denis Thornton, sharply suited, with a gold pin thrust through his collar ends under the knot of his tie, standing waiting with an official smile.

"Good afternoon, Mr. Cavendish. Do please take a seat. Will you have coffee? No? One coffee only then, Heather—"

The dean sank down. Denis Thornton sat down neatly and folded his arms on the desk. He wore several rings, all on unorthodox fingers.

"Now then. What can I do for you?"

The dean's voice seemed to him to come from a long way off.

"I am sure you are aware of the appeal we are having to mount for the cathedral roof—"

"Well, yes, I—"

"It appears the damage is very much greater than we feared. Very much. It appears we have beetle to contend with as well as water."

Denis Thornton made sympathetic noises but said nothing.

"I am not sure how far the suggestion has gone in the council, but I believe you were anxious to have some kind of centre, for the people, in the close—"

He looked up. Denis Thornton was watching.

"It was Mr. Ashworth's project," he went on, too quickly, "and I must confess that at first I could not bring myself to see things his way. The house he had in mind, the headmaster's house, you see, is so very—"

"I'm afraid," Denis Thornton said, "that I know nothing of this."

"But I thought—"

"I'm not saying, Mr. Cavendish, that it isn't a proposal we might entertain. But it isn't on the current agenda." He smiled at the dean. "I can see it might be a very attractive proposal."

"I understood Mr. Ashworth had proposed it already."

"Perhaps privately, but not in council, Mr. Cavendish. Explain to me, if you would, what you have in mind."

"The sale of the headmaster's house to the council," the dean said. "It has recently been valued at three hundred thousand pounds. Of course—" He stopped.

Denis Thornton picked up a pen from the rack in front of him and held it lightly between his fingers.

"Suppose you write me a letter, Mr. Cavendish, outlining your proposal."

The dean sighed.

"I feel that as the project began with Frank Ashworth—"

Denis Thornton laid his pen down with precision.

"It would be better to address the letter to me. Frank Ashworth is nearing retirement after all."

"Retirement! But I thought—"

"Oh yes indeed. Younger shoulders, you know."

The dean stood up.

"We live in a harsh world, Mr. Thornton."

Denis Thornton escorted him back to the lift and saw him into it with slightly showy courtesy. He was borne downwards, and stepped out into the echoing foyer with a righteous tread. Duty, he told himself, duty, authority, and the cathedral.

"OK, then?" the girl on the desk said cosily to him as he passed.

He bowed very slightly.

"Thank you."

She came round the desk and tapped past him on her high heels to open the heavy outer door for him.

"Mind how you go," she said.

Disgusting expression, overfamiliar, *chummy*. He passed through in silence and sought his car in the park.

He came in through the garden door of the deanery. Bridget was on the telephone.

"My dear, I can't promise anything just now. I've got to *devote* myself to Hugh, you know, he has so much on his plate—of course I will, the moment I can see a day ahead—I couldn't agree more, all politics and money—I'm sure you understand—"

She caught sight of the dean.

"My dear, he's just come in. Will you forgive? Absolutely, as soon as ever I can. Bye—"

She put the receiver down and came towards him with a curious expression on her face which, he would have said if he had not known her better, contained a trace of uncertainty.

"Huffo, where have you been? And no lunch! Let me make you a sandwich. And after such a morning—"

He moved past her.

"Thank you, but no sandwich. I had things to see to in the city, but really I am not hungry."

"Some tea, dear, then—"

He gave a tiny sigh.

"Tea would be very nice."

She gave a step towards him as he opened the door to the study. "Huffo . . ."

He turned in the doorway and said quietly, "Tea. Thank you. Tea," and then he closed the door gently in her face.

13

AT THE END OF TERM, A STAND-IN CHOIR ARRIVED FROM A SURREY parish church, and the singing boys were sent off on their various summer holidays. Henry took Chilworth to his grandmother's for a week, most of which they spent building an elaborate camp in the small wilderness Jean permitted to the garden beyond the regimented vegetable patch. Both boys were very happy being orthodox by day and experimenting with hair gel and pop music on their Walkmans by night, when Jean supposed them in bed with the innocent copies of Anthony Buckeridge and Captain W. E. Johns she had left for them to read.

Behind them, despite the provisional choir, a lull fell upon the close at Aldminster. Alexander and Felicity, elated at the growing fund for the choir and the promise of secure tenure of their house, borrowed Sam's Herefordshire cottage for a fortnight and drove away to walk the Malvern Hills. Half the school closed down entirely; the other half was taken over by two hundred Scandinavians on a summer English course. They were, on the whole, very quiet, and when a group of them, cornered while gazing conscientiously at the cathedral, were asked by Bridget Cavendish what they most enjoyed in Aldminster, they answered her gravely, "The cheapness of the alcohol." Gallantly, she tried to pass this off around the close as an amusing story, to show her lightness of heart, but nobody was taken in. That she was suffering in some way was visible to everybody, but she remained essentially unreachable. One morning, Janet Young found her inexplicably weeping in front of a scarlet sprayed slogan on the deanery wall; "Judge Dread," it said, "says YES to the choir."

"It is only a piece of silliness," Janet said, putting a tentative, solacing hand on Bridget's arm. "It is no real menace."

Bridget stood very upright at once and blew her nose authoritatively.

"It's for Hugh, of course. I can't bear him to be exposed to any more of this."

Janet made kind and murmuring noises, but was brushed off when she tried to help Bridget into the house.

"Please say nothing of this. I try to keep all these feelings from Hugh because I do not wish to add to his burdens."

"At least *then*," Janet said later to the bishop, "she was speaking the truth. But she wasn't weeping for him, I'm sure of that, at least not for his pain. It's some pain of her own—"

"Those children?"

"No. No. She looked too vulnerable for that. The last person she would ever confide in is me. Her pride wouldn't allow it."

The bishop bit the earpiece of his spectacles reflectively.

"The dean is not himself either. Much more withdrawn—"

Intellectually, the dean pitied his wife. He saw her misery and he was sorry for it, but emotionally he could do nothing to alleviate it. His own afflictions in the years they had spent together had not so much hardened him as alienated him, so that he could not regard Bridget with any imaginative sympathy. She had defied him, day in, day out, for almost thirty years in matters of love and life, over children and parish, and although he could not identify which straw it was that had finally broken the camel's back, he knew his docility was ended. He was, he told himself hourly, daily, as a kind of mantra, dean. He held as dean an administrative and spiritual authority that was not only his privilege but which he would make his gift to God. Nobody, any longer, should defy that authority, not Bridget, not Alexander Troy, not Leo Beckford, not his own daughter. He felt there was a kind of purity in his authority and in the strength he saw in it; he had inklings of a reforming zeal. When he and Bridget took their customary ten days' fishing on the Dee, he would make the new pattern of their life very plain to her; while they were thus occupied, Cosmo, he resolved, whether he liked it or not, would go to an adventure centre in North Wales. Out of the muddle and compromise of life in the close as it had become, he resolved, a new clean, strong order should rise, with all disruptive forces subdued. Living in the undistinguished second master's house—Mr. Vigors, a bachelor, would surely be no trouble to move into the school—would effectively subdue Alexander Troy.

Once the choir had dispersed, and their substitutes and Martin Chancellor had shaken down together, Leo took himself off to record, at the invitation of a significant company, pieces played on the organs in private chapels in some of the great houses of the north. The invitation had come, slightly irritatingly, through Mike Perring, of Ikon, who used the same pressing plant for records as did other and more celebrated companies. In a telephone conversation rich with incomprehensible references to lacquers and stampers, Mike had told Leo that not only was this invitation to be forthcoming, but that Henry's album, "Singing Boy," was to be given rush release through a whole lot of pop music channels. He sounded far less laconic than usual, almost enthusiastic.

Leo was relieved to leave Aldminster for a while. He thought he might have time and sufficient peace of mind to compose—a plan for a short choral work based on the story of Jonah had been gathering force in his mind ever since Henry's recording—and he hoped he might not think too much about Sally. At least there was no chance of seeing her suddenly among the hills of Northumberland and Derbyshire. And yet he longed to see her; every day in Aldminster he hoped he would, and since he had kissed Ianthe, he had feared it too.

He told himself repeatedly that he made too much of that kiss. It was only one kiss, after all, a sort of impulsive celebration of the end of the recording session, when Mike had edited a master tape for them all to hear, and they had all been so thrilled. Everybody was hugging and kissing then, so kissing Ianthe wasn't in the least significant, because she was, after all, the only girl there. She had come into the organ loft and put her arms round him from behind and said, "Oh, Leo, it's going to be so great—" and he had turned round and kissed her in the way you kiss someone when you are serious. He couldn't hide that from himself, even when he tried. Of all the people in the world, he shouldn't have kissed Ianthe like that. He didn't even like her very much, and her wild and faintly grubby dark charm wasn't to his taste at all. But he had done it, and he was in despair to find how much it affected him, chiefly— and he tried not to think this—because he felt himself committed to Sally.

He attempted to tell himself that Sally deserved it. She hadn't been near him in weeks, had never commented on or tried to get in touch over the recording, had insisted that she be left strictly alone to make the next move. After his initial angry resentment of her attitude, he had come to see that her childish and ineffectual attempts at independence were actually the result of an enforced self-sufficiency learned *inside* a lonely marriage. What she was struggling to persuade herself was that her choice of Leo was made out of freedom, not as an escape. She had to show the world, for the sake of her self-esteem, that she could manage without any man before she elected to live with another. Sally's pride, Felicity had said to him, had suffered at the hands of a careless husband.

"Society won't allow a woman pride," Felicity said. "Men are allowed it and society respects it very much and regards it as wrong that it should be damaged. But why shouldn't a woman suffer the same loss of self-respect, the same humiliation, if she is betrayed, as a man does? Sally has had a lot of that."

He saw all that, yet at the same time he perceived himself to be very patient and he wanted his patience rewarded. He couldn't believe she could let so many weeks go by without seeing him; he couldn't credit her with being other than stubborn, even cruel. He missed her. Kissing Ianthe had nothing to do with missing Sally, he was sure of that, but then kissing Ianthe had been the impulse of a suspended moment when none of his normal, important faculties had been on duty. And as it was Ianthe, a land mine had now been buried in the sand, which somebody, probably himself or Sally, would step on and set off one day. Ianthe had written to him twice. He had hardly read the letters; he had thrown them away and hadn't answered them. Ianthe had forestalled him there. "I know you won't answer these," she had written, "you wouldn't be you if you did. But it doesn't matter, now that I know." The word haunted him. Know what . . . Of course, he told himself half the time, Sally will understand—we aren't children, after all; and of course, he told himself the other half, it will hurl her away from me even further, just when I am, by superhuman patience, proving myself trustworthy.

To go away seemed a clean, if temporary, solution. Ianthe would not find him, might calm down; Sally might come to the end of the long walk she had set herself. He, breathing an air clear of the quarrels and complications that had poisoned the air in the close for months, might come back with revived spirits and energies to find the musical way ahead for him clear again, as well as a personal future to build.

He took his house keys round to Cherry Chancellor. She was very nice to him because she liked to see Martin in sole charge; to her mind, Martin's sense of responsibility made him a better man for the job irrespective of his talents at the organ. When Martin had described Leo's way with Bach as flexible, she had no idea what he meant—she would never, sitting in the cathedral, have known whether it was Leo or her husband playing, even though she admired Martin's profession and thought of him as an artist. Now, surveying Leo in corduroy jeans and an elderly jacket of a different corduroy, she asked playfully if that was what he planned to wear to meet the duchess. Leo looked at her regular, pretty, unexciting face and said, deadpan, he thought he was rather overdressed for that.

The taxi to the station took him, with unintentional unkindness, along Blakeney Street. The house looked very blank, the windows empty of flowers or cat. He had a sudden clutch of fear that she might just up and off and he would never know, but he thought of the necessity of Henry's return to the choir and to school. Henry was at last an anchor—wasn't he? Panic at going overtook the relief.

Leo screwed round in his seat and watched devouringly the amiable brick façades of the Blakeney Street houses dwindle behind him.

"Forgotten something?" the driver said.

"Probably. I forget things all the time—"

At the station, he discovered the train was delayed half an hour. He bought a writing pad and envelopes from the bookstall, and took them to the cafeteria and settled himself in a corner, hedged about with his luggage—"I could have lent you something suitable, you know," Cherry Chancellor had said, eyeing his battered grips and holdalls—and wrote furiously.

"Sally, darling Sally, I'm going away for a couple of weeks, on a job. I meant to say nothing of it, just to go, but I find I can't. I'm at the station. I just want you to know that I do understand what you are afraid of, the losing of 'I' to become 'we.' Of course it's a price to be paid, a kind of gamble, but you don't get the big prizes without it. And remember that the 'I' of you will be safe with me just as the 'I' of me will be with you. I want to live with you, not own you or exploit you. We can only live half lives without love, but I think you know that. Cherry has my keys and all my telephone numbers—stupidly I've given her my only list."

He wanted to write "Ring me, *ring me*," but he stopped himself. Instead he just wrote "Leo," and his name looked bald and sad there, alone at the end. He put the letter in an envelope, addressed it, and persuaded the woman in the newspaper kiosk to post it for him.

"Important, is it?"

"Very—"

"OK, dear."

They were announcing his train. He thrust twenty pence at the newspaper woman, gathered up his bags again, and dashed for the platform. The train was full. He was forced to pile his luggage in the swaying section between two carriages and to settle himself there somehow, his back against the lavatory wall while the train drew slowly away from the cranes and the tower blocks and the terraces and the cathedral, riding high and imperturbable above them all.

* * *

A disc jockey on Radio Two liked Henry's recording of the shepherd boy's song. He played it every morning for four mornings and then, because of the clamour of calls begging to hear it again, he played it twice on the fifth morning. Nicholas and Mike went down to the plant at Wimbledon and cajoled them into pressing five thousand extra copies and then, a week later, ten thousand more. Three national newspapers came to Blakeney Street and took photographs of Henry and Mozart, and then a television programme asked for him. Sally said no. Henry was outraged.

"Mum, please, *please*, why not, it'll sell heaps more—"

"It's bad for you. You're too young and your voice isn't even finished yet."

"But I promise I won't get big-headed, I promise, just once on telly—"

"Television. No, Henry."

He whined a little.

"I'll ask Dad—"

"It's nothing to do with him," Sally said without thinking. "You are eleven, singing in the choir is serious, your voice is serious. Because you're a pretty boy you'll just become a sort of silly toy for the public."

He was very angry with her. He went upstairs and chucked things about his room for a while and then kicked his bean bag too hard and split a seam and a million uncatchable little white granules rolled out and ran everywhere. He tried to scoop them up in his toothmug but they were light and elusive and blew away from him and clung to his curtains and bedclothes. He began to cry, out of excitement and frustration. He cried as loudly as he could, swooshing the granules about with his feet so that they swirled up and stuck to his socks. Sally stood at the bottom of the stairs and listened to him, restraining herself from going up. After fifteen minutes or so, blotchy with tears and speckled with mysterious little white bobbles like some kind of fungus, he came downstairs and said with difficulty, "Would you just ask Mr. Beckford?"

"Mr. *Beckford*—"

"Please."

"If he thinks you should, I wouldn't agree with him, Henry."

"Just ask him—"

"As long as you understand what I've just said."

He nodded and then came tiredly over and put his arms round her. She said, holding him in return, "R.I.P. one beanbag?"

"Sorry—"

"Doesn't matter. We mustn't fight over this wonderful old voice, you know."

He said, "It's not just about me—"

"I know. But I don't want you being exploited. It's fun at the beginning and then it's exhausting and then you miss it when it stops. Henry—"

He looked up at her.

"Don't cry," he said sternly.

She shook her head. "No, no—"

"*Will* you ring Mr. Beckford?"

There was a pause.

"All right."

Henry drew away, comforted.

"You don't like him anymore, do you. But he's nice."

Sally rang Chapter Yard. There was no reply. She rang later in the day and again in the morning and this time Cherry Chancellor, who had gone in to be neighbourly about Leo's domestic disorder—a generosity inspired by seeing Martin, if only temporarily, in what she considered his rightful place—answered it.

"Oh, he's away," she said complacently to Sally. "He's gone north to record in some stately homes. Didn't he tell you?"

"No—"

"How odd. Well, you know how chaotic he is. But I expect he'd be pleased to hear from you."

"I need," Sally said with rigid self-control, "to talk to him about Henry. I need his advice. About a television interview."

"My *word*. You will have to be careful he doesn't get spoiled. Would you like to speak to Martin about it?"

"Thank you but as Mr. Beckford was in charge of the recording I must speak to him."

Cherry's voice grew frosty.

"I'll ring you back when I'm back at home with the numbers."
Henry was sitting at the table painting a model aeroplane.

"Was that Ianthe?"

"Ianthe? No, it was Mrs. Chancellor. Why should it be Ianthe?"

"She's there quite a lot."

"But it's midweek—"

"She doesn't do ordinary things," Henry said, and after a pause, "Hooper really likes her."

Cherry left it until teatime to telephone with Leo's numbers. She gave them to Henry, who wrote them down painstakingly with a purple felt-tipped pen but without noting which one applied to where, so that Sally had to make three calls—she was very nervous—before she tracked him down. A pleasant woman's voice at the far end said he was actually recording right now but that she would give him the message and ask him to ring back. Sally could settle to nothing. When the telephone rang, she let Henry answer it and it was Chilworth, wanting him to share some tennis coaching, and then it rang again, and it was her mother to say she would be in Aldminster tomorrow and would return all the things Henry had left behind.

"I can't imagine how he's managed with only one sandal, I must say—"

"He's got other shoes—"

"And little James left a tin of some dreadful hair spray. He seemed such a nice boy. I wonder if his mother knows."

After that the telephone was quite silent. At nine, Henry went up to bed and Sally went to talk to him to show the telephone she didn't care. At ten, she had a bath on the principle that if you are longing for a call, it will come only when it is really inconvenient to take it, and at eleven, she went downstairs and laid breakfast round the bits of Henry's aeroplane. She lay awake until one in the morning, very miserable, and then slept fitfully, to be woken at seven by Leo ringing from Derbyshire.

"Sally? Oh, Sally, I couldn't ring last night because we were still at it until after midnight and I thought you'd be asleep. Did you get my letter?"

"Your letter? You *wrote* to me?"

"Yes, when I left. In a panic. I gave it to some stupid woman to post. Sally?"

"Yes—"

"It's so wonderful to hear you. I've been hoping and praying you'd ring, after you got my letter—"

"But I didn't—"

"I love you," Leo said. "D'you know that?"

She nodded furiously.

"Sally? Are you there?"

"Yes."

"Are you crying?"

She said angrily, "I *keep* crying—"

"I wish I was with you," he said fiercely. "It's all wrong, my being here and you there. I can't believe you wanted to ring me, I can't get over it—"

"To be truthful, it was about Henry. But to be even more truthful, I wanted to. When will you be back?"

"At the weekend. I'd come *now* if I could."

"I had an awful call from Alan. He's so *untouchable*, you can't make him mind about anything. I went berserk afterwards. How *could* I be married to a man like that?"

"Why didn't you ring me?"

"I tried to. You weren't there. And then in the morning I couldn't."

"But yesterday you could."

"I had an excuse. Henry's had a television offer."

Leo transmitted himself instantaneously from lover to choirmaster.

"Absolutely not."

"That's what I said."

"It would wreck his voice, overexpose it, get him into bad habits. He's got at least two years to go before he's ready and even then I'll object."

"The record's doing wonderfully. It's being a sort of hit—"

"Heavens," Leo said, "really?"

"I promised Henry I'd ring you and ask—"

"Give him a clip on the ear from me and say Mr. Beckford gives it the big no."

"All right," she said happily.

"Meet me. Come to the station on Friday."

"Yes," she said. "Yes—"

She felt lifted, flying.

"Till Friday—"

She put the telephone down with infinite care. Henry came in and flumped himself down across her.

"I've got all those bobbly white things in my bed and now they're inside my p.j.'s—"

"Mr. Beckford says no."

Henry eyed her.

"Did he?"

"Actually he said to give you a clip on the ear as well as no."

"Sounds familiar—"

"Sorry, Henry."

He leaned across her and twiddled the knobs on her bedside radio.

"*Not* Radio One, please—"

Henry's voice, clear and mysterious, sang out at them suddenly from some anonymous station. Henry's hand froze on the knobs. He turned to look at Sally and they regarded each other with awe.

Nicholas Elliott, feeling his emotions all over in a gingerly sort of way, thought that he was happy. Steven and Jon had both left the company, and although that meant their capital had gone with them, Ikon seemed to be doing so well that its bank manager, a man who prided himself on his nose for the right kind of private enterprise, had increased their loan with no trouble. Mike had doubled Nicholas's salary and had moved in with a currently much-sought-after model, so that Nicholas had the temporary loan of the flat. With his slowly increasing confidence and visibility, he began to make friends, and Mike, who remained half embarrassed to have had anything to do with the Aldminster world, was only too happy to allow him the credit for Henry's record, selling not only at a steady rate but selling far better than anything Ikon had produced before. Even to Nicholas, peering anxiously in the mirror for signs of the cool image he hoped for, it was noticeable that his air of weedy vacuity was diminishing. He took a couple of girls out, he gave a handful of interviews, he was asked to parties without Mike or Ianthe. Everybody asked him about Henry's next record, told him he must cash in on this newly tapped vein of appreciation for a quality oddity. He realized that he wasn't just enjoying things now, but that he looked forward to them as well. A high moment came when a school leaver from Ealing was taken on to sit in the office in the Charing Cross Road and take the telephone calls. It rose even higher when, dropping into the office on the fifth day of the boy's employment, he discovered there had been four calls for him alone. He was friendly to the boy; he remembered his own time there too clearly not to be.

He didn't see much of Ianthe. She was on a real high and out all the time. Like Mike, though not for the same reasons, she was generous in giving Nicholas the credit for "Singing Boy," in her case because she wanted to strike a bargain with him. She said that she wanted to be the one to break the news of the sales figures to Leo, she wanted to go down to Aldminster alone. Nicholas found that he minded that. The choir, Henry's choir, was *his* choir too. He wanted to see Leo look at him with something other than his weary half-smiling pity. He had even visualized a rather emotional interview with the bishop. But he was no match for Ianthe, and he wasn't going to push his luck; Leo was too intelligent to give all the praise to Ianthe. Leo and Ianthe. Nicholas didn't know what to make of that but he didn't like it. He couldn't think what Leo had been about, making up to Ianthe; she'd probably chucked herself at him—she was like that.

Two days after the rights in the record had been sold to America, France, and Italy, and the English sales had topped a hundred thousand, Ianthe went down to Aldminster. She travelled first class, and bought a glossy motoring magazine to choose the car she would now buy when she had learned to drive. Ikon had suddenly acquired an accountant, a friend of Mike's father's, and he had been very stern with them and said not one single Mini, let alone a Porsche, until he was sure they understood what they were doing and he was sure about their financial position. In her mind Ianthe had pooh-poohed him, because she was so close to her own goal it made her reckless. She smoked long American cigarettes in the train and flipped the pages of her magazine and knew with pleased certainty that people were looking at her.

She took a cab straight to Chapter Yard and sent her case on to the deanery in it. Leo was at home, alone, looking well and happy, and she liked it that he didn't kiss her at once but was pretty cool and stood back for her to go into the sitting room. It was tidy and there was a vase of marguerites on the coffee table.

"Hey—"

"Cherry Chancellor," Leo said, "and she's put a purple whirly thing in the loo that smells worse than any human smell could ever do."

Ianthe walked round the room, leisurely, so that he could look at her, and shook back her hair.

"Want to know the good news?"

"Of course," he said politely.

She put her hands on her hips so that armfuls of bangles clashed dramatically down to her wrists.

"The choir'll be OK."

"What—"

"It's selling and selling. Mike signed up the States and France and an Italian company this week. It's worked."

Some tiny danger light began to glow at the back of Leo's brain.

"That's wonderful. That's absolutely marvellous. I do congratulate you, really, it's terrific. What are the figures?"

She told him.

"Have you told Alexander?"

"Not yet." She eyed him. "Just you."

"You must tell Henry."

She said, very softly, "Don't I get a reward?"

His battered sofa was between them. He put his hands on the back of it, leaned forward and said in the resolute voice he had used long ago to the Iranian girl at St. Mary's, "You and Mike and Nicholas get my thanks. And everyone else's too, I should think."

She was smiling still.

"Don't play games," she said.

He straightened.

"I am not going to kiss you."

She glared.

"What's all this—"

"I should not have kissed you in the cathedral. I didn't intend to and I regretted it the moment I had. I shan't kiss you again."

She began to scream like a beast. She seized cushions off the chairs and the sofa and flung them at him, and then books, and newspapers. Her bracelets clanked and clashed. He came round the sofa, and hit her on the side of the head. She spat at him. He gave her a rough push backwards into a chair and stood hard against her knees so that she couldn't get up. She scowled up at him, breathless and glowering.

"What a show-off you are," he said and walked away.

She began to cry.

"How could you *do* that to me, you mean bastard—"

"You wanted me to and I did it. I'm not going to repeat myself. I'm very pleased indeed about Henry's record, but frankly, given the lot of you who run Ikon, I think it's a fluke, and I'm not going to grovel with gratitude to you or anyone else. The point is the choir."

She screamed, "You're not telling me the truth!"

He turned.

"The truth is, Ianthe, that I am in love with Sally Ashworth, I have been since I met her, and I mean to marry her. I have never been within a million miles of being in love with you, and you know it. I'm not responsible for your adolescent fantasies."

She began to rock herself about and wail.

"You're a first-class *shit*—"

Leo went out to the kitchen and plugged in the kettle. The plates and mugs from his and Sally's breakfast were still in the sink; she had met him at the station and come back for the night with him until it was time to go and collect Henry from the Chilworths', where he had spent the night. Leo put a finger on the rim of the mug Sally had used, for reassurance. He made tea and took the tray back into the sitting room.

"I hate you," Ianthe shouted.

He put the tray down.

"Do you want some tea, or do you want to go, straightaway?"

She sniffed.

"I don't know—"

He handed her a mug.

"Here."

"Leo—"

"We aren't talking about it any more. Will you tell your father about the choir?"

"I might."

"I think he'll be pleased, in his heart of hearts."

"*You* don't know anything about hearts."

Leo sat down on the edge of the sofa with his mug between his hands.

"I'm pleased for poor old Nicholas over this—"

Ianthe slammed her mug down and leaped up.

"I'm going!"

"As you wish."

"I hope you have a bloody awful marriage!"

He closed his eyes. She banged out of the sitting room and then out of the front door with equal violence. Leo heard her unsteady feet running over the cobbles, across the yard to the close. The bomb had exploded and he was still alive.

Ianthe went in through the back gate of the deanery, observed that the car was gone and so was Cosmo's bicycle. She stopped and blew her nose tremendously, tousled her hair, pushed her sleeves up above all her bangles and opened the door of the house.

"I'm back!"

There was silence. The kitchen was perfectly tidy; Benedict's basket was empty. The house was holding its breath in the afternoon quiet. She went through to the drawing room. It was empty. Anticlimax began to descend heavily upon her. She climbed slowly up the stairs and, on the landing, found her mother sitting with folded hands on a little sofa, looking at nothing in particular. Ianthe peered.

"Mum?"

Bridget turned slightly.

"Hello, dear."

"You OK?"

"Perfectly, thank you."

Ianthe moved forward.

"Isn't that a bit of a funny place to sit?"

"I felt rather tired. I'm simply longing for Scotland this year, you can't think—"

Ianthe dropped on the floor beside her.

"I think the record's making so much money the choir'll be all right for a while. Should I tell Dad?"

Bridget seemed to come out of some kind of trance.

"No, Ianthe. We mustn't trouble him with anything. He's quite exhausted by it all."

"Where's he gone?"

There was a silence. Then Bridget turned a sudden, beseeching gaze on her daughter and said, "I don't know."

It was too much for Ianthe. She put her head down on her mother's expensive print lap and began to sob out her story over Leo, never doubting that whatever ailed her mother, she would have enough to herself to spare to comfort her.

14

When the dean asked the bishop to switch on the first part of the new lighting at a special ceremony, the bishop felt he could not refuse. He disliked any kind of ostentation himself, as well as the dean's slightly flamboyant touch with such occasions, but this was no time for personal scruple. The dean and the Church required his support and they should both have it. He even allowed the dean and the architect and the lighting designer to give him a preview of the eighteen concealed floodlights now mounted on the clerestory shelf and flinging a great sweep of light up into the vault of the nave, and the strip lights hidden below the triforium arches, which gave an almost theatrical glamour to the bays behind them.

"And you will observe," the dean said, spreading his arms, "the vast improvement in the appearance of the masonry after washing. The Friends of the Cathedral have given us the most splendid new washing equipment—we are simply racing along. South transept next, eh, Mervyn?"

Despite his enthusiasm, the bishop did not think the dean looked well; his enthusiasm was staccato. The bishop had tried, on two or three occasions, to suggest that, as brothers in Christ, they might open their hearts to one another, and he had been sharply rebuffed on each occasion. On the contrary, the dean had said to the smallest suggestion that all might not be well, the close had never looked forward to a more promising or united future. All was under control, all differences and difficulties had been sorted out. The bishop knew this was not so, but there was, in the face of the dean's insistence upon his satisfaction with the state of things, nothing for it but patience. He would at least not add to the dean's burdens by being in any way disobliging, even if he could not but reflect how infinitely more difficult and elusive his ministry in an English diocese was than it had ever been, somewhat naturally, in India. His life seemed to be too often one long struggle to get across the distance imposed by his position and back to the people whom he loved and missed. When the dean was being human like this, even extra human because he refused to admit to any trouble, the bishop found him very lovable indeed.

"You," Janet said to him, "are really just an old busybody in a mitre."

"Oh dear—"

"An immensely sympathetic one. But you do always want to sort people out."

"Of course—"

"You must remember their pride."

"I do," the bishop said firmly. "Otherwise why am I spending a large part of Saturday afternoon being instructed as to which switch to switch? If that isn't being mindful of the dean's pride, I can't think what is."

The ceremony was, to his relief, peculiarly dignified. The stand-in choir, rehearsed by Martin, sang two English anthems, and Leo played part of Elgar's First Organ Sonata, and then his Vesper Voluntaries. During the first anthem, obediently switching switches and spinning dimmers under the watchful eye of the lighting designer, the bishop caused the cathedral nave to wake into a wonderful dawn. The gasp from the congregation was audible above the strains of William Byrd. The dean was observed to be extraordinarily moved, and said his prayer of thanksgiving in a voice that was not at all steady. Frank Ashworth, halfway down the nave, remarked this to himself with a kind of disgust; to him, the dean's hypocrisy knew no bounds.

He did not quite know why he was in the cathedral except as a result of instinct, a really strong instinct, which had risen up in him unbidden and demanded to be indulged. He told himself that he wasn't fooled, he knew people automatically sought a sanctuary in time of trouble, and the traditional sanctuary was a church, and he, Frank, was in trouble. But he wasn't going because of God; he made that very plain to himself. He was going because he needed calm and quiet and time in a place where the outside world didn't obtrude. He needed a setting where he could allow his flayed-raw mind to come gently to rest upon the fact that his days as a councillor of Aldminster were, to all intents and purposes, over.

He had risen at the last meeting to withdraw, for the time being, his proposal that the council should buy the headmaster's house. He had been told that in an extra session of a newly appointed public facilities committee—sprung up without his knowledge, empowered, it seemed, to spend money at will—the council had offered the dean and chapter three hundred thousand pounds for the house, and it had been accepted. Completion of the deal was to be hurried through in six weeks; by autumn the house would have become a community advice centre, open to all the oppressed people and groups in the city. Frank objected strenuously to such a use and was overpowered. Even his old colleagues, men whom he had worked alongside for twenty years, gave him apologetic glances and voted against him.

"If we don't, we're out," one neighbour whispered to Frank. "It's our only chance of staying around. I'd advise you—"

Frank looked at him with disgust. He rose. He made a short speech about the folly and mendacity of the present council and was treated in return to repeated gibes about his own part in the scheme to save the choir.

"You should," Frank said to the chamber in the ancient phrase of morality from his childhood, "you should be ashamed of yourselves."

There were jeers and catcalls. Denis Thornton remarked that perhaps Frank would be happier to disassociate himself from a progressive group he clearly could no longer keep up with.

"There are many people in this city," Thornton said, "who are keen to take up the burden of public service. Perhaps it's only right you should make way for someone younger. No pressure from us, of course; it's quite up to you."

For the second time in a month, Frank walked out of a meeting, but this time he walked in utter silence. Even when he closed the door behind him, there was silence. He went up to his office and collected the personal things off his desk—a photograph of Henry, his father's old brass ink-pot and pen tray, a few mementoes of great civic occasions—and went out to his secretary.

"Got a box?" he said.

She stopped typing.

"What d'you want a box for?"

He indicated the clutter in his arms.

"Moving offices, are we? First I've heard—"

"No."

She looked straight at him then. He couldn't recall that she had ever looked at him directly before.

"Oh, Mr. Ashworth—"

"Can't be helped."

She found him two carrier bags and packed his belongings into them. They didn't speak, and it was only when he said goodbye that he noticed she was crying. He said, "Thanks for everything. I'll keep in touch," but she only shook her head. He went down the great boastful Victorian staircase, treading deliberately in the centre of the steps, a bag in either hand, and walked across the foyer and out into the car park. The attendant came, as usual, to open the door of his car and make remarks about the weather and Aldminster's slow progress up the second football division. Frank made his usual replies, put his bags on the back seat of the Rover, and climbed into the front. The attendant gave the roof a pat.

"I've washed her for you, Mr. Ashworth. Might give her a wax Thursday."

Frank put the car into gear.

"It'll never have another friend like you, Ron. Thanks for everything."

He drove home to Back Street and found he was so tired he wanted to lean against the wall of the lift and close his eyes as he was carried upwards. The sitting room of his flat was filled with callous sunshine. He put the bags down, and lowered himself into an armchair and lay there, wondering if this was what a bereavement felt like, this lopping off of a limb, this falling away of the foundation of things. He could do nothing all afternoon and evening, and when night came, he could not sleep. He got up as dawn rose, and sat by his sitting-room window and watched the luminous light strengthen behind the city, and looking at the cathedral, he discovered that he wanted to be in it. Somehow it took him all morning to get there, impeded as he was by this peculiar inertia, and when he did arrive, he found himself mixed up with some sort of ceremony to do with a new lighting scheme. He was irritated and felt trapped. He had only wanted to come to be alone in the cool dim space and think a bit. But the irritation itself proved healing, if only because it was a distraction, and he left the cathedral after the service with a brisker step than he had entered it.

He had left his car at the small park across the close at the top of the Lyng. A path ran across the grass towards it, and he was about thirty yards down it, away from the cathedral, when someone, coming up quickly behind him, said his name. He stopped and turned. Ianthe Cavendish, her hair flying away from her face, said rather breathlessly, "I saw you in the cathedral—"

"I'd no intention of getting mixed up in a service. I went in for a bit of quiet—"

She looked extremely overwrought. She came very close to him and said in a rush, "There's something you ought to know."

Ianthe conformed to no ideal of womanhood Frank had ever cherished; girls of her sort hardly seemed to *be* women, but rather sexless darting insect forms, waiting to grow up into something more substantial. He had scarcely exchanged ten words with Ianthe all her time in Aldminster; there was not, and never had been, the smallest reason for communication between them. He said now, suspiciously, "I don't listen to gossip."

Ianthe seemed to hesitate for a minute, but she said, all the same, "It isn't gossip. It's true and it affects Henry."

"Henry!"

"I'm not a sneak," Ianthe said, "and I wouldn't say anything except—" She stopped, took a breath, and said very clearly, spacing her words, "Henry's mother is having an affair with Leo Beckford and they are planning to get married."

By nothing did Frank betray he had even heard her.

"I haven't made it up," Ianthe said. "Leo told me so himself yesterday. You can ask him if you don't believe me."

Frank said, "I believe you." He looked woodenly ahead.

"Henry doesn't know," Ianthe said confidingly.

"That wouldn't be any of your business."

"Look, I'm not a troublemaker. I just thought you ought to know—"

Frank made to move away.

"Just make sure," he said, "that you don't think everyone else ought to know too."

She said nothing. He took a step away.

"No doubt you have your reasons for telling me such a thing."

She turned and began to walk quickly back towards the cathedral, her head bent as if she were crying. It occurred to Frank that she might have been in love with Leo Beckford herself. It wouldn't have surprised him; nothing seemed to surprise him. After all, he'd half known all this for weeks, half known that some very rough waters lay ahead for Henry, whatever happened. He was angry with Sally for dawdling, for not making up her mind, but he felt no pity for Alan, son or no son. To his mind, Alan had walked away from his human responsibilities, step by step, these last few years, into his own peculiar freedom, and he was about to be asked to pay the price for that. But Henry, there was Henry. Only Frank's essential fair-mindedness, which remembered his own behaviour to Alan thirty years before, checked his rising tide of fury against Henry's parents. But he wouldn't sit still and watch anymore; he wouldn't allow it to take its own wandering course, as Sally seemed to allow it to. He would make something happen; he would telephone Alan and insist that he come home.

He reached his car and let himself into it. Late-afternoon light was settling over the close, gilding the walls of the cathedral, and beyond it the russet bricks of the headmaster's house, and farther still, the smooth eighteenth-century face of the deanery. He looked at the deanery for some time. "Vengeful little bitch," he said to himself and turned the key to start the engine.

In the last night of their stay at the cottage near Wyche, Felicity woke with a premonition. It seemed to her so clear and possible that she remembered her new resolve to be as unseparate as she could, and woke Alexander. She thought it was typical of his essential niceness of character that his first half-waking question was to ask her if she was all right and had she had a bad dream. She said not exactly, just a foreboding so real she knew it would happen.

He put on his bedside lamp.

"About what?"

"The house."

"My darling—"

She turned her face towards him.

"I'm perfectly certain that we shall get home and find it sold behind our backs."

"Heavens—"

He lay down again.

"But Frank Ashworth withdrew his proposal and it would break Hugh's heart to sell it anyway."

"I don't think it has anything to do with promises or logic."

"If you're right," Alexander said, feeling for her hand under the bedclothes, "shall we be broken-hearted all over again?"

She thought for a bit, staring upwards.

"Not—quite so badly." She turned back to him. "Would we have to go to the second master's house?"

Stanley Vigors was a bachelor, an efficient, upright, unimaginative man whose personality had rendered his house as inviting as a medical waiting room. It was an unprepossessing house in any case, an insubstantial-feeling brick box put up in the fifties with metal window frames and mean proportions. It had a long, bleak sitting room, which faced the games fields, and the back of the house looked down into an unfriendly strip of garden planted with trouble-free shrubs. Stanley Vigors would be just as happy, no doubt, to move his serviceable and charmless possessions into the empty flat at the top of the school building—in fact, he might even prefer the extra involvement of life there.

"You could make it lovely," Alexander said.

"Not *lovely*—"

"Well, a lot lovelier."

"If it is happening," Felicity said, "why don't we seem to mind more, even at three in the morning?"

"I think we know it would be good for us."

"What, morally—"

"No, no. Us. You and me."

She propped herself on one elbow.

"Has it been bad for us to live somewhere lovely, then?"

He said bravely, "It's been extremely *difficult*."

"Our marriage, you mean."

"Yes."

She lay down again.

"How very *odd* to feel like this. Not frantic."

"Not odd. Just the usual thing. Of having one's prayers answered in a way one never thought of."

She said warningly, "Alexander—"

"When am I going to be able to mention God again?"

"You do all the time."

"Of course."

He reached out to switch the light off. In the darkness Felicity said musingly, "I wonder if I could write there."

"When we got here," Alexander said, "you said you wondered if we could ever make love in this bedroom. Well, we have. Several times."

"I do appreciate you—"

"Go to sleep," he said, but she could hear that he was smiling.

In the morning, they packed the car, handed the key in to the pub in the village, and drove south to Aldminster. On the way, they didn't mention the house at all, but instead talked of Daniel and how their Christmas present to each other must be air tickets to America to see him. They discussed the probability of their having been rotten parents and the certainty of Daniel's having been a very difficult child, a child who had seemed to want to pull away from them even at the moment of birth, arching his back away from embraces and screaming with all the force of his brand-new lungs. Alexander confessed how dreadful he had always felt at being able to love some of the boys he taught so much more easily and comfortably than Daniel, and Felicity said that she loved him, all right, but it was a kind of love that wore one down to the bone and seemed to get nothing back. In a mood of intense harmony and closeness, they arrived back in the close to find that Sandra had left a pot plant on the kitchen table to welcome them home, and that among the letters that had accumulated in their absence was one from Hugh Cavendish formally announcing the imminent sale of the house.

Nobody boarding the plane with Alan Ashworth at Jeddah could have failed to notice his distress. He seemed like a man in deep shock and, for all his years of travelling, needed to be buckled into his seat by an air hostess and then didn't seem able to see her when she offered him sweets to suck for take-off, or hear her when she asked if he would like headphones. He was wholly unused to introspection, wholly unused to denying himself whatever he wanted at the moment he wanted it, wholly unused to thinking through the consequences of his actions. He had actually been summoned to the telephone while at the hospital, to be told by his father that if he didn't hurry home, he might have no home to hurry back to. Honesty had compelled Frank to add that it was probably too late anyway. Alan had gone back to the delicate and miraculous machinery they were installing in the new intensive care unit and, to his crew's horror, he had burst into tears. He told them that because he had worked so long away from home, his wife was leaving him. It was a dreadful scene and no-one knew what to do with him except find him a smuggled paper cup of illicit brandy from somewhere and take him back to the house in the expatriates' compound where he had lived for over a year, and where most of them had been frequently and vividly entertained. The air conditioning had been on full blast as usual, and Alan had sat shivering in one of his imported Italian armchairs, clutching a framed photograph of Henry, while people battled with the Saudi telephone system to make arrangements for him. He kept begging for reassurance.

"You're not a bad man," one girl said to him, a girl whose best friend he had slept with, "but you are a bloody fool."

It was, thank heavens, a British Airways flight, so there was drink. After a double brandy and a half bottle of claret with lunch, he felt a little better, sufficiently better at least to feel a growing anger at Sally for walking out on him. He had only taken this job so that they could pay off the mortgage on Blakeney Street and move a rung up the housing ladder, and he had, by so doing, sacrificed two years of watching his son grow up. He was just beginning to make a name for himself as a wizard at this kind of thing—only last week, he'd had an offer of an even bigger installation in Oman—and it was hard to feel that Sally couldn't be even a little bit proud of him, proud of a husband who was now summoned by sultans. When he thought of her in bed with someone else, he wanted to kill her. For her to sleep with another man was a betrayal, the worst wound. They'd sometimes discussed affairs—usually in the calm after a storm over some little philandering of his—and he always knew she wasn't really the type, she took relationships too seriously. That, of course, could be his strength now, Sally's seriousness. He drained his glass. Perhaps there was a glimmer of hope yet. He couldn't, frankly, *see* Sally with another man, and in any case, Henry had always been everything to her, she'd never do anything that would harm Henry.

His eyes filled with tears at the thought of Henry. When Alan himself had been taken away by his mother to live with her and Peter Mason, he had felt, through the inevitable alarm at the upheavals and the rows, a secret relief. Alan had always feared his father, feared him and felt him to be a stranger. Peter Mason was an accessible, indulgent man who liked to talk jocularly of "the family," meaning Gwen and Alan, and who had never frightened anyone in his life. But as Alan grew up, he perceived there was little to admire in Peter Mason beyond this jolly kindness, that his stepfather believed in getting by in human terms and no more, and that his own exacting and often unapproachable father at least lived by principles and aims greater than those dictated by personal convenience. Neither Frank nor Alan knew, by then, how to come much of the way towards each other, but the worst gulfs were bridged, and their closest moment came when Henry was born, and they drank brandy together in the pub outside the hospital gates and felt fond of the whole world. Alan, who had inherited too much of his mother's shallow sentimentality, made emotional avowals of the life he would give his son—"No offence to you, Dad"—and declared that they had all learned from past mistakes. Before Henry was two, he had accepted his first foreign job, four months in Cairo, and it had gone on from there. "Not again," Sally had cried, too often, and always he had said, eyes wide with hurt, "But it's for you and Henry!"

Why else, he told himself now, head back against the seat, eyes closed, would anyone stay in Jeddah for two days, let alone two years? Couldn't Sally see, or was she too spoiled by what he had given her and the freedom of her life to do what she wanted—she didn't *have* to work, she chose to—to care anymore? He saw himself suddenly alone and comfortless and the picture was quite overwhelming. Sally would *have* to care, she was bound to, it would be all right when he saw her again. It was all a nightmare, really, and soon he would wake up and find it had been no more than a salutary fright. Perhaps he should change his ways and freelance in England for a while, less money of course, but he'd be prepared to sacrifice that, even though the injustice of what was happening to him smote at his heart painfully.

The journey from the airport exasperated him, overcrowded and complicated, as did the thin grey greeting of an English summer day. He went into the lavatory on the train to Aldminster and washed and brushed his hair and regarded his sad, strained face in the little looking glass. You could see he was pale, even under his tan. Sally couldn't fail to see how deeply and honestly he was affected; she mustn't fail to, because the thought of losing her, standing there in the train's unpleasant and swaying little cubicle, was suddenly so terrible he thought he might be going to faint. He felt sick and sweating; he could not believe that it was possible to suffer like this; he could not believe that he was still alive while having to endure such pain.

Aldminster station looked exactly the same; it didn't even appear that the estate agents had changed their notices since he went away. He went out of the station like an invalid and found a taxi and asked for Blakeney Street. He sat in the back, shivering from time to time in his tropical-weight suit, looking out with alarm at the sheer familiarity of the roads and streets down which they were passing.

Sally opened the front door while he was paying the taxi, and stood waiting at the top of the steps. She had grown her hair and she was wearing a long buff cotton skirt, very full, and a white T-shirt, and she wasn't smiling. He went up the steps slowly, crooked because of carrying his bag in one hand, looking up at her.

"Sal?"

She stepped back into the house and he followed her and leaned forward for a kiss.

"No," she said.

"I should have brought you some flowers—"

She gave a little snort, and walked into the big room.

"Come on, Sal," he said, "there's no need for such a big deal now. I'm home."

He dumped his bag on the floor and began to tramp about the room, admiring things, commenting on changes. Sally stood by the stove, fiddling with coffee things, ignoring him until she held a mug out towards him and said, "Alan, it's *over*."

He took the mug and said in a voice whose airy tone implied that she hadn't uttered, "Where's our Henry, then?"

"He's with a friend. He'll be back later. We have to talk before we tell him."

Alan came up to her suddenly and held a threatening forefinger close to her face.

"Tell him what? Tell him I'm going to live at home now and he'll have a father around from now on, if you like. At least that's true. Tell him that while I've been slaving out there for you and him, you've been amusing yourself with another man. That's true, too. We'll tell him both those things together."

Sally held on to the stove rail and bowed her head and begged fiercely for self-control. Leo had taken her into the cathedral early that morning—"Not for anything godly," he said, "but just to remind you of the eternal stuff of things, the great enduring human qualities that get people through crises like this. You'll be all right the other side and so will Henry. If I have anything to do with it, you'll both be better, not just all right." He had walked her up and down the great aisles and round the shadowy curve of the ambulatory, and when they parted, he took her by the shoulders and said, "Now, don't get angry. Don't put yourself in his power."

She raised her head now and looked at Alan.

"No changes in your life will affect my decision. It's over. I don't want to be married to you anymore."

He shouted, "OK, OK, just chuck it all at me before I've even had time to wash, before I've even been in the house five minutes—"

He sank into a chair and put his free hand over his eyes.

"It'll be different, Sal, I promise. I'll do whatever you want."

"I only want a divorce."

"But you've given me no warning, you've just taken and taken all I've given you and suddenly out of the blue you turn around and say you're bored with me and you want a change—"

"That whole speech," she said, interrupting, "is a lie."

His voice sank to a whisper.

"You can't do this to me—"

She said nothing.

"You can't do this to Henry!"

She walked rapidly past him to the pine table and picked up a tabloid paper.

"It's all in here."

"What, what is—"

"Henry is something of a nine days' wonder because of the record he has made and the close has been in an uproar because the dean has tried to get rid of the choir. And somebody has now gone to the press and told them that Leo and I are having an affair, and the whole story is here, richly embellished with adjectives. Henry hasn't seen this, and I've asked Susan Hooper to be sure he doesn't while he's with her today, but we have to tell him ourselves, first."

Alan snatched the paper. It was half an inside page, with a photograph of Henry, singing in the cathedral, and a headline that ran, THE BITTER EXPERIENCE BEHIND THE INNOCENCE.

"We haven't got time to argue each other's rights and wrongs," Sally said, "because there's Henry."

"I won't have anything to do with it. I'm not leaving. I'm not giving you a divorce. I've nothing to tell Henry except I'm home and I'm staying."

"Then I'll tell him without you. I only waited for you, to be fair."

He gave a yelp.

"Fair! After what you've done behind my back! *Fair!*"

"You disgust me," Sally said.

She went out of the room and upstairs to her bedroom. She had made a bed up for Alan in the spare room and knew that that would be yet another hurdle to be got over, later. There was no sound from downstairs. She brushed her hair and then went into the bathroom and washed her hands and brushed her teeth. Mozart, who had been asleep on Henry's bed, came in and made a few enquiring remarks and twined himself round her legs. She picked him up and he covered the front of her T-shirt in an instant with speckled hairs.

"We must get through this," she said, "somehow."

He purred. She put him down and he walked quietly back to his dent in Henry's duvet. Sally brushed at her front to remove his hairs, took a deep breath, and walked downstairs. Alan was sitting where she had left him, the paper slithering off his knees, staring out of the window. He looked to her a complete and utter stranger.

"Look," she said, in as friendly and steady a voice as she could manage, "we have got to talk this through. Haven't we?"

Henry had a good day with Hooper. They gave the puppies obedience lessons—not particularly successful, since their pupils only had a concentration span of a few minutes at a time—and Mrs. Hooper let them make shortbread and chocolate fudge, and two of her friends who came in during the day told Henry they had bought his record and that they thought it was wonderful. They had chicken drumsticks for lunch and in the afternoon they made a rope ladder out of two old washing lines and some chair legs they found at the back of the garage, and tied this to the copper beech Hooper was lucky enough to have in his garden, even though it was a town one. Mrs. Hooper gave them tea in a carrier bag to take up their ladder and eat in the darkness of the tree. The puppies danced round the bottom of the tree and yapped and so they chucked bits of biscuit and crust down to them. When Mrs. Hooper said it was time to take Henry home, he rather hoped Hooper would beg her to let him stay the night, as he often did, but this time he didn't, and Henry didn't feel he could ask. He said thank you enormously effusively, to see if that would prompt her, but although she was very nice to him, and had been really kind to him all day, she didn't seem to get the message. At the back of his mind lurked his apprehensive knowledge that his father would be home, and he rather wanted to postpone seeing him. It was all right for people like Hooper and Chilworth, who saw their fathers all the time, but he just felt a bit jumpy. His father seemed to be coming home in a rush, and Grandpa had something to do with it, and all in all, Henry would have given a great deal to be curling up in a sleeping bag on the floor of Hooper's bedroom and playing the signalling game with torches that they had got down to a fine art.

When Mrs. Hooper dropped him at Blakeney Street, his father came out to meet him; it was a great help that she was there to prevent there being any big deal of any kind. "No heavy scene," Henry said to himself in the phrase he had learned from Wooldridge; Wooldridge used it all the time just now. He and Alan went up the steps together into the house and Alan asked him about his record and said what was it like to be famous. Henry blushed.

"Just the same—"

The table was laid for supper, and there was a big bowl of salad in the middle of it, and Sally was feeding Mozart, who was crying loudly, as he always did when he caught sight of the tin opener. Henry rather wanted to pick him up, but that wouldn't have been fair when he was so longing for his supper. Both his parents seemed rather jerky and peculiar, so he told them about the rope ladder and the puppies and Sally got a baked ham and potatoes out of the stove and they all sat down at the table. It looked perfectly ordinary but somehow it wasn't *being* ordinary. Neither his mother nor his father wanted to eat much, and he was so full of tea he wasn't very hungry either. His father kept asking him questions about the choir and the record and teasing him about being famous and when he said could he get down and go up to bed, they both said no, not just yet, they wanted to talk to him.

He thought he was going to have a lecture about not getting big-headed about the record, but instead they said a great deal about their not staying married anymore and Mum marrying Mr. Beckford, and how he wasn't to worry, because nothing would change for him. His father was crying. Henry said, "Will we still live here?"

His mother said probably not, and then he felt very much that he was going to cry too, and then he did, and then he didn't want to stay downstairs with them anymore, but rushed out of the room and upstairs and banged his bedroom door. He pulled his duvet off his bed and wound himself into it, like a padded caterpillar, and lay down on his bed, drawing up his feet and pulling down his head until he was quite obliterated in the soft bedfuggy darkness. He couldn't stop crying; he thought he could probably cry for ever. When Sally came up to him he screamed, "Go away, go away, go away" at her out of his cocoon and went on crying. It was hot and horrible inside his duvet but he wasn't coming out for anyone; his eyes felt like burning footballs. His parents stood outside his door, on the landing, and listened to him, muttering and sobbing, and when at last he stopped, his mother came in and unrolled him and peeled off his clothes and put on his pyjamas, and he came out of his abrupt angry, anguished sleep to shout at her, "I'm never going to get married!"

When she came out and went downstairs, Alan managed not to

be accusing out loud, but his eyes were full of it. He said he was going to sleep at his father's and he took his bag and the car keys and went off. When he had gone, Sally picked up the telephone and dialled Leo's number and at the sound of his voice, she began to cry, like Henry had, as if she could never stop.

15

Cosmo Cavendish told his father that Ianthe had been paid four hundred pounds for telling the newspaper about Leo Beckford and Sally Ashworth. He then added that of course she hadn't done it for the money. The dean asked in a remarkably alarming voice what were her motives, then, and Cosmo said he didn't know but he expected she had some.

"It is difficult to know," the dean said then, "whether yours or Ianthe's behaviour is the more unpleasant."

Cosmo was dismayed to find he felt a little abashed by this. Rule-breaking was one thing, and a frequently glorious and reputation-enhancing one at that, but suggestions of being an unattractive character were quite another, and disconcerting. His life depended upon his pulling power over other people, his glamour upon rebellion, and he knew well that true distastefulness of personality had no glamour at all. He went away to seek consolation from his mother, who, to his astonishment, declared his father to be entirely right, and so, comforting himself with the knowledge that she wasn't at all well at the moment—you could tell that, just by looking at her—he went upstairs to his black eyrie to things through. He had misjudged the situation badly and must discover why. After ten minutes he was rather inclined to blame Ianthe for everything, which was fine except that such a conclusion failed to remove the troubling knowledge that he had let himself down somehow, been outsmarted. He went down for supper, after being called three times, to find only two places laid. Bridget said the dean had gone up to London and would not be back until midnight.

Ianthe was just going out when her father arrived. His appearance, in a dog collar, in her sitting room—the room, her brother Fergus said, of a vulgar theatrical landlady—which contained four friends, all bound for the same concert in Highgate, was extremely startling. Two of the men got instinctively to their feet and had a hard time later explaining this away. The dean, with immense courtesy and authority, emptied the room in ten minutes and then, without a single preliminary, said to his daughter, "And have you any explanation to offer for your disgusting behaviour?"

Ianthe was torn between tears and temper. She knew that most fathers in the nineteen-eighties didn't speak to their grown-up daughters in this anachronistic and peremptory way—indeed the Sunday colour supplements paraded frequent interviews with modern fathers apparently craving the approval and affection of their careless daughters—but for all that, she was not sufficiently certain of her ground to fight back. Tears would be an instant admission of guilt. She lit a cigarette and began to walk nonchalantly about the room.

"Sit down," her father said.

Compromising, she hitched one thigh on to the arm of a chair.

"It is rare in women, I believe," the dean said, "for reasonable intelligence, which you are fortunate enough to possess, to be allied to glaring emotional immaturity. It would seem to me that you are a member of that unfortunate exceptional group, your case being exacerbated by an unattractive exhibitionism. You are not alone among your brothers and sister in having devoted yourself to defying and ridiculing all the principles by which you were brought up and by which you know I live, but you have carried your campaign to the furthest lengths of damaging folly. While your insults were confined to your home and family they could, with pain and difficulty, be borne. When you involve the reputation of a cathedral close and its inmates your behaviour is to be endured no longer. Are you listening to me?"

Ianthe said, "Can't I speak?"

"By all means—"

She wished suddenly for her mother. She said, too emotionally, "You wouldn't understand about love, you wouldn't know what I've been through—"

"I know about love," the dean said with distaste. "I am fortunate enough not to know about infatuation. Leo Beckford never gave you, to my knowledge, the smallest encouragement and your feelings were the result of your own deliberate exaggeration and persistence. The more he rebuffed you, the more you clung. In a stupid girl, I should regard such behaviour with pity. In a clever one, I view it only with contempt."

"And you call yourself a priest!" she shouted.

"It is not, Ianthe, a priest's function to be a bottomless well of woolly uncritical forgiveness. That would only devalue virtue."

There was a pause. Ianthe went over to the window and leaned her forehead on the glass and looked down into the early evening street. She was very frightened and full of a self-disgust she was desperate to find a culprit for. The carapace of illusory independence she had shielded herself with since she inherited her five thousand pounds on her eighteenth birthday—refusing, simultaneously, the university place she had been offered—felt very thin and fragile. When the dean said, in a voice quite empty of warmth, "If you have made fools of us all, you have made a worse one of yourself," she tried to speak and could say nothing.

"We must all give ourselves time to recover from this business," the dean said. "Your mother and I go to Scotland next week and Cosmo goes to Wales. For all our sakes, we should not see each other for a while—"

She spun round.

"I can't come home?"

"Not for a while. A few months. Are you in financial difficulties?"

She blushed scarlet.

"No—"

"The weeks ahead are going to be hard ones for Aldminster and there will have to be changes. I have yet to speak to the bishop and the archdeacon, yet to consider Leo Beckford's position. But you must stay away. You have Fergus and Petra in London and you have work to do. The money you received for the imparting of information must be returned to the newspaper."

Ianthe had a flash of spirit.

"May I not give it to the choir fund?"

"I believe," the dean said, "the choir fund hardly needs it."

He went towards the door. He longed to be gone, out of this room with its musty pseudo-Edwardian clutter, away from this headstrong child of his, whose present unhappiness seemed to him just a symptom of the self-indulgent volatility of her whole temperament, away from London. Ianthe gave an odd little whimper. The dean crossed the room and put his arm about her. His heart was as heavy as lead. He said, "God willing, this will all pass," and then he kissed her briefly on the top of her head and went away to catch his train back to Aldminster.

"Any more grave faces round the close," the bishop said, "and I shall want to skip into the cathedral wearing a false nose. May I come in for a moment?"

Leo, who was laughing, said of course and led the way into his sitting room. He indicated the bishop's cassock.

"If you walked across the close to see me dressed like that, I should think curtains were twitching all the way."

"I haven't time to go back after seeing you and change for even-song. May I sit here? Now look, Leo, I've come to see you before the dean does. It isn't strictly speaking, being chapter business, any of my concern, but humanly speaking it's my concern all the way. I'm rather sorry that in the last few months, with all this coming to a head, you haven't been to see me. There Janet and I were, worrying away about the choir, and all the time you were busy on quite another tack. I'd rather hoped, you see, that we had established some kind of trust—"

Leo looked affectionately at him.

"The other man I trust tried to stop me."

"Alexander Troy?"

"Yes."

"You know they *are* to be turned out of their house?"

"I do—"

"Another sorry muddle. Another good idea perverted by the motives of self-interest. But Leo, what troubles me is that your relationship with Sally Ashworth seems to have been so sudden, and of course I am deeply anxious that all the upheaval it is causing really is for something—"

"It is."

The bishop took off his spectacles and swung them by one hinge.

"The impulses springing from loneliness are so powerful, as are those when our lives reach, as all lives must, some kind of plateau. Are you thinking of marriage?"

"And children," Leo said.

The bishop put the earpiece of his spectacles between his teeth.

"*Social* orthodoxy never troubles me, as you know, only the helping of forces for good, be they traditional or progressive."

"Sally and I will be a force for good. I thought at first that I was the one in greatest need, but I've come to think rather delightedly that it might be the other way about. In any case, there's plenty of building to be done. I suppose you wouldn't marry us?"

"There's a *blessing* service—"

"No. No, marry us. Marry us properly."

The bishop put on his spectacles and said thoughtfully, "In a year's time, I might. If you think it's really necessary. If it's what you really want—"

Leo smiled.

"Is this some kind of test?"

The bishop looked up at the ceiling.

"Dear me, how suspicious you are." He paused and then dropped his gaze directly on Leo. "I must say something else to you before I go, something that I don't much want to say." He leaned forward. "Leo, immense loss as you will be, you must resign from the cathedral before you are asked to do so."

There was a pause.

"Is the dean going to ask me to resign?"

"I haven't spoken to the dean, but I don't think he has any option but to ask for your resignation. You would be doing both him and yourself a service if you were to take the initiative."

"But—"

"The dean," the bishop said firmly, "has more to bear than we know of. If anything is amiss with cathedral or close—and nothing ever is amiss without repercussions ripping out all over the diocese—the blame is laid at his door. I shouldn't think there are many deans who have served their cathedrals as Hugh Cavendish has served Aldminster, and if it has brought him joy, it has also brought him suffering of which he has never complained. For his organist simply to make a quiet and dignified exit will mean much to him and to Aldminster and I think you underestimate how much he values your contribution." He stood up. "I seem to be sounding rather pompous. I really only meant to say with as much affection and simplicity as I could manage that you must leave Aldminster but that one of my greatest friends, headmaster of a significant school in Sussex, is badly in need of a director of music. They are regular performers at the Brighton Festival, I gather."

"And Sally?"

"The headmaster must be put entirely in the picture."

"Thank you," Leo said with energy.

The bishop waved a hand.

"Don't. Absolutely don't. Anything that gets this poor precious old ship back on an even keel is its own reward. Aren't you playing for evensong?"

"No, it's Martin—"

"Ah," said the bishop. "Well, there we are. There's *someone* who will benefit from all this—"

Alan stayed in his father's spare bedroom for a week. It was a week he felt he never wished to repeat, from the wretched nights on the old Victorian boat bed that had belonged to his great-grandmother to the grim days when he felt he had sympathy from nobody. His father, though not actively unkind, made it plain that Alan was facing what had been inevitable for some years, inevitable because of his and Sally's choices. In this life, Frank said more than once, you can only reap where you have sown, and if you don't like the harvest, it's no good casting about for someone else to blame for it. When Alan went up to Blakeney Street to try and sort things out with Sally, and the interview disintegrated rapidly into accusation and acrimony, he resolved to take his father with him the next time. For both Alan and Sally, Frank's bulk and impartiality were immensely comforting; for Henry they were a lifeline.

It was Frank who, without condoning what Sally was doing, or rebuking Alan further for what he had done, made it clear that there was no marriage left for either of them to build on. It was Frank who made solictors' appointments for them both. It was Frank who took Henry off for hours on end and was just ordinary with him. On one walk they met Leo coming rapidly across the close, and to Henry's relief and gratitude, neither his grandfather nor his future stepfather appeared to be anything other than normal. Leo came round to Blakeney Street later that day and Henry, who had said he wanted to do something in his room, sat on the stairs and heard Leo tell his mother that they were probably going to Sussex. Henry had only the haziest notion of where Sussex might be, but a very defined notion that he didn't want to go there, wherever it was. He went down to the big room straightaway and said so.

"It's a school," Leo said, "with a strong choral tradition and a famous chapel. Why should that be so different to here?"

"Everywhere's different to here. I don't want it to be different."

Sally said encouragingly, "It's always difficult to imagine a kind of life that you aren't living, but why shouldn't another life be better?"

Henry thought.

"I don't want it to be better or anything. I just don't want it to be different from now."

Leo had his arm round Sally. When Henry burst in, she had instinctively tried to move away but he had held her firmly.

"The thing is, Henry, that I have to leave Aldminster."

"Why—"

"Because there has been a lot of rubbishy publicity about Aldminster recently, including that bit in the paper about my marrying your mother. It's bad for the cathedral and the close if I stay—"

Henry said rudely, "Don't get married then."

"For whose sake?"

Henry went over to the dresser and kicked at the bottom of the doors for a bit.

"I don't see the *point*—"

Sally said, "Of course you don't. But you will, in time."

"Why do I have to go to Sussex?"

"Because we are going and you must live with us until you are older. Then you can live where you like."

Henry's throat was suddenly thick with angry tears.

"Why does all this have to happen? Why can't we just do what we were doing?"

"Because," Leo said, "human beings never stand still, and nor do their relationships. They either develop or die. Look at you and Hooper, hardly speaking a year ago and now best mates. That's change. It may change again, and if it does, you won't die of it. All your father and mother and I are doing is changing, but as we are adults, it makes bigger waves."

Henry shouted, "I'm not going to horrible Sussex!"

He stamped out of the room and went upstairs. He got out a drawing pad and his tin of paint sticks and wrote "NO NO NO" all over several sheets of paper in the most violent colours he could find. After a while his mother came up and said they were going out for half an hour, to walk, and did he want to come. He yelled no, he didn't. After they had gone, he went downstairs to the television and the telephone rang.

"Is that Henry?"

"Yes—"

"It's Nick Elliott."

"Oh," Henry said with warmth, "*hi!*"

"How are you doing?"

"OK—"

"Listen, I really rang to speak to your mum. Is she there?"

"No, she's gone for a walk—"

"Well, I'll tell you. How do you feel about making another record?"

"*Great,*" Henry said, and then, remembering, "but I can't. I've got to go to Sussex."

"*Sussex?* Why on earth—"

"Mum and Mr. Beckford are going."

There was a pause.

"Sorry," Nicholas said, "I forgot."

Henry was afraid he might be going to cry.

"Look," Nicholas said, sensing it, "d'you want to talk?"

"I don't know—"

"I know how you feel. My dad went off when I was five and I only ever had my mum and she's a nutter. Tell you what, I'll come down. I'll come down on Saturday. We'll go and have a pizza. OK?"

"Thanks," Henry said.

"Want some good news?"

"Yes—"

"You've sold, in England and Europe, one hundred and fifty thousand copies."

"Wow—"

"Pity they won't let you give any interviews."

"Well, I'm a chorister, you see, I'm a chorister really."

"You hold on to that," Nicholas said. "That'll get you through. I'll see you Saturday."

Nicholas took Henry to the pizza place where Ianthe had taken him three months before. Henry had the Super Special and a tall glass of Coca-Cola with a blob of ice cream in it, and Nicholas thought for the thousandth time how amazing it was to have money in his pocket that he had earned and that was entirely his own to spend. They talked mostly about the choir, and Nicholas told Henry how he had nearly died of envy that morning, coming into the cathedral and hearing them singing "Tu es Petrus" and Henry remembered coming down the steps and finding him, because Harrison had swiped him with a flute case and his leg really hurt. They did imitations of Leo—"Now keep that note really *clean* to the end," "Come on, you little horror, open, open, *open*"—and compared memories of choir outings and Henry said they were going to Norway next term and then he remembered about Sussex and for the first time he looked terribly depressed.

"Don't go. Don't go to Sussex. If you stay here you'll be head chorister in under two years."

"I've *got* to—"

"Why?"

"Because of Mum and Mr. Beckford."

"You could board at school."

"Yes," Henry said dejectedly.

"Come on—"

"None of my friends do."

"You'd make new friends."

"I don't want *anything* new," Henry said.

"Look," Nicholas said, "the most important thing is the choir. Right? You can't leave that. But if you're going to stay in it, you'll have to think of some other way of staying in Aldminster. Boarding isn't too awful, and then you could spend the holidays with your mother and Mr. Beckford."

Henry looked unconvinced.

"What about your father?" Nicholas said.

"He's going back to Saudi Arabia soon. That's where his job is."

"Oh. Well you can't live with him *there*—"

"I don't think he likes being in Aldminster much."

"But he's your dad—"

"Oh yes—" Henry looked away.

"When I have kids, I'm going to stay right with them."

Henry said nothing. Nicholas summoned the waitress for the bill, and went over to the cash desk to pay. Henry stayed on his chair and felt very full. When Nicholas came back he said, "That was *superb*. Thanks a lot."

Nicholas walked him home. He very much wanted to put in a word for Leo, but there didn't seem to be the right moment, with Henry in the mood he remembered all too well himself feeling, that the world was deliberately trying to make you miserable. Instead, as they went along Blakeney Street, he said that the only way to feel better was to make something happen that you wanted, and he knew he was a fine one to talk but he was convinced it was true all the same.

"Like what?"

"Well, you want to stay in Aldminster so you've got to make that happen."

Henry went into the house and found his mother and his grandfather sitting at the big table, talking about him. In case they had been planning something while he was out, he thought he had better remind them that he wasn't going to Sussex.

"I see," Frank said.

"Nicholas said why don't I board—"

Sally looked at her father-in-law.

"I've thought of that. But even with an assisted place—"

"Alan could afford it."

"I don't want to board," Henry said.

Frank looked at him.

"Look here, young man. All these shan'ts and won'ts and don't wants. You'll have to compromise somewhere."

Henry thought he sounded like Mr. Beckford. At least Leo and Frank never apologized to him or got all wet about things. He said suddenly, the words leaping from his mouth without the idea seeming to have entered his brain first, "Why can't I come and live with you?"

In ten days, the dean caught four salmon and Bridget one. They stayed in the usual lodge with the usual group of friends—a consultant at a large provincial hospital, an antiquarian bookseller, and a Queen's Counsel, with all their wives—and the signs of strain visible upon the Cavendishes were put down by almost all of them to the difficulties of Aldminster life in the last few months. The wife of the bookseller, who was extremely astute and infinitely more interested in people than salmon, observed to her husband that she thought the Cavendish marriage was not looking healthy and, what was more, that Hugh seemed to have the upper hand. The bookseller, who had spent five fishing holidays with the dean and his wife, and who had, like all the others, come to regard Bridget's supremacy in the marriage as the kind of joke they were all glad they were not part of, said nonsense, impossible, she was making it up. Charlotte Knight took Bridget to Ballater to stock up on groceries and boldly asked her outright if everything was all right as they drove.

Bridget said you simply couldn't imagine the strain of the last few months, seeing Huffo so gravely misunderstood when all his endeavours were for the cathedral, and to be defied by his own organist and, worse, by the headmaster of the King's School, who hadn't scrupled to use a public platform most improperly, had made life at times frankly unbearable. All the time she was speaking, she was adjusting her silk headscarf with funny little nervous plucking movements. Charlotte Knight said, probing, "Yes, I know. I should think it's frightful to be in a public position and have stones wrongly thrown at you, but at least you have each other. I mean, almost any trouble is bearable if you have someone to share it with."

Bridget did not reply to this. Glancing at her, Charlotte saw she had turned her head away. They drove on a little in silence and then Charlotte said, "And how awkward that Ianthe has helped to save the day with the choir."

Bridget said sepulchrally, "It has almost broken her heart."

"Twenty-year-old hearts do mend—"

"Oh yes," Bridget said, "I imagine twenty-year-old ones have a better chance than older ones."

It had gone far enough.

"Now come on," Charlotte said, "you're the cook. Think of something simple and interesting we can give that hopeless girl to cook for us tonight. And don't say salmon—"

On the banks of the Dee, allotted a favourite beat, the Dean and the QC were assembling their rods.

"I do congratulate you on saving the choir," John Claremont said. "It's been a marvellous effort. That splendid little boy. I hear Rochester's thinking of axing theirs now. It's the most awful prospect, frankly, cathedrals without choirs. I often wished we'd tried Mark for a choir school—marvellous classical education for almost nothing and all that music too. May I borrow your gaff? That looks pretty heavy water to me."

The dean, who had hoped rather vainly that in Scotland the talk would all be of fish and not at all of Aldminster, said of course, but unfortunately the choir had got all the publicity the fabric of the cathedral should have got. If the cathedral roof was to be repaired, some grave sacrifices would have to be made.

"Sacrifices?"

"My dear John," the dean said, spinning the drum of his reel, "what the public doesn't know is that I'm being forced to sell the best building in the close to keep water out of the nave."

"You don't mean it—"

"I do indeed. Thousands pour in to keep the choir going while another precious part of our heritage passes into the hands of a very dubiously motivated city council—"

The ghillie came up at this point and said there were two big fish under a ledge at the bottom of the pool. John Claremont said jocularly, "All ready for me to bounce a worm on their noses, Angus!"

The ghillie looked disapproving.

"It must be a frightful strain. No wonder poor Bridget—"

"Well," the dean said, cutting him off and moving down the bank after the ghillie, "when things mean a lot to you, they're bound to take their toll."

That night, Bridget burst into tears at dinner. The talk had turned inevitably to Aldminster, and the dean was gravely explaining the impossible juggling act he had to perform between the cathedral's income and the insatiable demands made upon it, when she cried, "Oh I wish I'd never even heard of the wretched choir! It's all because of that—" and rushed from the room in tears. Charlotte Knight followed her upstairs and sat beside her on her bed, patting her heaving, solid shoulder and saying soothing nothings about the healing effects of time.

"We had such a wonderful marriage," Bridget said between sobs, "never a cross word and I knew I was such a help to him, I knew it. I know the children have been rather naughty and perhaps I was a little inclined to take their parts, but surely a mother may be forgiven for that!" She rolled over and gazed at Charlotte in sudden terror.

"Do you suppose he would like to leave me?"

"He won't do that."

"But would he *like* to?"

Charlotte, who was not a soft-hearted woman, looked at her peach-powdered face, messily ravaged by tears, with real pity.

"I think he's in as much of a state as you are. He doesn't know what he wants."

Bridget sat up and pulled pink tissues from the box by her bed.

"I don't think I have ever been afraid before." She blew her nose loudly and a well-trained hand moved up instinctively to pat her hair into place. "I only want to be a good wife."

"It doesn't look to me as if Hugh's being a particularly good husband just now—"

"Suppose it is all my fault?"

"The choir isn't your fault. You've always bossed Hugh around, of course, we've made a bit of a joke about it, but if he didn't like it, couldn't he tell you so?"

Bridget swung her legs to the floor. Unexpectedly she said, "Perhaps I wouldn't have listened."

"Well—certainly you've always had to be right—"

Bridget went over to the chest of drawers and looked at herself in the glass on top of it. Her expensive jersey dress was rucked up at the back and she looked strangely ludicrous and inappropriate without her shoes on. After a while she said to Charlotte in her more usual voice, "I wonder if you'd explain that I have a shocking headache. And I should be more than grateful for a cup of tea."

"Would you like me to talk to Hugh?"

Bridget turned round.

"Oh no. Thank you but certainly not. We get by quite civilly just now and so it will remain until he chooses to speak to me more—intimately."

"And if he doesn't?"

"I am not," Bridget said, "thinking about that just now."

Charlotte stood up and went over to the door.

"I'll get your tea."

Felicity said that if she had to live in the second master's house she felt that being asked to live with the school bursar's choice of wallpaper was overdoing it. Stanley Vigors, mellow at the happy prospect of actually moving into the main school building, said how funny she should mind, he hadn't noticed them at all somehow.

"How *could* you not notice," Felicity said, making sweeping gestures in the sitting room, "vinyl tweed and Regency stripes. I'm going to get the entire house painted, every corner, and banish every plastic doorhandle and all the lavatory glass."

"Well, it *is* a bit of a comedown for you—"

"No it isn't," Felicity said, "it's a high old challenge."

"I suppose," Stanley said, feeling that this was a remark his mother would appreciate more than Felicity, "that it will be easier to keep—"

She laughed and gave him a swift kiss, which made him blush. He didn't think he'd ever seen her in such good spirits, or so confident, so that seeing her whisking about his house in her tremendous skirts while she measured and considered made him realize, with a curious alarm, how boring he had made it. She had left a red shawl lying in his sitting room, among the beige and olive green, and it was quite amazing the difference it had made. She had never been his idea of a headmaster's wife, but seeing her here made him think that she was very much his idea of . . . He stopped himself, blushed ever more darkly, and asked her if she would like some coffee.

"No thanks. I had it at the deanery. In a bone china cup with homemade shortbread."

"The *deanery!*"

"Olive branch," she said airily. "I'm not sure it isn't rather irritating of Alexander and me not to mind as much as we were supposed to. It's certainly very *surprising*, and nobody is more surprised than us. But then, you see, the choir is safe for now and Daniel wants to come home for Christmas and I shall bend this nasty little house to my will if it kills me."

Stanley put a reassuring hand on the nearest woodchip-paper-covered wall.

"Not *nasty*," he said, in case it was listening.

"Very nasty."

She had said as much to Bridget Cavendish, who had lost a lot of weight and who was undeniably less authoritative. When Hugh had come in, she was almost, astonishingly, nervous. Felicity said to him, "I hope you are properly sorry for us over our dismal new abode."

He looked briefly outraged, but he recovered himself sufficiently to say, surprisingly, "I am."

Bridget had looked as if she were bursting to say something in his defence, but she had restrained herself and just blown her nose instead. Felicity hadn't meant to feel sorry for either of them and found she was sorry for both. When she left, Bridget had kissed her unexpectedly and said she knew a frightfully good woman for curtains, immensely reasonable and very quick.

"I've always made my own—"

"Perhaps this time," Bridget said, "you deserve not to have to."

Felicity had gone across the close, musing on this. Had Bridget tried to say she understood Felicity's feelings and admired her courage, or had she even gone so far as to hint that she thought Hugh wrong in selling the house? Whichever, it made her feel gentler towards the Cavendishes than she had since her return, and more determined than ever to make of her new house a symbol of some kind of fresh start. When she had finished bemusing Stanley Vigors, she went lightly home, to find Sandra Miles crying in her drawing room, with Alexander hovering over her with a bottle of sherry and a crumpled snuff handkerchief. He looked unspeakably relieved when Felicity came in.

"My dear Sandra—"

She tried to get up from her chair.

"Oh Mrs. Troy, I'm so sorry to behave like this, but I thought I must tell you in person and then I just couldn't—"

"Couldn't?"

"Help myself," Sandra said with difficulty.

Alexander put down the handkerchief and poured sherry into a tumbler.

"Oh Mr. Troy, I couldn't drink all that—"

"Well, try. Drink a bit, anyway. It's really very good news Sandra has brought, although it's sad for us. Her fiancé has been promoted and is being sent to the head office in Reading, so of course, after they are married in December, Sandra will wish to go with him."

"I've been so happy here," Sandra said. "I'll never have such a lovely job again. I mean, of course I'm proud of Colin doing so well, but it's really come as the most awful blow. I did wonder whether to postpone—"

"Oh no," Alexander said hastily, "you mustn't do that."

Felicity sat down by Sandra.

"You can always come and see us. Your mother's here, after all."

Sandra looked at her and then said in almost a whisper, "I know it's for the best. Really—"

Felicity said gently, "Yes."

"Look, I don't want to drink by myself," Sandra said. "I feel ever so silly—"

"Are there two more glasses? We ought to toast Sandra's future."

"Of course," Alexander said. "I'll go and get some." He paused. "There's quite a lot to toast, in fact—"

When he had gone, Sandra said, "I feel everything's breaking up, Mrs. Troy, I can't help it. I mean Leo's going and this house and now I am. It's a bit scaring. I said to Colin last night that ever since the choir business came up, we've all been at sixes and sevens—"

"But we've saved the choir."

"Yes," Sandra said, but her thoughts were clearly on something else. "I know that. I just don't think anything will be as—as wonderful as it was."

Alexander returned with two glasses, filled them, and handed one to Felicity.

"Now, come on. The future!"

Sandra gave them both a watery smile.

"The future," she said, but her voice was very small.

16

IN THE FIRST WEEK OF SEPTEMBER, LEO LEFT FOR SUSSEX AND was, at the last moment, quite stricken to be going. This was not helped by Cherry Chancellor, who was visibly burning to move in behind him, since, although the houses in Chapter Yard were absolutely identical, the left-hand one was traditionally the home of the organist. The new assistant organist, just graduated from Cambridge and dying to begin at Aldminster, came in while Leo was packing his music and said enthusiastically that he didn't know how Leo could bear to leave that organ.

"At this moment," Leo said, "I hardly can."

"What do they have the other end?"

"An 1885 Walker. Very good, of course, of its kind but only forty-eight speaking stops, so I shall miss the size. Nice solo stops, though—"

He went into the cathedral for his own private farewell to the organ. He simply sat at the console, lightly stroking the ivory of the keys and the thumb pistons and the stop controls. He took his shoes off to feel the pedals better. He had spent hours in that organ loft, probably some of the best as well as the happiest hours he had ever spent in his life, hours in which he had sometimes felt himself so much part of the great central life force of humanity because of the music he was making that he had been moved to tears. It was a terrible parting. He had no wish at all to relinquish this extraordinary instrument, at once passionately human in its capabilities and superbly indifferent in its historic permanence, into the hands of anyone else. Its vast old personality seemed to engulf him, dwarf him, and at the same time to be withdrawing itself, inch by inch, and holding itself apart, ready for the next man. He drew the beechwood cover down over the console and laid his cheek against it and listened to the huge ancient breathing quiet of the place. He must go. If he stayed any longer, he would hardly be able to.

Sally helped him to load the car he had bought. She intended, until the house in Blakeney Street was sold, to divide her time between Sussex and Aldminster and Leo and Henry, until all four could somehow—she very much trusted to time in this—be harmoniously merged. She only said ordinary, administrative things to Leo, like "Careful when you pull the duvet out because I've filled it with records" and "There's a bottle of Scotch under the dashboard" but he knew she knew of his state of mind. The removal van dwarfed Chapter Yard, and the piano had to be put in a special crate and circled with mattresses and it seemed to Leo that it groaned as it was wheeled up the ramp. The goodbyes were hard too, and despite having Sally beside him, Leo was filled with a bitter loneliness. Like so many before him, he stood on the stone stairs leading up to the practice room and heard a Bach chorale being broken off and Martin Chancellor's voice saying, "Now, you didn't really think about the accent. Did you?" and it took him a long time to open the door and go in. They all stopped when he entered and turned to him their composed musicians' faces, and although he knew they were, most of them, sorry to see him go, he knew too that their lives would go on, the song would always outlive the singer. He glanced at Henry, and Henry, whose attempts at coming to terms with the new shape of his life were very much impeded by his fundamental liking for Leo, dropped his gaze to the floor. He walked down the room to the piano, said "Excuse me" to Martin, and turned to the men and the boys to say goodbye. Several said "Good luck" and Hooper said irrelevantly that his aunt lived in Sussex and got shushed by everyone else.

"I want you to enter the Brighton Festival," Leo said, "so that I can bring my new choir and beat the hell out of you."

There was uncertain laughter.

"I'll let you get on," Leo said, moving back to the door. "Mind you make the canticles in evensong the best I've ever heard. Or Mr. Chancellor will want to know why."

He closed the door behind him.

"Quiet, everyone," Martin said. "Now I want each of you bang *on* the note. One, two—"

Leo went down the steps. Sally was waiting for him and together they crossed to the palace. Janet Young said she never said goodbye to anyone unless she was sure she was going to see them later in the day, so she wasn't saying it now.

"I'm amazed at how much I *mind*," Leo said.

"We *all* mind," the bishop said, "but of course you'll be back—"

"I don't think I will."

Janet took Sally's hand.

"But you're leaving us a hostage here—"

"Only for a few days a week. I need her."

"I'm hoping to get a job there," Sally said. "And Henry must come for the holidays. To break us all in."

"And now," the bishop said with just a hint of firmness, "now you are going to the deanery."

They all shook hands and Janet and Sally kissed each other.

"God bless," the bishop said, and gave a valedictory flourish of his spectacles.

They went out through the palace gates.

"This is awful," Sally said. "Why should it be so painful?"

"Because you don't realize how important your human landscape is until bits drop away." He gripped her hand. "It's worse when you get older. In your twenties, you never think—"

"Talking of twenties," Sally said, "I had a letter from Ianthe."

"Oh my God—"

"I didn't mean to tell you, but I think I will. I so don't want us to have no-go areas. She said you had made her believe you were in love with her."

Leo stopped walking.

"And what do you think—"

"Look at me," Sally said. She was smiling. "You forget it was me who told you she fancied herself in love with you in the first place."

"Sal—"

"I wrote back. I wrote and told her the best cure for a broken heart was to give it to someone else to mend. It was a phrase I found in an agony aunt's column. What do you have to say?"

He kissed the hand he was holding.

"You *know* what I have to say."

"Just don't go kissing anyone else. I'm a bit raw on the subject."

"If *you* did," Leo said, "I'd go bananas. So I know."

The dean was out. Bridget opened the door to them with very much less than her customary assurance and led them into the drawing room. The fireplace was filled with Michaelmas daisies and there was a bowl of chrysanthemums on a sofa table, as big as white mops.

"Hugh does so love flowers," Bridget said, "I like to keep as many in the house as I can. I'm afraid chrysanthemums really aren't his favourite and I should so have preferred gladioli but Mr. Cheeseman only had a dreadful salmon pink so I thought—"

"I've really just come to say goodbye," Leo said, wondering whither this floral byway tended. "I leave early tomorrow for Sussex. I'd hoped the dean would be in."

Bridget spread her hands and shook her head. It seemed to Sally a strangely appealing gesture, incongruous in this well-dressed woman against a backdrop of silver photograph frames containing all her unsuitably, improbably mutinous children. Sally put out her own hand.

"Would you tell the dean we called?"

"Of course," Bridget said, "of course." She seemed to recollect herself a little. "I do hope you will be very happy in—"

"Sussex."

"In Sussex. Such a pretty county. So lovely to have the sea."

"And I hope," Leo said, with an edge of asperity, "that you and the new assistant organist get on well."

A moment of the old Bridget returned.

"Too extraordinary. He is the grandson of such a dear friend of my father's. Such a wonderful family, so charming and all very musical. A real coincidence." When Ianthe was allowed to return to Aldminster she had high hopes of Simon Prescott for her, with his lovely manners and his entirely *right* sort of upbringing, but those hopes, like so much nowadays, had to remain secret. She smiled stiffly at Leo. "Of course, poor Simon has a lot to do to live up to your playing—"

Leo did not smile back. He gave a tiny bow and put his hand under Sally's elbow. Bridget led them back to the front door, opening it to a flood of chatter about the autumn and a new term and so many fresh starts and do mind the second step from the bottom, where Cosmo had accidentally dropped a stonemason's hammer, Heaven knew why he needed such a thing or where it had come from, but there was a whole half-moon out of the step and the poor archdeacon, only that morning . . . In midsentence, she shut the door.

Leo said, "Patronizing old—"

"No," Sally said. She was looking back at the closed deanery door with its glossy white paint and brilliantly polished knocker. "She *was*, but she isn't anymore. She's either having, or heading for, a nervous breakdown."

"Come *on*—"

"I mean it. Perhaps the dean is being horrible to her."

"He wouldn't dare."

"Worms turn," Sally said, "don't they?"

They walked back to Chapter Yard in silence. The removal van had finished and driven off, and nothing remained but Leo's car, and the mattress and sleeping bag Cherry was lending him for his last night. She was in the house, plastic-aproned and rubber-gloved, attacking Leo's kitchen with a scrubbing brush.

"You might have waited until I'd gone," he said mildly.

"We have to be in by Monday," Cherry said, scrubbing on, "and you couldn't put a *child* in here."

"Thank you," Leo said, but he was too tired to care. He went back into his empty, echoing sitting room and found Sally squatting on the floor, talking to the baby, jiggling idly in its bouncing chair.

"It smiles." She dropped her voice. "Luckily it smiles just like its father. Come down to Blakeney Street. You can't stay here or you'll get disinfected."

Henry was ahead of them. He and Mozart were in their customary places on the floor watching television, and the table was littered with the usual detritus of Henry's having found himself something to eat, but somehow even Blakeney Street didn't feel familiar either, as if the house, knowing it was to be sold, was, like the organ, withdrawing itself in readiness for a new relationship. Henry was perfectly friendly. He got up and kissed his mother and said hello to Leo and sorry about all the crumbs but the bread wouldn't cut properly because of being new.

"There's a new probationer," he said. "He's called Froggett or something and he's got kneesocks."

"Any good?" Leo said.

"My goodness," Henry said, putting his hands in his pockets, "we wouldn't *have* him in the choir if he couldn't sing—"

Outside the headmaster's house, a new varnished board with a metal plate screwed to it proclaimed that Aldminster City Council would shortly be opening an advisory centre in the building. Inside, the house was complete emptiness and silence. The house, being Grade One listed, was proving intractable about being made into offices because the rooms could not be altered, the doorways and passages provided a fire-prevention officer's field day, and the frailty of a great deal of the original plasterwork was making the Historic Buildings people dubious that many areas could actually weather public use. At the town hall, the subject had become a very sore one indeed, and Denis Thornton, only weeks before acclaimed as a public benefactor, found himself now accused of spending three hundred thousand to achieve a personal victory in his vendetta against Frank Ashworth.

From Back Street, Frank watched it all with more detachment than he had felt in weeks. It no longer seemed beyond the bounds of possibility that he might, some not too distant day, just drive the grey Rover back to the town hall car park, deliver it to Ron for its promised wax, and walk peaceably back up that extraordinary staircase to his old office, past a secretary who, knowing her, wouldn't even look up from her typing to say, "So you're back, Mr. Ashworth, are you," in tones of exasperating matter-of-factness. In the meantime, while he revolved this half-fantasy in his mind, he had Henry. He had even, at Henry's request, painted his spare bedroom the colour of a chocolate bar, and anything more depressing he thought he had seldom seen, but Henry was entranced. They went shopping together for curtains and posters and an imitation art-nouveau bedside lamp with a pink-petalled glass shade that Henry much admired. When Henry went back to choir practice a fortnight before the official start of term, Frank insisted on collecting him from Blakeney Street and driving him up to the cathedral, which Sally found at once touching and irritating and Henry thought was wonderful because it saved him an uphill walk.

While Henry sang, Frank paced the cathedral and the close. He went often to stand in front of the headmaster's house and look, with a certain grim satisfaction, at the imperturbable old soft red façade and the raw new board. When Alexander Troy met him there by chance, he was standing with his arms folded looking up at the house with his head slightly on one side, as if according it an amused and reluctant admiration. He said as much to Alexander.

"Do you think this old bugger has us all beat?"

"There's no justice," Alexander said, surprised into a perfectly natural reply, "if it hasn't."

Frank turned to look at him and Alexander thought how changed his face was from the weary, beaten air it had worn at their last meeting.

"Between you and me," Frank said, recalling with a strange little jerk of pleasure that this man was his Henry's headmaster, "do you think the dean and chapter would buy it back?"

Alexander hesitated and then said no, he didn't.

"Money?"

"Yes," Alexander said quickly, and then added, "no. It's—too late. It's too complicated—"

"Perhaps the council would give the dean a mortgage—"

"Mr. Ashworth, forgive me, but you are an old schemer—"

Frank beamed.

"Force of habit. We learn all the time. I'm not ashamed to admit a mistake when I've made one. Can't the dean do the same?"

"No," Alexander said, "in this case I don't think he can and I don't think he should be asked to."

"Odd—"

"Not very. Just human."

"No," Frank said, "odd. Here you all are, at loggerheads for months, open war declared over the choir, schemes and deceits, not one with a good word to say for another and now, when you've lost the house, and the dean has had a slap in the face over the choir, you all rally round him and say nobody must make life hard for him."

Alexander looked away from him, back at the house, but he was smiling.

"My wife has an image for what has happened. She says that sometimes you plant an acorn, and you plant it in good faith and instead of finding yourself with an admirable sturdy single oak tree, you're landed with a terrible mad forest that won't stop growing in all directions and develops an uncontrollable life of its own. The dean set out to mend the fabric of the cathedral. That's all."

Frank grunted. He looked at Alexander.

"And you? You're not bitter?"

"The reverse. I've won what I needed to win."

"I shall," Frank said with a little show of pride, "be helping to take care of Henry this winter."

"So I gather. It seems a good solution. And the choir is, oddly enough in this kind of situation, a sort of substitute family. But no more showbiz for Henry just now. One thing at a time."

Frank said slowly, "You've only to ask, you know, if you think Henry needs anything—"

"Yes. Thank you."

"I must be getting along to collect him—"

"Get him a kitten," Alexander said suddenly. "His cat has to go to Sussex. He'll find that hard. Get him a kitten."

Frank thought about this as he went slowly back into the cathedral. He had never liked cats, but then, he had always thought he didn't much like children either. Could you have a cat in Back Street? Would it learn to use the fire escape? He walked slowly round the ambulatory, where the hazy sunshine fell through the circling windows in soft dusty bars across the stone floor. He passed the first bishop in his little granite tomb and the marble cartouche of Bishop Fielding's menagerie—three cats there at least—and the bronze bust of the Victorian bishop who had founded the city orphanage that Frank remembered still going strong in his boyhood. The chapels were all empty, except for flowers here and there, and a solitary grey-haired man in a tweed jacket kneeling in the chapel dedicated to the patron saint of the old country yeomanry. Frank paused to look at him and wonder why he should be kneeling there alone at nine o'clock on a weekday morning, and then the man turned his head slightly to the eastern window, as if instinctively wanting the sunlight to fall on his face, and Frank saw that he was the dean.

Henry had thought that he would create a fuss, rather, about not being allowed to make a second record; but even if the adults around him seemed anxious to placate him over most things, they were united and adamant about this. Even his father, who had taken his uncomfortable emotional displays back to the Middle East, wrote to him to say he wouldn't allow it either. Leo said to him that not only had he a lot to learn, but that a record made by a chorister in conjunction with a tiny rock record company being a hit was a chance in a million that they had taken and, amazingly, succeeded in, but it wasn't the sort of thing you could do twice. Henry was nettled by this.

"It wasn't *just* a fluke—"

"The unlikely combination of you and Ikon working *was* a fluke. When Mr. Chancellor thinks you're good and ready, you can record with a proper professional company experienced in choral music."

"But then it wouldn't be a *hit*—"

"That remark," Leo said, "proves to me that you shouldn't make another. The rock world is horrible."

"What sort of horrible?"

"Hype, hysteria, and duplicity," Leo said.

"What's—"

"The answer, Henry," Leo said, "is no."

When he got back to it, Henry could not help noticing that the choir were more inclined to squash him than cheer him. In fact the squashing reached proportions that made Martin Chancellor send Henry out of practice one morning, in order to remind the others that Henry had played a significant part in saving their choral lives. When Henry came back in, his eyes were pink but he kept his head up. As they resumed the "Magnificat," Wooldridge, who was next to him, slid a packet of chewing gum quietly along the music stand towards him. Gratefully Henry covered it with his psalter and sang on until it was safe to transfer it to his pocket. Harrison had been made head chorister and was briefly being very officious about it, darting disciplinary glances about the room, but he never noticed. The new probationer could hardly see the music on his stand, he was so small, and Harrison's thirteen-year-old majesty loomed over him as a guide. Henry's hand closed in relief about his chewing gum in the secrecy of his pocket and he leaned slowly, slowly sideways until his shoulder touched Wooldridge.

"Henry," Martin Chancellor said—he had begun to call them all by their Christian names—"Henry, are you too tired to stand up by yourself?"

"No, sir."

"And is Charles too feeble to stand up by *himself*?"

"No, sir."

"Then behave yourselves."

Being ticked off, Henry found to his relief, rehabilitated him. The choir, the routine, the discipline, everything went blessedly back to normal. Only home wasn't normal. Mozart had gone—that had been a parting, however temporary, of true misery for Henry— and every room had a series of wine boxes in it, begged from Quentin Small, that Sally was slowly filling with possessions, hers and Alan's apart, with a scrupulous, idiotic fairness. People came to look at the house and Henry regarded all of them with hatred; they seemed to love the big room but when they got upstairs they said to each other, "Well, *I'd* push that wall through to make a decent-sized bedroom" and "Of course the boy's room would make a perfect second bathroom," the insensitivity and arrogance of which sometimes reduced him to tears of helpless rage. He tried to punish Sally by taking all his photographs and posters down to Back Street, but three days later he brought them all back again. Frank told Sally she should just go, and let him and Henry sort out life after a clean, final break, but she went on obstinately, sorting and packing, making lists and telephone calls. She wanted to hug Henry a lot, which he liked usually but at the moment felt uneasy about because hugging anyone had become suddenly so much more complicated. When Frank had said gruffly to him that perhaps they'd better not embrace anymore in public, Henry had been truly grateful.

He spent several nights, for practice, in Back Street. He liked it. At night, because it was a flat, he could lie in bed with the door open and actually see Frank reading in the sitting room, and if thoughts of Mozart and Sally came to him, as they too often did, he could pad through and ask nonchalantly for a drink. Frank said to him one night, "One thing you've got to learn is that in this life you've got to make your own happiness."

This struck Henry because it seemed to him that his life was not of his own making at all, but something other people arbitrarily made for him, happy or unhappy. The notion that he might have his own kind of power was more than pleasing. He lay in bed with a torch and sent its beam whirling in the dark and felt, briefly, mighty. The mightiness, however, could not survive Sally's first departure for Sussex, two weeks after term began, and he broke down in choir practice, to his infinite chagrin, and had to be comforted ignominiously by Harrison, who saw it as his duty.

In break, he borrowed ten pence from Chilworth and telephoned his grandfather.

"I'm coming home from school on my own. I've got something to do on the way—"

He paused. Frank said, "I was going to meet you."

"I'd rather come on my own. Everyone else does. I'll be fine."

"Six—"

"No later."

"Bangers tonight," Frank said, "and you keep your word."

After school, he went down to empty Blakeney Street and let himself in. It was oddly quiet, and Sally had turned everything off, so that not even the fridge was humming, and the house didn't seem to smell quite normal. Henry went into every room and opened every cupboard and drawer and looked at everything in them very carefully before he closed them again. He found two chocolate digestive biscuits and ate them, and the Asterix comic book he thought he had lost, and Sally's big black sweatshirt he was sure she wouldn't mind him borrowing. He went into the big room last and played chopsticks on the piano. Then he put the book and the sweatshirt in his sports bag and carefully locked the house up behind him.

The light outside in the street was dusky blue and there was a little sharp frosty bite to the air. Grasping his bag, Henry set off, not downhill to catch a bus to Back Street, but uphill again, back to the close, through the small streets where he had walked every morning of his school life. The proper shops were shutting and the takeaway-food places and wine bars were putting on their outside lights and opening up, and when he crossed Lydney Street he saw the first hot-chestnut seller of the autumn standing by his brazier outside the pizza place Nicholas had taken him to. The close was almost empty when he reached it, and the grass was turning dark blue in the dusk, specked with white scraps of litter, and the cathedral looked as big as a mountain with just a few lights glowing from the chancel.

The public door would be shut by now, and anyway, Henry preferred to use the medieval bishop's door that the choir always used when they came in from the cloisters. Once inside, he leaned against the ancient oak of the door and listened. Someone was playing the prelude to a Bach fugue, but the rest of the cathedral seemed to be quite empty. Henry closed his eyes. It was probably the new organist, because everyone knew Mrs. Chancellor liked Mr. Chancellor to be at home around this time so he could play with the baby before it got put to bed. The prelude came to an end, there was a short pause, and then the organist began on the Agnus Dei. Henry clicked his tongue. Mr. Beckford would not have approved. He had always said that the sixteenth century had got it right by having choral contrapuntal music unaccompanied and he didn't except his hero, Bach, *either*.

Henry left the bishop's door, and began to walk up the shadowy nave. At the sanctuary steps, he turned left and made his way round the edge of the choir screen to the steps that led up to the organ loft. He left his bag at the bottom in the care of a slim stone angel whose face and folded hands shone from touching, and climbed up to the organ loft and found Martin Chancellor, baby or no baby, alone in front of the console. He glanced in the mirror that hung above it and said without any surprise, "Hello, Henry."

Henry crossed the little panelled space and stood behind him.

"Can you remember this?"

Henry made a doubtful noise. Martin played peaceably on for a little while and then he said, "Have a crack at it anyway."

Henry drew himself up to see the score clearly over Martin's shoulder and took in an immense breath. The notes came rising up at him out of the organ, swelling all round them both.

"Ready?"

Henry nodded, opened his mouth, and sang.

About the Author

JOANNA TROLLOPE, a descendant of nineteenth-century English novelist Anthony Trollope, is the author of a number of historical novels and *Britannia's Daughters*, a study of women in the British Empire. However, she has become best known for her marvelously readable contemporary novels, often centered on the domestic nuances and dilemmas of life in England. She has now written seven of these novels, and *The Choir* is the third of them to be published by Random House. Joanna Trollope was born and still lives in Gloucestershire, England.

About the Type

This book was set in Goudy, a typeface designed by Frederic William Goudy (1865–1947). Goudy began his career as a bookkeeper, but devoted the rest of his life to the pursuit of "recognized quality" in a printing type.

Goudy was produced in 1914 and was an instant bestseller for the foundry. It has generous curves and smooth, even color. It is regarded as one of Goudy's finest achievements.